# A–Z OF IRISH NAMES FOR CHILDREN

AND THEIR MEANINGS

# A–Z OF IRISH NAMES FOR CHILDREN

## AND THEIR MEANINGS

**DIARMAID Ó MUIRITHE**

Phonetic transcription by
Máire Ní Chiosáin

*Gill & Macmillan*

Gill & Macmillan Ltd
Hume Avenue, Park West, Dublin 12
with associated companies throughout the world
www.gillmacmillan.ie


978 07171 4008 4
Typography design by Make Communication
Print origination by Carrigboy Typesetting Services
Printed by Nørhaven Paperback A/S, Denmark

This book is typeset in Linotype Minion and Neue Helvetica.

The paper used in this book comes from the wood pulp of managed forests. For every tree felled, at least one tree is planted, thereby renewing natural resources.



A CIP catalogue record for this book is available from the British Library.

5 4 3 2 1

# CONTENTS

For

*Dáithí Ó hÓgáin*

who won't, I'm sure, mind sharing this dedication with my granddaughters

*Clodagh* and *Catherine* and my grandson *James*

# INTRODUCTION

Christian, or first, or given names are, among other things, badges of familial and cultural identity. Names come and go, and for sometimes obscure reasons may come into vogue again centuries after they have fallen into disuse. Most names fluctuate in popularity, even those hardy perennials John and Mary, but they never die out.

In Ireland parents have a wonderful selection of personal names to choose from. We have our own Irish versions of biblical names such as Adam and Aaron, Simon and David as well as the names of the evangelists and of continental saints who have taken our fancy at various stages in our history.

The Vikings left us some of their personal names, such as Raghnall and its female counterpart Raghnailt; Lochlainn and Íomhar, which in either their Irish or their anglicised forms have proved to be as hardy a growth as those names bequeathed to us by the Anglo-Normans, names such as Risteard, Mártan, Annábla or Nábla; scores of them are included in this book.

And of course we have the great repository of our old Irish native tradition to choose our children's names from, and it is a source of delight to me, at any rate, to know that children are being given names such as Émer, Fergal, Dairearca, Dairíne, Donncha, Órnait, Colm and even Setanta once again.

The names of the great Irishmen who brought a high civilisation to Continental Europe in the so-called Dark Ages have been discarded there over the years, as have these Irish names from twelfth-century Iceland, recorded in the *Landnáma bók*, the Icelandic Book of Settlement: Dufan, Dufniall, Feilan, Gilli, Kaðall, Kaðlín, Kaillakr, Kalman, Kiaran, Kiarvair, Konall, Kormloð, Kylan, Lunan, Meldun, Melkorka, Melpatrikr, Niall, Parak, Patrekr, Raforta.

I hope this book may be of help to parents and prospective parents in choosing names for their offspring.

I must offer my thanks to professors Dáithí Ó hÓgáin and Donnchadh Ó Corráin for their generosity, two men whose knowledge of ancient lore is unsurpassed. My thanks too to Canon Séamas de Bhál of Bunclody for allowing me to use unpublished material on Wexford's saints, and to Karin Lach of the Fachbereichs-bibliothek Anglistik und Amerikanistik der Universität Wien for her generous help. My thanks too to the librarians in the Österreichische Nationalbibliothek in Vienna for supplying me with other indispensable works of reference. I am grateful too to Fergal Tobin and Deirdre Rennison Kunz of Gill & Macmillan for helping to bring the book to its finished form. The responsibility for the book's flaws and foibles are mine alone and I hope that whatever measure of illumination it contains makes up for them.

Diarmaid Ó Muirithe
Vienna, Autumn 2006

**AARON** (m) This biblical name is now used in Ireland more frequently than in the past. The reason why biblical names such as Abigéal, Ádhamh and Aaron are beginning to be used again is unclear. The name was used sparingly in early Ireland by monks. There was a St Aaron, a Welshman, martyred in the reign of Diocletian. Could his death have had an influence here, I wonder?

Aaron was the brother of Moses. He was appointed by the Almighty to be Moses' spokesman on earth and according to *Exodus* he was the first high priest of the Israelites. The current thinking on the name's origin is that, like Moses, it is of unknown Egyptian rather than Hebrew origin. Hanks and Hodges regard the oft-quoted derivation from Hebrew *har-on* (mountain of strength) as mere folk etymology

**ABBÁN** (m) This sixth-century saint was and is still venerated in Co. Wexford in the Adamstown area. He was of noble lineage and was abbot of Magh Arnaidhe (Adamstown). Félire Óengusso refers to him as Abbán Ua Cormaic and Féilire na Naomh nÉireannach says he was descended from the race of Labhraidh Lorc. He was sent before his teens to St Iobhar (Ibar), said to have been his uncle, at the foundation of Begerin in Wexford Harbour. Later he was said to have founded monasteries at Cill Abbáin (Kilabban), Co. Laois, and in other places. His feast day is 16 March. He is sometimes confused with another *Abbán*, also a Leinster saint whose feast day is 27 October, but of whom nothing else is known.

**ÁDHAMH** earlier **ÁDAM** (m) The biblical name *Ádam* was used by clerics of the early Irish Church. A seventh-century Irish abbot of Fermo in Italy bore the name. Afterwards it became quite popular when it was reintroduced by the Anglo-Normans. The name probably comes from the Hebrew *adama* (earth); in the creation legends the first human beings were created from earth or clay, and life was breathed into them by a god.

**AIBHISTÍN, OISTÍN** (m) Irish forms of the name of St Augustine of Hippo (from *Augustinus*, a derivative of *Augustus*) who lived from 354 to 430; and of St Augustine, the sixth-century bishop of Canterbury. The Augustinian friars had some important monasteries in pre-Norman Ireland, notably at Lady's Island, Co. Wexford, a house sacked by Cromwell's soldiery but still an important place of pilgrimage. The Augustinians brought with them one interesting custom which still survives in the Anglo-Norman baronies of Forth and Bargy in Co. Wexford. On the road between the church and the graveyard one may see little wooden crosses piled on whitethorn trees, an interesting fusion of the Christian symbol and the pagan symbol of resurrection and new life in nature. The custom, it is said, can be traced to Charlemagne's time.

**AIBIGÉAL** (f) This name was very common in nineteenth-century Munster, particularly in west Cork. Its diminutive in most places was *Abaigh*, anglicised *Abbie*, and strangely it was the 'translated' version of the name *Gobnait* (p. 101). The English is, of course, *Abigail*, a biblical name which means 'father of exaltation' in Hebrew. It was the name given to one of King David's wives who had earlier been the wife of Nabal, and to the mother of Absalom's commander Amasa. There is evidence that in Munster the name Aibigéal pre-dates the nineteenth century when it was at the height of its popularity; perhaps its popularity among the Puritans of England in the seventeenth century may have had an influence here. In the literature of England of that time Abigail was a name commonly given to a maidservant; an example is the woman in *The Scornful Lady* by Beaumont and

Fletcher (1616) who calls herself 'thy servant'. The name seems to be gaining a little in popularity again.

**AIFRIC** earlier **AFFRECA** (f) The name of two abbesses of Kildare, one of whom died in 738, the second in 833. The name meaning 'charming, pleasant' is found in Scotland, where there is a Lough Afric, and in the Isle of Man as well as Ireland. Aithbhreac was the Scots Gaelic form of the name. The most famous Aifric or Affreca was the daughter of Godred, King of Man, who married John de Courcy, the ruler of east Ulster for 27 years from 1177. She founded Grey Abbey in Co. Down. Columba Mansfield, Augustine poet, wrote this about her:

Daughter of the raven ships
Affreca, brought a warrior fleet
As dowry to her lord, de Courcy,
Knight of the eagle standards.
On Man's Isle they kissed as
Hawks swooped above them.
Later they smiled across a
chessboard.

De Courcy castled Ulster
While Affreca smiled and
Won Dunleavy's conquered heart.
Bishops and abbots graced her
table
And lived in homes she granted.
Later, de Lacy crushed Affreca's
eagle,
Shattering her king-father's ships.
The widow Affreca lived on,
Remembering.
Does she still smile on Ulster?
Eagles vanish while sparrows
survive.
Affreca was, I think, a skylark.

**AILBHE** earlier **AILBE** (m, f) Ailbe was one of the great pre-Patrician saints of Munster whose feast day is 12 September. The *Annals of Innisfallen* record his death in 528. His foundation was at Imlech Iubhair (now known as Emly), Co. Tipperary. Legends about him abound. Like many another Irish saint he was fond of wild animals. One story has him suckled by wolves. In his old age it was said that the local people organised a great wolf hunt. One of the wolves came in distress to Ailbe who told it not to be afraid as he himself was suckled by a wolf in infancy. He fed the wolf every day and when the people saw this, they called off the hunt.

Some famous women bore the name, among them the legendary Ailbe, daughter of

Midir, the fairy king. Mention should be made as well of Ailbe, the daughter of Cormac Mac Airt, who was said by Caoilte, the Fenian warrior, to be one of the four best women to have ever slept with an Irishman. Ó Corráin and Maguire connect the word with the old root *albho-* (white) and with the Gaulish *Albiorix* (world-king).

**AILLINN** (f) A name given to girls during and immediately after the Irish revival movement of the late nineteenth and early twentieth centuries. It seems to have fallen into disuse since then. Aillinn was, according to a story written down in the eleventh century, a Leinster princess. For her story see *Baile.*

**AINDRIAS, AINDRÉAS, AINDRIÚ** Irish equivalents of English *Andrew*. From the Greek *Andreas*, whose first element is *andr-* (man or warrior). St Andrew the apostle was a very popular saint in the Middle Ages and is the patron of Russia, Greece and Scotland. The popularity of his name in its Irish forms from the Middle Ages is probably due to the influence of the Scottish planters in the first instance.

**AINGEAL** (f) This is the Irish form of the English and Italian given name *Angela*, which is the feminine form of *Angelus*, from the classical Greek *angelos* (messenger). *Aingeal* is a fairly new translation of the name which gained popularity during the Irish revival in the twentieth century.

**AISLING** (f) The name, quite popular now, is of recent origin. It is not found in medieval times but is a product of the Irish revival movement in the late nineteenth and early twentieth centuries. *Aisling* is a genre of vision poetry which flourished in the eighteenth century; it means 'dream, vision'. Sometimes the name is anglicised *Ashling* and *Ashlin.*

**AMHLAOIBH** (m) This name, very popular in Munster, was introduced into Ireland by the Vikings who called it *Olaf*, a name still popular in Scandinavian countries. The Old Norse personal name was composed of *anu* (ancestor) and *leifr* (heir, descendant). St Olaf,

King of Norway (995–1030), is given credit for spreading Christianity in his country. The Irish form was anglicised as *Auliff* and, ludicrously, *Humphrey*, a name still widely given to children in west Cork and Kerry. The Scottish cognates are *Amhlaidh* (Gaelic) and *Aulay* (anglicised). Amhlaoibh Ó Súilleabhain, a Kerry-born schoolmaster residing in Callan, Co. Kilkenny, in the first half of the nineteenth century, wrote an interesting diary which has been edited and published in Irish, and translated into English as *The Diary of Humphrey O'Sullivan* by Tomás de Bhaldraithe.

**ANLUAN** (m) This name was borne by a brother of Brian Boru. It means, probably, 'great hound' or 'great lord'. The northern surname *Ó hAnluain*, acceptably anglicised as *O'Hanlon*, derives from it. In the nineteenth century the name was ludicrously rendered *Alphonsus*.

**ANRAÍ, ANNRAOI, ANRAOI, ÉNRÍ, EINRÍ** (m) Irish forms of *Henry* or *Harry*. It was introduced into Ireland by the Anglo-Normans who called it *Henri*. It quickly became very popular even among the native ruling clans, particularly among the O'Neills of Ulster. The name is of Germanic origin, containing the elements *haim* (home) and *ric* (power, ruler). No less than eight kings of England bore the name, six kings of France and four of Castille and Leon; Heinrich der Vogler, Henry the Fowler (fl. *c.*900), Duke of Saxony and King of the Germans, became the first in a long line of kings and princes in Europe to bear cognate names. *Harry* was the accepted standard vernacular form in England until the seventeenth century, when it was supplanted by *Henry*. *Anraí* now seems to be the standard used in Irish.

**AODH** earlier **ÁED** (m) This ancient name, the commonest of all male names in olden times, is now anglicised as *Hugh*, a name with which it has no connection. Ó Corráin and Maguire say that it is cognate with the Latin *aedes*, *aestus*, and with the Gaulish *Aedui*. It is very common among the northern families, particularly among the O'Donnells. There are many men called Áed mentioned in the old stories; one in particular, Áed Allán, who is said to have reigned as high king in the 730s, had a particularly dramatic conception and birth. His father was High King Fergal; his mother was a nun, the daughter of Conghal who was king before Fergal took over the throne. Conghal was a strict man, and having got wind of the word that the pair were secret lovers, raided what he believed was their love nest. His daughter hid her lover by sitting on top of him in the bed, but Fergal paid a price. A big cat chewed his legs where he lay and Fergal was forced to strangle it as quietly as he could. Conghal was so furious with the man who told what he considered a lie about his daughter that he had him drowned. He apologised to his daughter, but she conceived and hid herself away until she gave birth in secret. She gave the baby to two women to drown, but they kept him. Four years later when the mother saw the child and admired him, the women told her that he was in fact her son. She brought the child to Fergal who, delighted with him, secretly reared him as his own.

**AOGÁN, AODHAGÁN** earlier **AEDUCÁN** (m) This name has been anglicised as *Egan*. It was a very popular name in ancient Ireland. It is a diminutive of *Áed* (above). The name of the great legal family of medieval Ireland, the Mac Aodhagáins, anglicised as Mac Egan, derived from the personal name. The great Kerry poet Aodhagán Ó Rathaille bore the name. Daniel Corkery called him 'the Dante of Munster'. Seamus Heaney has translated a few of his poems.

**AOIBHEALL** (f) This lovely name is seldom if ever used nowadays, simply because it is mispronounced 'Evil'. The lady was an Otherworld goddess whose base was in Co. Clare at a place called Craig Liath (Craglea) near Killaloe. The name means 'sparkling, bright', attributes of a goddess, especially of a goddess of sovereignty, in Irish culture. She was a prophetess and was said to have appeared to Brian Boru the night before his battle against the Vikings at Clontarf in which he was killed. She foretold his death and told him that the first of his sons to visit him the following morning would succeed him. That son was Donnchad, who indeed succeeded his father. Aoibheall was a favourite among the poets of the eighteenth century. Aodhagán Ó Rathaille mentioned her in a great aisling or vision poem, attributing the gift of prophecy to her. And Brian Merriman in his rabelasian *Cúirt an Mheón Oíche* (*The Midnight Court*) has her as judge in the trial set up by frustrated women who complain of male impotence and sexual neglect. She was the reputed sister of *Clíona* (p. 44).

**AOIBHINN** (f) This lovely name means something like 'delightful, radiant'. It is very old and has in recent times become popular again. The most famous lady who bore the name in the past was the mother of St Éanna of Aran (p. 75). The name has been anglicised as *Eavan*. It is the given name of the poet Eavan Boland.

**AOIFE** (f) This is a recurring name in the old literature and is very popular today, which is strange considering that most of the Aoifes one comes across in medieval literature were downright unpleasant people. Take the most famous Aoife, the one connected with the Children of Lir. She replaced her dead sister as the wife of Lir, a chief of the Tuatha Dé Danann. She hated her sister's four children so she struck them with a magic wand and turned them into swans at Derravarragh Lake in Westmeath. She told one of them that the spell would last until a noblewoman from the south would marry a nobleman from the north. Her husband found out what she had done and he changed Aoife into a demon whose punishment it was to float around the world for ever. The children stayed on the lake for 300 years. Afterwards they spent 300 years on the Sea of Moyle between Ireland and Scotland, and a further 300 years in terrible misery on the sea off Erris in Mayo. Then they flew home to their father's fairy dwelling but found the place deserted. Back they went to an island in the bay of Erris, Inis Glóire, where they met the Christian missionary St Mochaomhóg who was kind to them. Soon afterwards a noblewoman from the south married a nobleman from the north and that ended their banishment. They were turned back into three withered old men and an old woman. The saint baptised them and they died in peace. The story was never popular in folklore, but it, and Aoife, became widely known by being anthologised in schoolbooks. O'Rahilly thought that the name came from the Gaulish goddess *Esuvia*.

**AONGHUS** earlier **ÓENGUS** (m) Still a very popular name in Ireland, *Aonghus* or *Óengus* was a mythical chief of the divine race, the Tuatha Dé Danann. He lived at Brugh na Bóinne, the tumulus of Newgrange, Co. Meath. His father was the Daghda, the principal deity of ancient times; his mother was Bóinn, the goddess of the river named from her (now called the Boyne). Óengus means 'true strength or true vigour'. An alternative name was *Mac ind Óc*. Óengus was the young god of Irish mythology.

The story of his birth is related in a ninth-century text. It tells how the powerful god, the Daghda, coveted Bóinn, who happened to be married to Ealcmhar, also known as Nuadhu, who lived at the Brugh. The Daghda tricked Ealcmhar into going away for a while, and using his magic powers he relieved his rival from the pangs of hunger and thirst so that he didn't notice the passing days, weeks and months. During that time he seduced Bóinn who gave birth to a son in due course. Ealcmhar believed Bóinn's explanation that 'young is the son who was conceived in the morning and born between that and evening'.

In the course of time Ealcmhar brought the youngster to the fort of Midhir to be fostered. During his nine years there he became a great hurler. One day during a game he was playing he had an altercation with another who told him the true story of his conception and parentage. He confronted Midhir with this story; Midhir told him the truth and went with him to the Brugh to confront the Daghda at Uisneach, Co. Westmeath, and to seek his heritage. The Daghda told him to go to Brugh na Bóinne at Samhain to have it out with Ealcmhar. He advised him to seek ownership of the Brugh for a day and a night. He did this, and when the day and the night were over he refused to give back the Brugh. Ealcmhar insisted that they both return to the Daghda to seek his judgment on the matter. The judgment was that 'it is in days and nights that the world is spent'. This ambiguous statement somehow tricked Ealcmhar out of his Brugh, but Óenghus was kind enough to give him a rath near by to live in.

In late medieval literature Óenghus is transferred to the Fianna times, where he is made protector of the young lover Diarmaid (p. 66). Amazingly, given his fame in the Fianna tales, Óengus does not play a part in later folklore.

**AONNA** (m) A man of this name was successor to St Ciarán of Clonmacnoise (p. 41) and confessor to the great King Guaire (p. 102). Now Guaire could be a vindictive old man, and the story goes that he had a widow's son arrested for trespassing in his gardens. The widow was given a choice by Guaire: either pay a heavy fine or see her thieving son executed. She went to Aonna for advice. He gave her a verse of poetry to say to the king, a reminder of his last end and hell fire. It seems to have had an effect on Guaire because he released the boy. Some time afterwards a good horse belonging to Aonna was killed while in the care of a poor farmer, who immediately went to the king to appeal the heavy compensation Aonna demanded. Guaire gave the farmer a verse to speak to Aonna. The verse accused the monk of seeking unjust compensation and warned him of hell fire and damnation. When Aonna heard it, he accepted a single cow.

**ART** (m) This is an ancient personal name, sometimes wrongly anglicised as *Arthur*, a name with which it has absolutely no connection. The original meaning of Art is 'bear', but the word was used only as a personal name, and figuratively meant 'a champion'. Many of the ancient legendary kings had the name. Art Óenfer, son of Conn Céadchathach (Conn of the Hundred Battles), was the father of King Cormac mac Airt. Medieval literature has it that when this Art's brother, Connla, set off to the Otherworld in a boat, his disconsolate father

Conn looked on Art as 'óenfer' (the lone one). Literature also has a marvellous story of Art Óenfer's adventures seeking the beautiful Dealbhchaomh on the Island of Women, bringing her back to Ireland, and expelling his evil stepmother Bé Chuma for ever.

Another legendary king was Art Corb, supposedly the ancestor of the Déisi. Many of the great families of Ireland honoured the name: it was, and still is popular among the O'Neills of Ulster, the MacMurroughs and Kavanaghs of Leinster, the O'Connors and O'Haras of Connacht, and the O'Rourkes of Breifne, to mention some.

**ATHRACHT** (f) Known in English as *Attracta*, this saint, to whom devotion is still shown, lived in the late sixth or in the early seventh century. Nothing certain is known of her life. An Augustinian priest who lived on the Island of Saints in Lough Ree on the Shannon collected some fanciful stories about her in the fifteenth century. On the one hand he says that she received the veil from St Patrick, then goes on to say that she was a friend of both St Naith-Í (p. 136) who lived in the sixth century, and of a seventh-century king of Connacht.

Local tradition says that Athracht was a great healer, making up her own special potions from herbs she gathered locally. Her foundation at Coolavin was famous for its hospitality. She is patron of the parish of Killaraght (the church of Athracht), and there are holy wells that bear her name in many places in counties Sligo and Mayo. *Attracta* is still a popular name in her native district.

St Athracht's cross was formerly venerated in the diocese of Achonry. It was in the care of the Ó Mocháins who, it is said, took it around from place to place so that the people could venerate it, paying dues for the privilege.

**BAILE** (m) In the early days of the Gaelic revival this name was occasionally given to boys at baptism in Omeath, but has since fallen into disuse. Baile was the star-crossed lover in a story written down in the eleventh century. He was known as Baile Binnbhéarlach (the sweet-spoken).

He was in love with the princess Aillinn (p. 4), a Leinster woman, and they arranged a tryst at Ros na Ríogh (Rosnaree) on the River Boyne. On his way there from Ulster, Baile stopped with his retinue to water their horses and was visited by a loathsome-looking man who told him that he was the bearer of bad news: his beloved Aillinn had been murdered by the Leinstermen as she journeyed to meet him. Poor Baile fell dead with shock. He was buried where he died, at a place ever since called Tráigh Bhaile (Baile's Strand) at Dundalk. The stranger then went on to Mount Leinster and asked to see Aillinn at her dwelling there. There he told her that her lover had died on his way to meet her. Aillinn, like her lover, died of a broken heart.

A yew tree grew from Baile's grave and its top branches took the form of the young man's head. An apple tree grew from the grave of Aillinn and its top formed her likeness. Seven years afterwards the poets of Ulster made a writing tablet from Baile's yew, and the Leinster poets did the same with wood from Aillinn's tree. The high king Cormac mac Airt (p. 56) was told this story at the feast of Tara and was much taken by it. He asked to see the two tablets and as he held them in his hands they became so intertwined like woodbine on a branch that they could not be parted.

The story was invented to explain the origin of the name of the strand. The narrative plot is international: abroad, the tragedy is caused by parents who fall out with each other; whilst here it is replaced by the malicious stranger, an Irish invention from medieval demon stories.

Yeats made his own of the tragic tale. In *Baile and Aillinn* (1903) he wrote the following as an Argument: 'Baile and Aillinn were lovers, but Aengus, the Master of Love, wishing them to be happy in his own land among the dead, told to each a story of the other's death, so that their hearts were broken and they died.'

**BAIRBRE** (f) A very common Gaelic name in Connacht, also found in its short form *Báibín*. It is found all over Europe in the cognates *Barbara* (English), *Barabel* (Scots Gaelic), *Barbro* (Swedish), *Barbora* (Russian), and *Varvara* (Hungarian), to mention only some.

The name comes from Latin, meaning 'foreign woman', a feminine form of *barbarus* (foreign), from Greek, referring originally to the unintelligible speech of foreigners which sounded to the Greeks like no more than 'bar-bar'.

That Bairbre and its cognates are so popular is difficult to explain, especially as she may never have existed. The name itself sounds beautiful; maybe that's the reason for its universal popularity. The legends surrounding her are many and colourful. One has it that she was imprisoned in a tower and then murdered by her father, who was immediately struck dead by a bolt of lightning. This is why she is regarded as the patron saint of architects, stonemasons, artillerymen, fireworks makers and men who work with explosives.

**BAIRTLIMÉAD, BEARTLAOI** (m) These forms derive from Latin *Bartholomaeus*, the name of one of the Apostles. The Latin name is from an Aramaic formation which meant 'son of Talmai'; *Talmai* is thought to have meant 'of many furrows'. The Irish forms have been anglicised *Bartley*, *Batt*, *Bertie* and *Bart*. See also *Parthalán*.

**BALAR, BALOR** (m) This terrible tyrant of mythology was

known in some stories as Balar Bailcbhéimneach (the strong-beating Balar). His name, *Boleros* in ancient Celtic, may have meant 'the gleaming one', and there is a promontory in Cornwall tentatively identified as Land's End which, according to Ptolemy and Diodorus Siculus, was known as Bolerion. In one early text Balar is called *birugderc* (the piercing eyed), but is now generally called Balar of the Evil Eye, because one glance from it could destroy whole armies.

Ó hÓgáin relates a folk story connected with the Balar myth in which a smith called Goibhleann had a marvellous cow called the Glas Goibhleann which Balar tried to steal from him. Balar succeeded in driving the cow and its calf down into Leinster, but when they reached the coast near Dublin the cow tried to turn back. Balar tried to raise the lid of his eye to see what was troubling her, and immediately the cow and its calf were turned into rocks, which are now the two Rockabill islands off Skerries.

A folk account from Mayo states: 'He had a single eye in his forehead, a venomous, fiery eye. There were always seven coverings over this eye. One by one Balor removed the coverings. With the first covering the bracken began to wither; with the second the grass became copper-coloured; with the third the woods and timber began to heat; with the fourth smoke came from the trees; with the fifth everything grew red; with the sixth it sparked; and with the seventh they were all set on fire and the whole countryside was ablaze!'

Not many children were called after this monster, I should imagine.

**BEARACH** earlier **BERACH** (m) He was a sixth-century saint who, according to a late biography, was born in Gort na Luachra (Gortnalougher, the field of the rushes) in Co. Leitrim. His birth we are told was prophesied by St Patrick. He seemed to have a strange way of finding sites for his monastic foundations. Once when a woman and a boy refused him permission to use their mill, the boy fell into the mill and the woman died of shock. Bearach brought them back to life again and a thankful father gave him a site at the place, Raon Bhearaigh, near Iniskeen in Co. Monaghan. On another occasion he was refused a drink at Tara and after he left all the beer was found to be gone from the vats. When the king heard this, he sent for Bearach and gave him the site he was looking for, whereupon Bearach restored the beer.

After a spell at Glendalough he headed for Cill Bhearaigh (Kilbarry), in Termonbarry, Co. Roscommon, his chariot drawn by a stag. There, his extremely unreliable Lives say he performed many miracles, including turning a bog into a lake to drown an agressive army that was pestering people who had asked for his protection. His feast day is 15 February.

**BEARCHÁN** (m) This saint, founder of a famous settlement at Clonsast, Co. Offaly, lived in the sixth century. It was said that he was of the Dál Riada sept of Co. Antrim. He spent half his life in Scotland and thus earned the name Fear Dá Leithe (man of two halves). There is no biography of the saint, but he was known as a prophet who foretold the fate of the Irish until the end of the Elizabethan wars; no doubt his prophesies were amended and added to as the centuries went by. He seems to have been confused at times with Bearchán of Glasnevin, also known as Mo Bí (p. 129). An interesting piece of folklore about him survived in west Cork. This is it, as Ó hÓgáin relates it. He had a vision in which it was revealed to him that his death would come when three kings came uninvited to his house. Three such guests did indeed come and when he told them of his vision they promised to protect him. Placing him under an overturned vat, they stood on guard around it. Soon a cowherd arrived and lulled the kings to sleep with music. When they awoke in the morning they found nothing left of Bearchán but his bones underneath the vat. Bearchán of Clonsast is remembered on 4 December.

**BÉBÓ** (f) The beautiful and vivacious Queen of Iubhdán, King of Fairyland, in the story *Eisirt*, of which a modern Irish version written by An tAthair Peadar Ó Laoghaire exists, though it is no longer in print. The story relates the adventures and misadventures of Bébó and her husband in Ulster at the court of King Fergus Mac Léide at Eamhain Mhacha. The story was first written down around the thirteenth century. On the night that Fergus gave a great feast at Eamhain, Iubhdán gave another in his fairy palace. Iubhdán boasted during the banquet at his and his warriors' invincibility, at which his poet and wise man Eisirt burst out laughing, telling the company that one of Fergus's warriors could annihilate Iubhdan's entire army. Iubhdán was incensed but allowed Eisirt to travel to Eamhain to prove what he had just said. He was received with great amusement and was humiliated. He was so small that he could stand in the palm of Fergus's dwarf and poet Aodh. After three days and nights Eisirt and Aodh were allowed back to the court of the fairy king, where the dwarf Aodh was an object of terror. Iubhdán decided to see Ulster for himself, and accompanied by Queen Bébó arrived at Eamhain secretly at night. Hungry, the little king attemped to eat porridge from a cauldron, fell into the mess and was rescued in the morning by disbelieving courtiers. After many misadventures Iubhdán and Bébó were given places of honour in Fergus's household, but were refused permission to go home. Not forgotten, their army of tiny men came to rescue them, and after threats and offers of ransom, the pair were allowed to leave Ireland for ever. The ransom accepted by Fergus was a pair of Iubhdán's shoes. Fergus, while swimming, had been attacked by a monster and had suffered a terrible blemish: his mouth had been twisted around to the back of his head by the monster's breath. He was sure that a pair of Iubhdán's shoes would repel the monster, should he ever again confront him. A sequel to the story tells that when they did meet, Fergus slew the monster, but the beast in his death throes tore his heart out and killed him. It has been suggested that this story, contrasting a land of giants with a land of pygmies, was the basis for Swift's *Gulliver's Travels.*

**BÉIBHEANN** (f) This lovely name is associated with the Finn tales. Not all of these have a happy ending and the story of

*Béibheann* is very sad indeed. It is told in *Agallamh na Seanórach* (the Colloquy of the Old Men), written down in the tenth century, and this is the bones of it.

Finn Mac Cumhaill (p. 91) and his warrior Goll Mac Mórna were taking their ease under the greenwood trees one day when they saw a woman approaching. Goll was amazed at the woman's size; he had never seen the likes of her in all his life. As she drew near they asked her who she was and where she came from. She told them that her name was Béibheann and that she was running away from her husband for the third time. His name, she said, was Áed. She begged Finn to protect her from this man and Finn and Goll promised her refuge and protection; the Fianna would look after her, they said. Later that evening after supper, as somebody played the harp, Béibheann let down the seven score tresses of her voluminous golden hair, and all the men were amazed at its luxuriant beauty. Then the company saw in the distance a man approach the party. If the girl Béibheann was big, this man was immense. Who is he, this giant of a man? they wondered. 'It is he,' said Béibheann. 'It is the man I have run away from.' Striding towards them, spear in hand, he suddenly flung the spear at Béibheann. It passed through her body while the man strode nonchalantly through the mesmerised Fianna. Gathering up their weapons they followed the stranger to a great ship, but he was aboard and away before they could capture him. The Fianna performed their funeral rites over poor Béibheann and buried her at a place subsequently known as The Ridge of the Dead Woman. Her sad death did not stop people from naming children after her; the name was found in Co. Clare in the eighteenth century and it became popular again during the Gaelic revival at the end of the nineteenth century. There is no acceptable anglicised form.

**BEIRCHEART** earlier **BEIRICHTIR** (m) This saint is not Irish at all but an Anglo-Saxon monk who came here in the eighth century, probably with a company of monks from some foundation across the water. He was by no means the only English holy man in those days to be attracted to Ireland. He settled in Tullylease in north Cork in a place sheltered by the Mullaghareirk mountains, and he is remembered to this day at the old church set between two holy wells on his feast day, 18 February. 'Rounds' are performed at the wells and at the church. In Tullylease he is known today as *St Benjamin* or *St Ben*. There are some beautifully carved cross fragments at the place.

The two holy wells are known now as St Mary's and St Ben's, Tobar Mhuire and Tobar Bheircheart in the old days. The only surviving tradition relating to the saint is a story about a deer that used to come every day whilst Beircheart's little church was being built and milk herself into a bullaun so that the workmen might have a nourishing drink. They had no idea who was bringing them the milk, so they decided to place a man to spy. The deer became so incensed that she kicked a hole through the stone and never appeared again. The bullaun may still be seen with a hole through its base.

Beircheart is venerated elsewhere in Munster. There is a Kilberrihert near Aghabullogue not far from Macroom in west Cork, another place of the same name in Truaghanaicmy, Co. Kerry, and a third in the Glen of Aherlow.

**BEOC, MOBHEOC, VOGUE, VAUK** (m) Four names for the man who may have been *Vouga*, a sixth-century bishop of Brittany, thought to have been an Irishman. He is venerated in Carne in the south-east corner of Co. Wexford. The fame of his miracles in Brittany was propagated here by the Anglo-Normans and by the Augustinians. In the townland of St Vauk there is a holy well and the remains of a little church dedicated to him.

**BLÁTHMAC** (m) This eighth-century poet wrote a set of lovely, simple poems about the Nativity. He came from an area between Monaghan and Louth, in the district where the modern poet Patrick Kavanagh was born and reared. His work has been edited by James Carney. His name means 'beautiful son' or 'the flower of sons'.

**BLÁTHNAID, BLÁTHNAIT** earlier **BLÁTHNAT** (f) The

name means 'little flower'. She was the unwilling wife of the west Munster hero Cú Rói. She fell in love with Cú Chulainn, her husband's great enemy. Cú Rói's palace was so constructed that its door was magically concealed. Bláthnat poured milk into a stream which ran through the fortress and she and Cú Chulainn watched and found the place where the milky water emerged. Cú Chulainn found the door and in the ensuing skirmish Cú Rói was slain. Cú Rói's poet, Ferchertne, survived the attack and followed Cú Chulainn and Bláthnat as they left the scene of the battle. He caught up with them as they paused to look out to sea on the cliffs of the Beara Peninsula in west Cork. He crept up to the pair and, taking hold of Bláthnat, carried her with him over the cliff to their deaths.

Kildare chefs might consider Bláthnat as their patron. She was St Brigit's cook.

**BLINNE** (f) This name is associated with both Co. Louth and Co. Wexford though it is no longer in use in either place. The name seems to be a modern form of *Mo Ninne*, and her original name was supposed to have been *Dar Erca* (p. 61). She was reputed to have been baptised by St Patrick and to have founded a convent composed of a widow who was raising a child, and eight virgins, in Faughart, Co. Louth. The story goes that she found it difficult to live so near her home place, and so she set off to Wexford, where *St Ibar* gave her a home at Begerin Island. Her feast day is 6 July.

**BRAN** (m) Bran was a character in a fine story written around A.D. 700. The name *Bran* (raven) was not confined to Ireland; a mythical king of the name is found in Welsh literature. The story is the earliest Irish example of the *imram* (rowing story). A beautiful Otherworld woman came to the palace of Bran bearing a silver branch. From the branch came lovely music. She explained to Bran that the branch was from an apple tree in Emhain, a faraway island in the Otherworld. She sang its praises and invited Bran to follow her there. She disappeared then and Bran and three times nine men set off in a boat to find the island. After two days at sea they met Manannán, the god of the sea, who told them how to navigate to the island. When Bran and his crew came to the place they rowed around it, and were surprised to see the island's inhabitants standing on the shore laughing at them. When one of Bran's men went ashore to meet the people, he too started laughing and giggling incessantly like the rest. Then Bran set off for the Island of Women, and there they had a great time for what they thought was a year; in reality it was many years. One of Bran's men got lonely; he wanted to go back to Ireland and Bran decided to accompany him. His lover warned him not to do so, but if he insisted he was on no account to set foot on dry land. They made landfall at Sruibh Bhrain (Stroove Point) in north Donegal, and the people who came to see the strange boat told them of old stories they had heard of the voyage of Bran long ago. Bran's companion, Neachtan, jumped from the boat, and as he did he became as withered as a man who might have been centuries old. Bran wrote the story of his voyage in ogham and then departed, never to be seen again.

**BRANDUBH** (m) The name means 'black raven'. He was a Leinster king who died, it is thought, around 605. He is a very prominent character in the stories about the kings. One such story in which he himself figures has to do with popular lore about babies being given to the wrong parents at birth. The story goes that King Eochu was once exiled in Scotland where his wife Feidhilm gave birth to twin boys. A lady called Ingheanach, the wife of a king called Gabhrán, had twin girls in the same house on the same day. They decided to swap babies; Feidhilm gave the other woman one of her boys in exchange for a girl, but before she did so she inserted a grain of pure gold in the baby's shoulder so that he might be identified later. Eochu returned to Ireland and his son Brandubh became king of Leinster. The other boy was given the name Áedán. As Áedán mac Gabhráin he became a leader of Dál Riada and king of Scotland. Áedán decided to wage war on Leinster, and when his real mother heard this she went to meet him and told him who he really was. She identified him to his satisfaction by plucking the grain of gold from his shoulder. War was averted and Brandubh and his brother became friends.

Brandubh was, another story goes, killed by a man called Sárán. When St Maodhóg heard the news that Brandubh had died without confessing his sins to him, he fasted and prayed, and Brandubh was restored to life. He received the last rites from the saint, and announced that he had no interest in living in this terrible world. He thereupon died, and Maodhóg buried him at his church in Ferns, Co. Wexford.

**BREAC** earlier **BRECC** (m) This was a common name in the Middle Ages. It means 'speckled' or 'freckled'. It was especially common among the Déise of Munster. There is a St Breac's well near Ardmore in Co. Waterford. His feast day is 15 January.

**BREACÁN** earlier **BRECCÁN** (m) This is a diminutive form of *Brecc* or *Breac* (above). It was a favourite name among the early clerics and there are some 13 saints who bore the name. One, Breccán of Kilkeel, Co. Down, was a patron saint of local fishermen. His feast day is 7 May. Other saints of the name are Breccán of Dál Cais, another patron of seafarers and one of the saints of Aran, whose feast day is 1 May; and Breccán of Moville whose feast day is 27 April.

**BREACNAIT** earlier **BRECCNAT** (f) There is a saint of this name whose feast day is 3 July. The name *Breacnait* (freckled girl) was known in west Waterford until the end of the nineteenth century. It is a pretty name and it seems a pity that it has fallen into neglect.

**BREANDÁN, BRÉANAINN** earlier **BRÉNAINN** (m) The oldest form of the name, *Brénainn*, is from the Welsh *breenhin* (prince); the modern form *Breandán* is from the latinised forms *Brendanus* or *Brandanus*. Of the many Brendans mentioned in the old annals, Brénainn of Clonfert was by far the most important. He was a mountaineer and seaman and his *Voyage* became a medieval bestseller. He was born in Kerry in 486, according to the *Annals of Inisfallen*, founded Cluain Ferta Brénainn

(Clonfert) in 561, and died in 578. It is claimed that he was fostered by St Íde of Killeedy (p. 104) and then went on to Clonard and also the foundation of St Iarlaith (Jarlath) of Tuam (p. 104). He took over the already established monastery of Ardfert in his own county and then founded the great abbey on the Shannon between Banagher and Shannonbridge. Today all that is left of Clonfert is the great Romanesque west door of its church, built long after Brendan's time. The 3,000 foot Mount Brandon is named from him. On its summit, still a place of pilgrimage, the Voyage legend has Brénainn praying and fasting before he sets out to seek the Promised Land he sees in a vision.

The story of the Voyage is told in the *Vita Brendani* and in the *Navigatio Brendani*. The former has him making two trips, one in skin-covered boats, the second in boats with wooden hulls. The first was unsuccessful, as St Íde told him it would be, because the boats he used were made from animals whose blood had been spilled in their construction. The second voyage was a success. But it was the *Navigatio* which became a bestseller all over Europe and made Brendan the Navigator a medieval hero.

He did sail from Ireland and perhaps some of the stories contained in the *Navigatio* are based on fact. He certainly did not say Mass on the back of a whale, but other incidents suggest a knowledge of volcanoes and icebergs. It should be remembered that Irish monks did make it to Iceland in the seventh century. So the Voyage to the Land of Promise is really a thoroughly enjoyable but fictional romance written in the tenth century by some exiled Irishman writing in the tradition of the Imramma, voyage romances which had their origin in pagan Ireland and in which the hero goes out to seek adventure. They were not confined to Ireland—think of Sinbad the Sailor. Brendan of Clonfert's feast day is 16 May.

Brendan of Birr, whose feast day is 29 November, was also a formidable man. Both Brendans studied at Clonard and both were friends of Colmcille. Brendan of Birr was called chief of Ireland's prophets in the *Martyrology of Óengus*. Nothing survives at

Birr except the holy well of Brendan.

In the account of Adamnán in *Vita Columbae*, it is related that at a synod convened at Teltown to excommunicate Colmcille, Brendan of Birr rose up and kissed Colmcille before defending him. He said that he had seen a pillar of fire and angels going before his friend. Colmcille was found not guilty of whatever offence he was accused of. Years later, when Brendan died in Birr in 573, Colmcille, who was in Iona, saw a vision of angels descending to escort Brendan to heaven. So said Adamnán. One thing survives to remind us of the glory of Brendan's monastery at Birr. It is the great gospel book of Mac Regnold, the scribe of Birr, who died in 820 as bishop and abbot of Brendan's foundation. The illuminated book, a copy of Jerome's text, was taken to England and a literal translation in Anglo-Saxon was added by two English monks, Farman and Owun, who belonged to the monastery of Harewood on the marches of the kingdom of Mercia and Northumberland.

**BREAS** earlier **BRES** (m) The Otherworld race, the Tuatha Dé Danann, has a king of this name. The word means 'handsome' or 'beautiful' and is the king's sobriquet, his real name being Eochu Bres. A text on the second battle of Moytirra gives an account of the life and times of this mythical king. According to it a young woman of the Tuatha Dé Danann called Ériu (that is Éire) was walking by the sea when a ship made of silver approached. On board was a very good-looking young man who, when he disembarked, told Ériu that he came to make love to her. She raised no objections. Afterwards he gave her a present of a ring and told her that she should give it to nobody but the man whose finger it fitted. He was, he said, Ealatha, king of the Fomhóire (the Fomorians), and that she would have a son by him. What he told Ériu came true, and when the boy came to manhood he replaced the king of his people, Nuadu, who was forced to resign because of a blemish. Bres was warned that he could remain king so long as his rule did not become oppressive. But oppressive it became, as he connived with the Fomhóire in levying taxes on Ireland. He was also guilty of not lavishing hospitality on his people, as a king was expected to do.

Then a poet named Cairbre wrote a satire about him and the poem had such an effect that the Tuatha Dé demanded that he resign. He agreed that he would do so after a seven year period had elapsed. What he had in mind was to assemble an army of the Fomhóire in the meantime, so he went to his mother for advice. She gave him the ring she had received from his father Ealatha and it fitted his finger perfectly. But when she took him to the land of the Fomhóire, where they were heartily welcomed, Ealatha declined to help him personally because of his tarnished reputation in Ireland, but did introduce him to two other Fomhóire kings who assembled a huge army. They set off to conquer Ireland but were heavily defeated at the great battle of Moytirra. Bres or Breas was captured after the battle, but his life was spared by Lugh because of agricultural advice he gave. He returned to the fortress of his father and, much to everybody's delight, never troubled the Tuatha Dé again.

**BREASAL** earlier **BRESSAL** (m) This fictional high king belongs to pre-history. He was an Ulsterman it seems, and he was said to have ruled for 11 years, during which time the cattle herds of Ireland were decimated by a great pestilence. Indeed at one point only one bull and one heifer remained of all the livestock in the country. He was known as Breasal Ró-Dhíobhadh (Breasal, lacking in stock) because of this calamity. He is sometimes confused with a Leinster Bressal who made a name for himself for refusing to pay the cattle-tribute called bóraimhe to the High King Cairbre Lifeachair. And we read of yet another Breasal, son of High King Diarmaid Mac Cearrbheoil, making a name for himself in the cattle business in the sixth century by taking a cow from a nun. Bressal means 'brave in warfare'. The name was common from early times to the later Middle Ages, and under its anglicised form *Brazil* (emphasis on the first syllable) was known along the Barrow valley until comparatively recent times.

**BREASLÁN** earlier **BRESLEÁN** (m) The Donegal surname

*Ó Breasláin*, the name of an important legal family in the Middle Ages, derives from this given name, which is a diminutive form of *Breasal* or *Bressal* (above). The name has been anglicised as *Breslin*.

**BRIAN** (m) Scholars differ as to the origin and meaning of this name. O'Rahilly's theory is that it was borrowed here in Ireland from people who spoke a Celtic language such as Welsh or British. The original form would have been *Brion*, a word of two syllables which developed at a later stage into *Brian*, with a genitive *Briain*. The original Celtic form was *Brigonos*. If this theory is correct, the name originally meant 'noble, high'.

The man responsible for the name's continued popularity here in Ireland is *Brian Boru*, who died after the Battle of Clontarf on Good Friday 1014. He had by then achieved a degree of authority over most of Ireland. He was the ancestor of the great Munster family the Uí Bhriain (the O'Briens), who were the sworn enemies of the MacCarthys. The latter, as you can imagine, did not give their children the name Brian.

In the nineteenth century, due to the rules that governed the National Schools, this illustrious personal name was changed into *Bernard*, *Barnaby* and *Barney*, but this nonsense was usually confined to the classroom rollbook and ignored in the home. The name began to be mispronounced and written *Bryan*. That form is still popular.

Why, one might ask, is the name so popular in the north of England? Consider the late loquatious soccer manager Brian Clough. Ó Corráin and Maguire point out that an exactly similar name, Brian, had been popular in England since the Middle Ages when it was introduced from Brittany. It survived in northern England until the eighteenth century although it died out elsewhere. Mr Clough's name probably had its origin in northern France and not in the territory of Thomond.

**BRÍD, BRIGHID** earlier **BRIGIT** (f) The chief saint of Leinster and second to St Patrick in importance among the saints of Ireland. Indeed it could be said that her foundation at Kildare was almost as important as Armagh in seventh-century Ireland. She is also known as *Brigid, Bridget, Breed, Bride* and *Breege*. She had her origin in the Celtic goddess *Brigantia*. She was known as Muire na nGael (Mary of the Irish), and had two Lives written about her in Latin, one of them around the year 650. Nothing much of the saint herself may be gleaned from the Latin Lives, which were really a compendium of miracles attributed to her and a valuable description of the foundation at Kildare. In the ninth century a Life was added in Irish, written in Kildare. She is still venerated especially around her feast day on 1 February, which coincides with *Imbolc* (parturition), one of the four principal days of the Celtic year, and the beginning of Spring.

It is interesting that Cill Dara (the church of the oak tree), anglicised Kildare, was built near such a tree, a sacred place in druidic times. Brigit has always been regarded as a patroness of crops and farm animals, just what one would expect of a goddess of Spring. It is very probable that a pagan sanctuary at Kildare was Christianised by a holy woman called by the people after the Celtic goddess.

She is shown in the Lives to have had the power to multiply household items such as butter, bacon and milk, and to control the weather. Ó hÓgain shows that some narratives of the saint of Kildare were developed in the Middle Ages by additions from continental hagiography. A text from the ninth century tells of a man coming to woo the virgin Brigit. She is ordered to accept his hand in marriage, but she knocks out one of her eyes so as not to be attractive to him. When her family relents, she miraculously restores her eye. This story survived in the recent folklore of north Leinster and south Ulster. It was in fact taken from the lore of St Lucy and was suggested by the symbolism of light associated with both these holy virgins. It could also well be, Ó hÓgáin suggests, that some of the paraphernalia associated with Brigit in Irish folk life, such as processions of young girls with the leader dressed up as the saint, show the influence of the Lucy cult.

Foremost among the surviving customs associated with

Brigit is that of the Cros Bhríde (St Bríd's cross), woven from rushes or straw and placed under the rafters of the house and in cattle sheds, to ensure health and good fortune in the coming year. A piece of cloth is still left in places outside the door of the dwelling house from sunset to sunrise on the eve of 1 February, in the belief that it will be touched by the saint in passing; it is believed to have great curative properties. All over Ireland in years not so long gone by, it was the custom for girls in disguise to go from house to house, singing and dancing, collecting eggs or money. The leader of these girls was dressed as the saint and carried a doll known as a *brideog* (young Brid), in English a biddy.

**BRIOC** (m) About this saint, still venerated in Wexford, Georges Goyau wrote in the *Catholic Encyclopedia* (1913): 'An Irish saint, Briocus (Brieuc), who died at the beginning of the sixth century, founded in honour of St Stephen a monastery which afterwards bore his name, and from which sprang the town of Saint Brieuc . . . An inscription later than the ninth century on his tomb at Saint-Serge at Angers mentions him as the first bishop of Saint-Brieuc.' He is reputed to have been trained by St Germanus of Auxerre. Devotion to him spread to Ireland, England and Wales, and there is a holy well at the Burrow, Rosslare, dedicated to him.

**BRÓNACH** (f) *Brón* (sorrow); *brónach* (sorrowful). This was the given name of St Brónach of Kilbroney, Co. Down, of whom nothing much is known. She is revered in the district she lent her name to; her crozier is now in the care of the National Museum in Dublin and her bell is preserved in the Catholic church at Rostrevor, Co. Down. She is remembered on 2 April. Her name is acceptably anglicised as *Bronagh*, and this version is now quite popular. One Brónach told me that her mother gave her the name, thinking that it was an Irish translation of the Spanish name Dolores, which came from the Marian title *Maria de los Dolores* (Mary of the Sorrows), a reference to the seven sorrows of the virgin in Christian belief, *Seacht nDólás na Maighdine*

*Muire* in Irish. The feast of Our Lady's Dolours wasn't established until 1423. Our St Brónach lived 800 years before that.

**BUANAIT** (f) I have heard this name only once, in Co. Clare. *Buanait* (victorious woman) is a lovely old name. It comes from *buadh* (victory), probably. In the Finn stories, popular for many centuries until recently, *Buanait* was the daughter of the King of Norway.

# C

**CADHLA** earlier **CADHLAE** (m, f) This name for either a boy or girl means 'lovely'. The name was once very popular in Munster, particularly in Clare, Limerick and Waterford. In Waterford it was used almost exclusively for a girl in the nineteenth century. It gave the surname *Ó Cadhla*, anglicised as *Kiely* and *Queally*, common in the Déise territory. As a first name it was anglicised as *Kiely* or *Kylie*, and a well-known Irish-Australian chanteuse has made the name known the world over. As far as I know there is no saint bearing the name.

**CAILÍN** (f) The name Colleen is becoming increasingly popular in Ireland, having been confined to the United States and Australia until recently. It is from the Hiberno-English vocabulary word *colleen*, itself from Irish, *cailín* (girl). The name's popularity can be dated, it seems, from a fashion for Irish names in the America of the 1940s, particularly in Hollywood movies. I am told that Colleen is now being placed on some Irish school rolls as *Cailín*, which is the only justification for placing it as a headword above, as it was never previously used as a given name in Ireland. In Australia it is sometimes mistakenly taken as a feminine form of *Colin*.

**CAILLÍN** (m) This saint founded a monastery near Fenagh, near Ballinamore, Co. Leitrim, in either the fifth century or the sixth. His name means 'little cowl'. A fanciful account of the saint was written in the sixteenth century. When he returned from Rome after his ordination, he was greeted by St Patrick but was opposed by the local king Feargna and his druids. Caillín cursed both the king and the druids; Feargna was swallowed up by the ground and the druids were turned into boulders. The king's son was a forgiving fellow and he became Caillín's friend. He was extremely ugly, but the saint made him handsome as a reward for his friendship and conferred the kingship of the district on him. Caillín was regarded as a great sage and a prophet who could predict the fortunes of the great houses of the northern half of Ireland, including the O'Rourkes of Breffni.

**CAIMÍN** earlier **CAIMMÍNE** (m) This saint, whose name derived from *cam* (bent, stooped), is associated with the foundation of Inis Cealtra, also known as Holy Island in Lough Derg on the Shannon. It is one of the most important early Christian sites in Ireland, and Caimmíne was its abbot towards the middle of the seventh century. He died in 654. Nothing much is known of him, but his foundation is still impressive. A series of churches grace the place. One is dedicated to St Michael; another is Caimmíne's, which must have been a simple church to which a Romanesque chancel was added later; other churches are *Teampall na bhFear nGonta* (the church of the wounded men), St Brigit's and St Mary's. Given its position on Ireland's greatest waterway, it attracted the attention of the Viking predators, and some Irish predators as well; Brian Boru is given credit for carrying out reconstruction work on the site. A famous pattern was held there until 1838 when, according to John O'Donovan, it was suppressed because 'ill behaved young rascals', as he termed them, made a habit of kidnapping young women to use as 'fresh consorts for the ensuing year'. The pattern was held on Whitsun weekend. Caimmíne's feast day is 24 March. There is a lovely illuminated fragment of a psalm in the care of the Franciscan library in Killiney, Co. Dublin, which is ascribed to St Caimmíne, although it was written long after his time, in the late eleventh or early twelfth century. It may, however, have come originally from Inis Cealtra.

**CAINNEACH** The name means 'pleasant person'. This is the

saint who gave his name to Cill Chainnigh (Cainneach's church), now Kilkenny. He died around 600. His name is anglicised as *Canice* and *Kenneth*. He is one of the most important saints of the early Irish Church. He was well known and revered on the continent, and was invoked in the Pontifical of Basle in the ninth century, in a calendar of Reichenau in the same century, and in a psalter of Rheims a century later.

Here in Ireland he is generally spoken of as Cainneach of Aghaboe in Co. Laois. He was born, it is said, in Glengiven, Co. Derry. He was schooled at St Finnian's foundation at Clonard and at St Moibhí's at Glasnevin. He fled Ireland to Wales for a time when a plague struck; when he returned he set up foundations in both the north and south of the country. Cill Chainnigh, although it helped to preserve his name, was a minor monastery which did not gain fame until the coming of the Anglo-Normans. He was associated for a time with Colmcille's monastery at Iona, and while in Scotland he set up several foundations, among them Kilchennich in Tiree, another in South Uist, and another at Kintyre. He is said to have had his own little island in Scotland, near Colmcille's Iona; it is now called Inis Kenneth.

Dr Johnson and Boswell stayed there in 1773. Boswell got up during the night to pray to Colmcille beside a little chapel. On his way back he took fright at the thought of Scottish ghosts, goblins and things that go bump in the night, and fell, hurting his ankle. Johnson tells us that in the chapel 'is a bas relief of the blessed Virgin, and by it lies a little bell; which though cracked, and without a clapper, has remained there for ages, guarded only by the venerableness of the place'. Both bas relief and bell have since disappeared.

When Cainneach returned to Ireland his Lives say he had a run-in with the king of Meath, Colmán, who had abducted a nun and kept her on an island. When the king saw the saint come towards him in a fiery chariot, he repented and released the poor nun. Another story has Cainneach coming on a group of men about to kill a boy by dropping him from a height on to their upright spears. The saint caused the boy not to be injured by his fall, but, terrified by the ordeal, his eyes were crooked and never regained their focus. The boy's name was Dálua, and he afterwards became a famous saint, founding the monastery of Cill Dálua, Killaloe, Co. Clare. He was famous for seeking solitude, to be in the company only of birds and wild animals, especially the deer, much to the alarm of his monks at times.

Cainneach is described in the texts as bald and small, with great skill in both giving sermons and copying manuscripts, skills which, it was thought, were given to him by Christ himself. His feast day is 11 October.

**CAIREANN** earlier **CAIRENN** (f) *Caireann* is now being given to schoolchildren as a 'translation' of *Karin* and *Karen*. The names are in no way related. The Irish *Caireann* is a medieval borrowing of the Latin *Carina*, and the only woman in ancient times to bear this name was Cairenn Casdubh (of the dark, curly hair) who was, according to legend, the daughter of a king of the Britons and who became the mother of Niall of the Nine Hostages. This made her ancestress of the high kings of Ireland. Niall was the youngest of the five sons of Eochu, a slaver, the others being children of the king's legal wife Mongfhind. This lady hated her perceived rival, Cairenn, so she made a slave of the woman, entrusted with carrying water from a well all day long. Cairenn's baby was born near a well and she lay near the pail she was about to fill, because nobody dared to help her for fear of Mongfhind. Ravens were beginning to darken the sky above the new-born infant when the poet Torna came on the scene. He had the gift of prophecy and, recognising the greatness of the infant, he took the baby with him and reared him. When the child became a man Torna brought him to Tara, where they found Cairenn still carrying pails of water from the well. Niall caressed her and told her that never again would she be treated as a slave. He clothed her in purple, as befitted the mother of one who was to become the founder of one of Ireland's greatest dynasties.

**CAITRÍONA, CAITLÍN, CAITILÍN** (f) The Crusaders

brought home with them the name of a virgin martyr of Alexandria called *Catherine* who died about 307. Her cult flourished in Ireland through Norman and English influence, and by the fifteenth century the Old French forms *Caterine* and *Cateline* had been absorbed into Irish as *Caitríona* and *Caitilín*. There are many popular associated pet names, such as *Cáit*, *Tríona* and *Ríona*. The English versions of the name are very popular, especially *Kathleen*, *Kitty* and *Kay*. *Kate* was one of the most popular English pet names of the sixteenth century, and it has held its own since then both in Britain and in Ireland.

**CAOILTE** earlier **CAÍLTE** (m) It is surprising that the name of the great athlete of the Fianna declined in popularity after the ninth century; stories about him and his companions remained hugely popular in folklore until recent times. His name may mean 'hard'; others see in it a compound of *cael* (slender) and *te* (hot or fierce).

He was one of the greatest runners in literature; a text of the eighth century would give this impression. In this text Caoilte comes from the land of the dead in the south-west of Ireland to settle a row which had erupted concerning a warrior's grave in Ulster. He had to run all the way. His feat was reported again in the *Agallamh na Seanórach* (the Colloquoy of the Old Men), a tenth-century text, which has Caoilte running from Tonn Chlíodhna (Dingle Bay) to Tráigh Rudhraighe (Dundrum Bay) in a single day.

He ran other famous races. In one he bends the rules of sportsmanship somewhat. A hideous-looking hag challenged the Fianna to find a man to race her. Caoilte is chosen, and he sets off like the wind in front of her. When she catches up with him he turns around and cuts her head off with his sword.

Then there was the case of the beautiful woman from the fairy dwelling of Beann Eadair (Howth), who is beaten by Caoilte in a great race. Ó hÓgain points out that the contrasting images of hag and beautiful woman are those of the goddess of sovereignty.

Towards the end of the tenth century another story was written about Caoilte's prowess as a long-distance runner. When Fionn courted *Gráinne* at Tara, that *femme fatale* demanded the impossible: that he have delivered to her the male and female of every wild animal in Ireland in one single drove. Fionn asked Caoilte to help and he succeeded in bringing the great straggling herd to the woman.

Ó hÓgain quotes a late folk story concerning Caoilte the runner. 'The King of Ireland wished to have a fistful of sand brought to him every morning from each of the four shores of Ireland. By smelling the sand the king would know if an enemy had landed during the night. The first runner said that he would have the sands collected as quickly as a leaf falls from a tree. The king wasn't satisfied. A second said that he could do the job as fast as a cat slinking between two houses, but again this did not satisfy the king. Caoilte then offered to do the job as fast as a woman changes her mind. The king was impressed. "Off you go," he said. "Off you go and collect the sands."

"I have just returned with them!" said Caoilte.'

**CAOIMHE** (f) The name stems from *cáem* (dear, precious, beloved). It is a name which has grown quite popular in recent times. I know of only one saint of the name, a virgin associated with Killeavy, Co. Down. Nothing is known of this lady except her name and that her feast day is 2 November. Her name is anglicised as *Keeva*.

**CAOIMHÍN** earlier **CÁEMGEN** (m) This famous abbot and founder of the monastic settlement at Gleann Dá Locha (Glendalough) in Co. Wicklow has been anglicised as *Kevin*. It means 'beauteous birth'. Two biographies of the saint survive, in Irish and Latin, but they were both written centuries after the death of the saint around 618 and cannot be relied on. They state that he was born without any pain to his mother, which may account for the child's name. Twelve angels were present at his baptism, the biographies state, and he was reared on the milk of a mysterious white cow.

An angel advised him to become a priest and to go to Glendalough, the valley of the two lakes. There, wearing only the skins of animals and living in caves, he would use the bare stones of the place for a bed. He ordered a monster from the smaller of the two lakes into the bigger one, and from that day on man and beast could be cured of their illnesses by visiting the smaller lake. The illnesses were transferred to the bigger lake, where they entered the monster, rendering him so weak that he became harmless. Kevin was an animal lover, and it was said that while he prayed with his hands outstretched, a blackbird came and built her nest on the palm of his hand. The saint kept his hand in the same position until the bird's nestlings were fledged.

A herdsman, whose cow gave a marvellous milk yield through being in contact with the saint, helped him build his foundation in the beautiful valley, and soon he was joined by other men. He was credited with bringing the dead back to life. Most of the medieval legends about him have survived in local folklore. Perhaps the best known of these is the story of a young woman, beautiful of course, who fell in love with him and who, according to the medieval literature, was driven away by the saint with nettles. She afterwards became a nun. A surviving folk legend has the lady climbing up the precipice that rises from the larger lake to the saint's bed in a cave, only to be flung down into the waters below by an angry Cáemgen. They say that no larks ever sing in Glendalough because the saint, angry with them for waking the men who were building his church too early in the morning, banished them.

Beautiful Glendalough was one of the greatest centres of learning in early medieval Ireland. Though cruelly vandalised in the eighteenth and nineteenth centuries by visitors who stole many of its ancient artifacts, its remains are still beautiful, although its peace is shattered by busloads of tourists nowadays. Its founder's feast day is 3 June.

**CAOMHÁN** (m) The principal saint of this name is associated with Wexford, principally with Árd Chaomháin (Ardcavan), on the shores of Wexford Harbour, with Cill Chaomháin (Kilcavan) in Bannow, and with another place of the same name in the parish of Kilanerin. He is sometimes thought of as a brother of

St Kevin of Glendalough. Said in *Félire Óengusso* to have been looked after as a young boy by a queen of Leinster called Sanctlethan, his name means 'gentle, beloved, or friend'. His feast day is 7 June.

**CARA** (f) A twentieth-century coinage, possibly of Irish-American origin and invariably mispronounced kar-ah, it is the Irish word for 'friend'. The suggestion that it is from the Italian term of endearment *cara* (beloved) may be discarded, because the name was never used as a first name in Italy or indeed among Italian-Americans.

**CARTHACH** (m) The name means 'strong man, or lover'. A native of Kerry, Carthach was a hermit for some years before joining several communities in turn; around 595 he formed the community at Rathan in Offaly. His rule was very strict and forbade his monks to have any property, even horses or oxen to be used in tilling. The foundation seems to have caused jealousy among neighbouring monasteries, and at the insistence of a local chief, Carthach and his monks moved south to lovely Lismore, Co. Waterford, where he established one of the most famous monastic schools in Ireland. Carthach was also known as *Mochuda* and his name has been anglicised as *Carthage*.

He had a great way of recruiting women to the monastic life, if one can believe a story related of him. He was, it was said, the most handsome man in Ireland, and at one stage 50 beauties wanted to seduce him. He prayed and prayed, and all 50 were miraculously attracted to a life of piety and became nuns. A great secular bearer of the name was Carthach mac Saírbrethaig, ancestor of the powerful Munster family, the MacCarthys.

**CASS** (m) This old and lovely name means 'curly haired'. It was given as a nickname to boys no matter what their given names in Co. Clare while Irish was spoken in that county, according to Anraí de Blác, one of the last native speakers of the region. The most famous Cass was the supposed ancestor of the Dál Cais, comprised of the MacNamaras, O'Briens and O'Grady clans among others. There is a saint, Cass of Bangor, whose feast day is 26 April.

**CASSAIR** (f) A holy woman of this name, which probably comes from *cass* (curly haired), was said to be a follower of St Kevin. According to one legend she upbraided him for being dressed in tatters and instructed him to clothe himself properly. He refused. She was so impressed by his humility that she asked him to allow her to place herself and her women followers under his rule. The good man consented.

**CATHAL** (m) This old name has been anglicised as *Charles*; likewise the name Charles has been gaelicised as *Cathal*; but the names have no connection with one another. The most famous Cathal in history was probably Cathal Crob Derg (Cathal Mór of the Wine-red Hand), king of Connacht, who died in 1224. Cathal Mac Fionguine, who died in 742, was king of Munster. He is remembered as a patron of poets and as a most generous man, as well as living up to the meaning of his name, 'fierce in battle'. He was buried in St Ailbhe's (p. 3) foundation at Emly. A very interesting man who bore the name was Cathal or Cathaldus of Taranto in southern Italy who is remembered on 10 May. His cult is widespread, extending all over Italy, Malta, Sicily and parts of France. San Cataldo is invoked against plague, tempest and drought, and is prayed to by sailors. His image, Pochin Mould tells us, is painted on a pillar in the basilica of the Nativity at Bethlehem. The strange thing is that many of the legends about him, including his connection with Taranto as bishop of that see, may be simply that—legends. His liturgical cult stems from the discovery of his relics in 1071. When his body was found, a small pectoral cross was found with it, thought to date from the seventh or eighth century, bearing the inscription 'Cathaldus Rachau'. Where Rachau is, nobody knows. One continental scholar, J. Hennig, who has written about Cathal, thinks that it is simply an Italian's idea of what an Irish placename should sound like—a far-fetched notion, I think. At any rate the Benedictines and the Normans helped spread the cult of this saint, who was certainly an Irishman, and a much revered one at that.

*Cathalán* is a diminutive. It was once found mainly in southern Ireland.

**CATHAOIR** earlier **CATHAÍR** (m) This name, still popular in the north as *Cathair*, is anglicised in many places as *Cahir* and *Charles*. Scholars differ as to the name's origin. Some say it means 'battle lord'; others think that its origin lies in some language unknown to us. Cathaír Mór was claimed to have reigned at Tara, possibly in the fourth century. The medieval *Dindsheanchas*, the mythical geography of Ireland, has two accounts of him. In one, a drunken guest called Garman stole the queen's coronet after a feast hosted by Cathaír at Tara, and made off towards the mouth of the River Slaney, pursued by the king and his soldiery. He was caught and drowned when the lough overflowed. Hence, we are asked to believe, the place was named Loch Garman—a fanciful story. As is another quite beautiful one, told by the same author, Eochaid Eolach Ó Céirín, which connects Cathaír with the ancient sovereignty of Leinster.

**CEARBHALL** earlier **CERBALL** (m) This name possibly means 'brave in sword-play' or 'fierce in battle'. It is an ancient name and was given to many kings who distinguished themselves as warriors, among them an Ossory king of the Viking period, Cerball mac Dungaile who died in 888, and Cerball mac Muireacáin, king of Leinster, who died in 909. It became a favourite name among Leinster people in the later Middle Ages and was particularly liked by the Ó Dálaighs (O'Dalys), the famous bardic family who, the story had it, were given the gift of poetry by a Dálach, who was bequeathed it by the reputed founder of the early Christian monastery of Cloyne, Co. Cork, Colmán mac Leinéini, himself a poet.

There were some illustrious poets of the Ó Dálaigh family called Cearbhall. One who lived in the thirteenth century was a small boy who worked for a farmer. He was asked every evening after his day's work if he had seen anything strange during the day as he was herding the cows. He always replied truthfully that he hadn't, until one day he saw a wondrous cloud descend on a bunch of rushes; a brindle cow went among the rushes and ate them. The boy, Cearball, was told to bring the first milk from that cow to the farmer. He did so, but spilled some of the milk on his finger and sucked it off. From that day on he never spoke except in verse.

Another poet bearing the name Cearbhall Ó Dalaigh lived in Pallis, Co. Wexford, in the early seventeenth century. He is said to have fallen in love with Eleanor Kavanagh, daughter of Sir Morgan Kavanagh of Clonmullen Castle, Co. Carlow. Two love poems about Eleanor survive.

An extraordinary folk narrative has blossomed from this love of the poet for Eleanor. A beautiful love song which was popular since the sixteenth century was called 'Eibhlín, a Rún'; it was addressed by an unknown man to a lady of that time. Because Eibhlín sounds like Eleanor, the song was attributed to Cearbhall Ó Dalaigh from Pallis in the folklore.

The distinguished fifth President of Ireland was another Cearbhall Ó Dálaigh. A lawyer of international repute, he was born in Bray, and died in Dublin in 1978.

The name has been acceptably anglicised as *Caroll* and *Carl.*

**CEASAIR** earlier **CESSAIR** (f) This fictional woman, whose name is no longer given to children although it appears in some nineteenth-century Irish fiction based in the north of Ireland, was said to be the leader of the first ever settlement in Ireland. The popular pseudo-history of the Middle Ages depicts her as the grand-daughter of Noah, and says that she arrived in Ireland in an attempt to escape the Flood. Why Ireland? one might ask. Because 'she liked a place where no man or woman had set foot previously, which was therefore free from evil and free from sin. There were no monsters in Ireland and no reptiles, and she knew that the place would be free from the Flood.'

She landed in Kerry in the Dingle Peninsula, but two of her three ships broke up in a storm as she approached land. Fifty women and three men survived: Cessair's father Bith, son of

Noah, Ladra the pilot, and Fintán (p. 94). The men divided the women between them and Cessair was part of Fintán's share. The Irish climate obviously did not suit Bith and Ladra and they died, leaving Fintán to look after their women. The prospect daunted him and he fled from them. Poor Cessair missed him so much that she died of a broken heart. The other women followed her; Fintán alone remained.

Ó hÓgain gives another account. It states that Noah had refused entry into his Ark to the three men because he considered them robbers, and that Cessair offered to bring them to safety if they accepted her leadership. An idol she consulted told her to travel to Ireland.

Cessair is said to be the person who brought the first sheep into Ireland.

**CELLACH** (m, f) A male saint of this name was a great reformer of the eleventh-century Irish Church and patron of St Máel Máedóc, better known nowadays by his corrupted name, Malachy of Armagh. The name means 'bright-headed', according to Maguire and Ó Corráin, not 'frequenter of churches' as some think. His name was latinised as *Celsus*. Very little is known about Cellach except that he was adopted by Máel Máedóc as his vicar at Armagh. A consummate politician, he spent a lot of his time touring the country on visitations, with the purpose of collecting dues, asserting the position of Armagh and mediating in disputes between princes and local rulers. The country and the Church had suffered a lot from the Northmen, and reforms were needed. Cellach presided at the reforming Synod of Ráth Breasail in 1110 in which the reforms of the earlier Synod of Cashel were reinforced and the Church divided into formal dioceses with two archbishoprics. In 1121 Cellach went on a circuit of Munster. The following year, the death of the bishop of Dublin caused quite a rumpus. The Norsemen sent a candidate to Canterbury to be consecrated, but Cellach was able to get his own candidate appointed, much to the delight of the Irish of Dublin. In doing so he ended the dependence of Dublin on Canterbury. He died at Ardpatrick on 1 April 1129 on one of his travels through Munster, and was buried at Lismore on 4 April. St Bernard called him 'a good and holy man'.

There was a female *Cellach*, the daughter of Donnchad, an east Cork king, who died in 732.

*Cellachán* or *Ceallachán* is a diminutive of Cellach and was popular among Munster families such as the O'Herlihys of west Cork, the O'Callaghans and the MacCarthys.

**CIABHÁN** (m) In ancient lore he was the handsome man of the Tuatha Dé Danann who eloped with Clíona (p. 44) from Tír Tairngire (the Land of Promise), only to see her drowned in his boat by a gigantic wave in Glandore Bay, Co. Cork, as he was hunting for a meal for them ashore. Anglicised *Keevaun*.

**CIAN** (m) The name, which means 'ancient', belonged to two heroes of mythology, Cian Cúldubh (of the black hair), a Leinsterman, and Cian, son of Ailill Ólum, mythical king of Munster.

A Cian Mac Maolmhuaidhe married the daughter of Brian Boru, Sadhbh, and is the subject of an old romance called *Leigheas Coise Chéin* (the Healing of Cian's Leg). It deals with the journey of a man called Ó Cronagáin to the dwelling of Brian Boru at Kincora to seek promised redress for a wrong done to him. On his way home his hounds coursed a hare which, jumping on to his chest, was transformed into a beautiful woman of the Otherworld whom he promptly seduced. He brought her home with him, and she stayed with him for three years, his wife having conveniently gone away. He entertained Brian Boru and his son-in-law Cian, and the latter fell in love with the fairy woman. He attempted to have his way with her, but she was transformed into a mare and ran away, kicking Cian in the leg and breaking it. All the physicians in Munster failed to heal it, but this was eventually done by a man who came from Rheims in France and told a convoluted story about once having a sweetheart from the Otherworld who banished him after he had slighted her. He tells Cian of his adventures in France, including his procurement of a woman for the king, and of his own success in marrying the daughter of the German Emperor. He was unfortunate. His wife was taken from him by a warrior who left him bound for a year. He then wounded himself in the leg with his own spear, but was healed by a lovely princess from Orkney who used a special poultice. He applied this poultice to Cian's leg, and lo and behold the leg was healed.

The name Cian is associated particularly with the O'Mahony clan.

**CIANÁN** (m) A diminutive of *Cian*, it is sometimes anglicised *Keenan*. One Cianán of note was the founder of Duleek, Co. Meath. Its history began about 450 when St Patrick set up a bishopric there and appointed Cianán to the see. Possibly because the first church in Duleek was built of stone, Cianán became a patron saint of stonemasons. He died on 29 November 489.

**CIARA** is an ancient name, and for some reason it is gaining in popularity in Britain among people who are not of Irish descent. It derives from the word *ciar* (dark or black). Anglicised *Kyra*, *Keera* and *Keerah*. The most famous and certainly the most saintly of Irish women bearing this name was St Ciara of Kilkeary, near Nenagh, Co. Tipperary. She was a friend of St Brendan of Clonfert. The old story has it that one day Brendan called on her to extinguish a fire that blazed out of control and threatened not alone his monastery but the surrounding district. The good woman said a prayer and the fire was miraculously put out. As her little community grew she decided to look further afield for a site, and was given one by St Fintan Munnu (p. 95) of Taghmon, Co. Wexford. She died in 679 and she has two feast days: 5 January and 16 October.

**CIARÁN** (m) There were two great saints of this name. One was *Ciarán of Cluain* who died around 550, the founder of the great monastery of Cluain Mhic Nóis (Clonmacnoise) in Co. Offaly, on the Shannon. The saint's biography, written there in the ninth century in Latin and Irish, says that his father was a carpenter called Beoán who was a member of the Dál nAraidhe sept of Antrim and Down, and his mother was Dar Erca (p. 61), a Kerrywoman. When Ciaran was in her womb his greatness was foretold, it was said, by Patrick, Brigid and Colmcille. The high king's druid announced that the chariot in which Dar Erca travelled sounded as though it carried a monarch.

In his youth Ciarán showed the traits of a hero. He restored a dead horse, the property of the high king's son, to life. He slew a huge hound which attacked him, as Cú Chulainn had done. He was trained at St Finian's foundation at Clonard, Co. Meath. He had asked his mother to allow him to take a cow from her herd with him, but she refused him. So he blessed a dun-coloured cow and it followed him. This was the famous 'odhar Chiaráin' (the dun of Ciarán); it gave enough milk to feed the whole monastery and the surrounding countryside. A later legend has it that *Lebor na hUidhre* (the Book of the Dun Cow) was written on parchment made from the skin of Ciarán's cow (in actual fact the book was not penned until centuries after Ciarán's time). Somebody wrote an irreverent limerick about the matter to win a prize offered by the custodians of the book, the Royal Irish Academy, some years back. It went: 'Said Ciaran to his cow after Mass / You're dun and you'll get no more grass, / For the scholars and scribes are descending in tribes / To write sagas all over your ass.'

Several legends of the saint from the folklore of the Clonmacnoise area are recounted by Ó hÓgáin. It was said that a local chieftain refused him food when he was very hungry, and Ciarán threatened that the man would die of thirst. And this happened, because every time the chieftain put a goblet to his mouth the drink disappeared. Another man had the temerity to tell Ciarán that he was no more a saint 'than the robin on that bush beyond'. No sooner had he said these words than Ciarán changed into a robin and flew to a hawthorn bush near by. The man fell on his knees and begged pardon; the saint returned to his usual shape.

Ciarán, founder of the great monastery and school at Clonmacnoise, is celebrated on 9 September. The name Ciarán means 'the little dark-haired one'. His name is anglicised as *Kieran* and *Kieren*.

The other famous Ciarán is *Ciarán of Saighir*, or Seir Kieran, in Co. Offaly. After schooling in Europe he became a hermit in the Slieve Bloom Mountains, where his only companions were the wild animals which roamed there. But his fame as a holy man ensured that disciples came to him from near and far, and in time his hermitage became a famous monastery. The two Ciaráns met occasionally. One legend has it that a landowner from Clonmacnoise quenched the perpetual fire that the monastery of Saighir had burning before it. He was eaten by wolves on the way home. Ciarán from Clonmacnoise went to Saighir and restored the flames with fire sent from heaven; he then restored the landowner to life. On another occasion when the two saints met at Saighir, Ciarán from Clonmacnoise prayed that the monastery of his friend would be always wealthy; the older man from Saighir prayed that Clonmacnoise would be famed for wisdom always.

The kings of Ossory were brought to Saighir for burial. Ciarán's feast day is 5 March.

**CIARNAIT** earlier **CIARNAT** (f) An ancient name this, and it has survived. I know of two Ciarnaits, luckily all brunettes because the name means 'dark lady'. The legendary King Cormac Mac Airt had a lady friend called Ciarnait.

**CILLÍN** earlier **CILLÍNE** (m) Acceptably anglicised as *Kilian* and *Killian*. There are many saints who bore this name, which derived from *cell* (a church, a cell): among them are Cillíne ua Colla of Fanad, Co. Donegal (3 January); Cillíne of the Déise (26 March); and Cillíne of Tallanstown, Co. Louth (27 May). Another Kilian left Ireland with 11 companions and landed at the mouth of the Rhine. Having made a Christian of Duke Gozbert, he went to Rome to see the Pope in 686 and returned to his mission to find that the Duke had married his brother's widow. A row followed and Kilian and two companions were murdered on the orders of the furious lady. Kilian's relics were transferred to Wurzburg and he quickly became one of the principal saints of that part of Germany. He is still revered there. His feast day is 8 July.

Yet another Kilian was a contemporary of Fiacre or Fiachra. He arrived in Meaux after a pilgrimage to Rome and the bishop of the place, Faro, gave him a hermitage at Aubigny, near Arras. He remained there for the rest of his life. His feast day is 13 November.

**CINNSEALACH** earlier **CENNSALACH** (m) This name, used in some Wexford families until around 1700, means 'proud, masterful'. The legendary Énna Cennselach was perhaps the most famous bearer of the name. He is the supposed ancestor of the royal house of south Leinster and of the Kinsellas, MacMurroughs, Murphys and Maddocks.

**CIONAODH** earlier **CINÁED** (m) It is said that this name was borrowed into Old Irish from Pictish, but this has never been proved. Hanks and Hodges say that the name may mean 'born of fire'. The name was that given by the Irish to the first king of the Picts and Scots, Cináed mac Ailpín, who died in 860. In Ireland it was the given name of the High King Cináed mac Irgalaig, who reigned about 724. He seems to have had an influence on the name's popularity.

The name was and is very popular among the planter stock of Ulster and in Scotland in its anglicised form *Kenneth* and in its diminutive *Kenny*. It also has the feminine forms *Kenna* and *Kenina*. The name has achieved popularity in Scandinavia where its derivatives are *Kennet* and *Kent*, and in the United States where it was brought by Scandinavian immigrants in the nineteenth century.

**CLÍONA, CLÍODHNA** earlier **CLÍDNA** (f) Reputed sister of Aoibheall (p. 6). A queen of the Otherworld, a medieval story has her falling in love with the god Aengus (p. 8) and going to meet him in a boat made of bronze. She was accompanied by a scoundrel who played magic music which caused her to fall asleep while a great flood drowned her at Cuan Dor (the Bay of Glandore), Co. Cork. Another story makes her one of the Tuatha Dé Danann who eloped from the Land of Promise with a man named Ciabhán (p. 40). They landed at Glandore strand and Ciabhán left her in his boat while he went ashore to hunt. A great wave came and drowned her. Ó hÓgáin points out that these accounts seem to have arisen from an actual designation of the tide at that place as the wave (tonn) of Clíona. Tonn Chlíona is one of the great waves of Ireland, according to the ancient topographical system. Clíona is, they say, still seen gambolling in the moonlight at the rock named after her at Kilshannig, near Mallow, and people keep well away from the place at night for fear of being abducted by her and her fairy friends.

**CLODAGH** (f) The name may have originated in that of a river in Co. Tipperary, the Clodagh, in Irish *Clóideach*. It is said that Henry de la Poer Beresford, Marquis of Waterford, was the first to give that river name to a child when he christened his daughter Lady Clodagh Beresford, born in April 1875.

There is also a Clodagh river in north Wexford. It rushes into the Slaney at the lovely village of Bunclody at the foot of the Blackstairs Mountains. Bunclody, in Irish Bun Clóidí, means 'the end of the little Clóideach, Clodagh or Clody river'. The river name is found in many places in Ireland: as Claudy in Derry, and in the townlands Clady Beg, Clady More and Clady Water in Armagh. There are also Clodiagh rivers in Waterford and in Tipperary, and there is a Clydagh river in Mayo. The root of the word means 'I wash, I clean', and so the meaning of the name of the river would be 'the clean one' or 'the one which cleans'.

**CÓILÍN** (m) This name is found only in Connemara. It may be a pet form of *Colmán* (p. 47).

**COLLA** (m) This ancient name means 'powerful chieftain' or 'great lord' and it was very popular among the people of Airghialla (Oriel), comprising the Counties Monaghan and Armagh and parts of Tyrone and Louth, until the beginning of the twentieth century. It was sometimes anglicised there as *Coll* and *Colley*.

*Colla* was the name of three mythical brothers, Colla Uais, Colla Meann and Colla Fochra, who were supposed to have lived in the fourth century A.D. The medieval pseudo-historians established the traditions surrounding them by the eighth century. They were supposed to be nephews of the High King Fiachu Sraibhthine, son of Cairbre Lifeachair. This Fiachu had a magnificent warrior son called Muireadach Tíreach who did most of his fighting for him. He once made a foray into Munster, and while he was away the three Collas decided to seize the high kingship for themselves. Poor Fiachu was warned by his chief druid that he had a momentous decision to make: either to win the war with the Collas but suffer the consequence of never having a king among his descendants; or to lose the war and be killed, which would ensure that his descendants would hold the throne. Fiachu chose the latter option, and was slain by the Collas at the battle of Dubhchumar, where the Boyne and Blackwater rivers meet. After the battle the three Collas fled before Muireadach Tíreach who, on hearing of his father's death, marched from Munster. The brothers went to Scotland where they spent a few years before returning to Ireland. Muireadach forgave them for slaying his father and advised them to go north and devastate Ulster. His ultimate aim seems to have been the total destruction of the royal seat at Emhain Mhacha. The Collas, aided by Connacht mercenaries, won seven great battles against the men of Ulster and set up a kingship for themselves in Oriel. The stories surrounding their conquest of Ulster became the stuff of medieval legend and literature.

**COLM** earlier **COLUMB** (m, f) This was a very popular name in ancient Ireland, given to over thirty saints, some of them female. The name is from Latin *columba* (a dove). The most famous saint of the name is *Colmcille* or *Columba* of Iona, the patron saint of Scotland whose feast day is 9 June. He is the object of a widespread cult both in Ireland and Scotland and legends surround his name, most of which may be marked 'of doubtful authenticity'. His sites at Iona, Durrow and Kells, with their magnificent high crosses, are proof of his legacy, best described in the *Vita Columbae* by Adamnán, ninth abbot of Iona, who wrote the work about 685.

Colmcille was born at Gartan, Co. Donegal, of royal blood, a descendant, it was claimed, of Niall of the Nine Hostages (p. 138). From the place known subsequently as Doire (the modern Derry), his first monastic foundation, he began his apostolate setting up foundations in many places in Ireland. He then went to Scotland to the island of Iona, where his courage and his political astuteness led to the success of Irish missionary endeavours. The story of his involvement in the copyright case with St Finian of Moville (p. 89) is thought to be fiction; but the *Cathach*, the battle book of the O'Donnells and carried by them in their wars, is real and may be in Colmcille's own hand. It is now in the possession of the Royal Irish Academy.

The *Vita Columbae* contains many fascinating stories about Columba. In the second section of the account we hear for the very first time the story of the world-famous Lough Ness monster. When Columba sat down to take his ease on the banks of the Ness he was approached by a group of people who were about to bury a man who had been swimming in the lake and was bitten by a water monster, 'aquatalis bestia'. They told the saint that the man's body had been recovered by a couple of boatmen using grappling hooks. Colm asked one of his own men to swim across the lake and bring him back a boat. As the man, who was named Lugne, was halfway to where the boats were bobbing in the lake water, a monster reared his head and rushed towards Lugne with its mouth wide open. Colmcille raised his hand, made the sign of the cross and commanded the monster to be gone. The beast did as it was told and disappeared into the depths of the lough.

Colmcille's feast day is 9 June.

**COLMA** (f) See *Colmán*

**COLMÁN** (m) This name is derived from Latin *columba* (a dove). The suffix *-án* is a diminutive; the name means 'little dove'. A very popular name in ancient Ireland, *Colma* was the female version. The most famous of the many saints of the name are Colmán of Cloyne whose feast day is 24 November; Colmán Mac Duach, patron of Kilmacduagh (2

January); Colmán of Kilcolman, Co. Offaly (20 May); Colmán of Lismore, Co. Waterford (22 January); and Koloman the Pilgrim who was hanged on an elder tree in Stockerau in 1012 because he was thought to be a Bohemian spy. He was the patron saint of Austria until 1663, and is venerated by mountaineers who ask for his protection against avalanches and storms.

There is a beautiful ninth-century Latin poem in the British Museum written by an old monk called Colmán to a younger one of the same name, who decided to abandon his mission and return to Ireland, probably because of home-sickness. He left with the old man's blessing. Here is his poem in Helen Waddell's translation:

So, since your heart is set on those sweet fields
And you must leave me here,
Swift be your going, heed not any prayers,
Although the voice be dear.

Vanquished thou art by love of thine own land,
And who shall hinder love?
Why should I blame thee for thy weariness,
And try thy heart to move.

Since, but if Christ would give me back the past,
And that first strength of days,
And this white head were dark again
I too might go your ways.

Hear me, my son; little I have to say:
Let the world's pomp by.
Swift it is as a wind, an idle dream,
Smoke in an empty sky.

Go to the land where love gives thee no rest,
And may Almighty God,
Hope of our life, lord of the sounding sea,
Of winds and waters lord,

Give thee safe passage on the wrinkled sea.
Himself thy pilot stand,
Bring thee through mist and foam to thy desire,
Again to Irish land.

Live, and be famed and happy: all the praise
Of honoured life to thee.
Yes, all this world can give thee of delight,
And then, eternity.

**COLUMBÁN** (m) This is the man described by one scholar as the man 'who hurled the fire of Christ wheresoever he could, without concerning himself with the blaze it caused'; by another as 'Ireland's greatest missionary to date'; and by Pius IX as 'the man who spearheaded the renaissance of Christian learning in Italy, Germany and France'. *Columbán* or Columbanus was born somewhere in Leinster, his biographer and near contemporary, Jonas, a monk of Columban's foundation in Bobbio, wrote. He went to school at Cleenish on Lough Erne and from there to St Comgall's foundation at Bangor. Eventually he headed for the continent with St Gall and 12 others and founded settlements at Annegray, Luxeuil, and Fontaine in the Vosges. He was almost deported for insulting Queen Brunhild's son for loose living, and he had to defend the harshness of his monasteries in front of Pope Gregory I. He eventually reached Bregenz on Lake Constance, where he engaged in vehement argument with another Pope, Boniface IV. His rule was very severe and its demise and replacement by the less strict rule of St Benedict was greeted with relief by the monks who followed him. He came to Bobbio in 614, and died there a year later.

His emblem is a bear, some say because of his fighting qualities, others because he was said to have been unafraid of wild animals. There were stories told of his attachment to one particular bear, which was forced by the saint to give up its lair in a cave to him as a temporary hermitage; other stories tell of his fondness for packs of wolves, and of their fondness for him. The great missionary is remembered to this day everywhere his travels took him.

**COMGHALL** earlier **COMGALL** (m) There are many saints who bore this name, but one is pre-eminent, Comgall of Bangor, a man who, according to the *Martyrology of Donegal*, 'kindled in the hearts of men an unquenchable fire of the love of God'. One scholar wrote of him that his monument is stamped on the history of Europe, for Comgall and his monastery of Bangor sent the party headed by Columbán and Gall to the continent, and Moluag of Lismore and Maelrubha to Scotland.

He was born in what is now Co. Antrim at the beginning of the sixth century and founded

Bangor around 555. He died in the early years of the seventh century. He is mentioned in Adamnán's *Vita* of Columba and in a twelfth-century Life, possibly a version of a much earlier one written in Bangor. One story has it that Comgall first studied with a cleric who kept a mistress and, disgusted, headed for a foundation which had a reputation for asceticism. After a time there he went home and was ordained by a bishop Lugaid. He then went to Lough Erne and founded on an island in the lake the monastery of Ely. His rule was so harsh that it was said to have led to the death of some of his monks. Some of the usual stories were told about him: that he prayed standing in the lake water; and that his cell was lit up at night by a mysterious glow.

Eventually he founded the great monastery of Bangor, an ideal location, as it was on the shores of Belfast Lough, on the shipping route to Scotland and the famous monastery of Candida Casa, and also on the route to the continent via Britain. An old litany of Irish saints speaks of 'four thousand monks under the yoke of Comgall of Bangor'.

The Ambrosian Library in Milan holds the greatest relic of Bangor, the famous Antiphony, which dates from between 680 and 691. It contains the beautiful *Sancti venite*, a long statement on the Church's teaching on the Blessed Sacrament.

Most of Comgall's poems are addressed to Christ, in reaction perhaps to the Arian heresy which denied Christ's divinity.

**COMHDHÁN** earlier **COMGÁN** (m) This extraordinary character is said to have lived in the seventh century. St Cuimmíne Fata's stepbrother, he was said to have been as wise as Solomon and as mad as a March hare in equal measure. One account describes him as 'the chief poet of Ireland and the chief fool of Ireland'. The stories relate that when he was mad he could walk on water and sleep at the bottom of a lake or river, where the fish would look after him. Above ground he could sleep out even in the worst of weather because the birds would build shelters for him. He became a fool as a result of an affair he had with the wife of his father's druid. This man cast a spell on a wisp of grass and flung it in Comhdhán's face, causing him to go mad and to be a perpetual wanderer. St Cuimmíne took pity on him and liked to converse with him. Such was his knowledge that he could solve the most abstruse theological problems for the saint. Many of his adventures are recorded in a humorous biography called *Imtheachta na nOinmhídhe* (The Adventures of the Fools). In one episode he sets off with the high king's jester, Conall Clogach, on a tour of Connacht. When they came to the king's fortress in Roscommon they were well received there, but at supper they complained about the quality of the butter. Conall flung it into the fire, where it blazed up threatening the roof. Comhdhán threw flax on the flames and Conall threw straw after it; the house went up in flames. They fled, and eventually after many adventures came to the house of King Finghein of Munster, who received them hospitably. Conall stole meat from the kitchen and his companion told him he was a disgrace. So they parted company, Conall going north to Ulster, while Comhdhán went to see his friend St Cuimmíne Fata. The saint gave Comhdhán a hermitage at a place named Inis Glinne, where he built a fish weir and lived happily as a hermit in prayer and contemplation until he died in the arms of the saint.

**CONALL** (m) The name means 'strong as a wolf'. This is a very ancient name, still found extensively in Ulster, especially in Donegal among the O'Donnells, O'Friels, Gallaghers, Wards and O'Dohertys. This is not surprising, as Conall Gulban, ancestor of the O'Donnells, gave his name to Tír Chonaill (now Co. Donegal). There were other legendary Conalls. notably Conall Cernach, the mythical hero of the Ulster Cycle. Some of the texts in which he is mentioned continued to be copied until fairly recent times, and so his fame came to the attention of modern oral storytellers. In Ulster folklore he is said to have joined the Roman army and was present at the Crucifixion. When he returned to Ireland he was so utterly dejected that people began to ask him why this was so. He answered that if they had seen what he had seen they would be as dejected as he was.

Conall Corc founded the kingship of Cashel, and Conall Echluath (as fast as a steed) was thought to be the ancestor of the O'Briens of Thomond. There are some saints of this name, notably St Conall of Iniskeen, near Glenties, Co. Donegal, whose pattern day is 22 May. He was said to be the Irish equivalent of St Jude, patron of hopeless cases. Conall is sometimes anglicised *Connell*.

**CONÁN** (m) A mischievous, thoroughly nasty member of the Fianna, the warrior band presided over by Fionn Mac Cumhaill. His name means 'little hound', but figuratively *cú* also meant 'warrior'. A brother of the great warrior Goll Mac Morna, he was noted for his scurrilous language. He appears in many weird tales associated with the Fianna. He was reputed to have had a magically destructive eye and folklore has preserved his reputation as a killer who destroyed his enemies by looking at them through his fingers. He was known as Conán Maol (bald Conán). There is an amusing story of the Fianna being stuck to the floor in a magic dwelling. They were released by the application of a magic liquid, but there was not enough left to free Conán; he was released by his companions by pulling him forcibly from his seat, leaving the skin of his backside behind him. Anglicised *Conan*, it is Sherlock Holmes' creator's middle name; and the name given to that extraordinary film creation, Conan the Barbarian.

**CONCHÚR** earlier **CONCHOBHAR, CONCHOBAR** (m) This ancient name which may mean 'hound-lover' or 'wolf-lover' or, as Calvert Watkins believes, may be a compound of *cú* (hound, figuratively warrior) and *cobhar* (desirous), has been popular from the later Middle Ages. It is still favoured among the people of west Cork and Kerry, although there it is used in some of its fifteenth-century manifestations, *Cornelius*, which later gave *Neilus* and *Con*. *Conor* is a more acceptable form found in many other districts.

Perhaps the most famous of those who bore the name was Conchobar mac Nessa, mythical king of Ulster in the time of the Red Branch Knights.

There are various legends about his conception and birth. One of these has Fachtna Fáthach, a high king, as his father. Another has Neas, his mother, as the daughter of a king called Eochu Sálbhuidhe. Her 12 foster-brothers were murdered by the druid-warrior Cathbhadh as they drank together. Neas, earlier Ness, went berserk as she ravaged the country looking for their killer; she was bathing in a lake when Cathbhadh came on her and took her. Their child was Conchobar.

The fact that he was a potent fertility figure is evinced by the myths of him sleeping with all the brides of his kingdom on the first night of their wedding; he also had his pleasure in every household he stayed in on his travels around Ireland. His sister Dechtine was the mother of Cú Chulainn, but another story has it that Conchobar fathered the great Ulster warrior with his own sister. The general picture of him that emerges is of a wise, generous king whose kingdom prospered during his reign, but this does not tally with his cruel role in the tragedy of Deirdre (p. 64).

Only the late story of his death survives in folklore. The Leinster king Meas Geaghra was slain by the Connacht warrior Ceat, who kept his foe's brain ball as a trophy. He used it in his sling in an attempt to kill Conchobar; the ball lodged in Conchobar's brain for seven years while he remained seated, ordered by his doctors not to exert himself. One day he noticed the earth trembling and the sun darkening, and his druid Cathbhadh told him that a good man called Jesus Christ had been killed in the East. Outraged, Conchobar got angry and the ball fell from his head, killing him. He was baptised in his own blood before he died.

**CONLAO** earlier **CONLAODH, CONLÁED** (m) The name is found in Irish prehistory but the Conláed mentioned in the early lists of saints died in 516, according to the *Annals of Inisfallen*. Conláed, son of Cormac of a sept of Crích Chualann, in modern times an area about the size of the diocese of Glendalough, Co. Wicklow, was much venerated in west Wicklow and in Kildare.

Very little is known of him except that the lore connected with St Brigid says that he was a hermit, and that the great Abbess of Kildare enticed him to come and live near her community. He gained fame as a skilled metalworker. He is known in English as *Conleth.* A well-known Dublin private school is named from him. So was the poet Conleth Ellis.

**CONLAOCH** earlier **CONLAÍ** (m) This man was one of the tragic heroes of the Ulster Cycle. His story first appears in the ninth-century text called *Aided Oenfir Aife* (The Death of Aoife's Only Son). The story has it that when Cú Chulainn was learning his trade in arms in Scotland, he fought and beat in single combat the female warrior Aoife. She consented to sleep with him after the fight. He gave her a present of a ring and asked her to promise him that if she had a baby boy to send him back to Ireland as soon as the ring would fit on his finger. He also made her promise that she instruct the boy not to tell his name to any warrior he might meet. Seven years later as the men of Ulster were taking their ease at the Newry estuary, they saw a boy coming towards the shore in a boat. On asking him who he was, he refused to give his name. One by one the Ulstermen challenged him to fight, and he destroyed all of them. Émer (p. 79), Cú Chulainn's wife, suspected who the boy was and she entreated her husband not to fight him. Cú Chulainn ignored her and demanded to know the boy's name. The young lad refused and a terrible fight ensued. In the water of the estuary Cú Chulainn shot his spear, the Ga Bolga, at him through the water; it pierced the child's entrails, his blood reddened the sea, and he died. Cú Chulainn immediately realised the horror of what he had done and he took the child's body and carried it before his army, saying, 'Here is my son for you, men of Ulster.' W. B. Yeats based his play *On Baile's Strand* on the story of Conlaoch and Cú Chulainn.

**CONN** (m) Scholars argue as to the origin of this famous name. Some say it may have meant 'wisdom', some say it meant 'chief', some 'head'; others see in it an Irish version of a Celtic word for 'sense' or 'intelligence', the equivalent of the Gaulish *condos*, also used as a personal name. It could also be derived from *cú* (hound), some have suggested.

The most famous bearer of this name was Conn, earlier Cond Cétcathach (Conn of the Hundred Battles). From this legendary king are sprung many of the great Irish families, according to legend: the O'Neills and O'Donnells of Ulster; and the O'Connors, O'Rourkes and the O'Flahertys of Connacht.

Conn, it was said, reigned for 53 years some time in the second century B.C. His was said to be the greatest reign ever known in Ireland. During it 'there was no robbery, no sickness, no bad weather; the trees were well foliated, the crops were copious, and the rivers were full of fish. No sharp weapons were carried, one ploughing in spring yielded three crops, and the cuckoo's cry was heard on the cows' horns. A hundred clusters grew on each stem, a hundred nuts on each cluster.' It is difficult to reconcile this peaceful picture with the reign of a man who is supposed to have fought 100 battles, many of them remembered in the stories of Conn's rivalry with Eogan Mór, king of Munster. Also known as Mugh Nuadhat, Eogan defeated Conn in ten successive battles and eventually they decided to divide Ireland between them, Conn taking the northern half and Eogan the south—hence the terms Leath Choinn and Leath Mhogha. Not all was peaceful between the pair. Once when Eogan went to inspect his territories, he saw many of Conn's ships in Dublin Bay. He demanded that the bay also be equally divided; Conn refused and war started again. Eogan's army was wiped out at Moylena in Co. Offaly, and Eogan was slain; Conn became the undisputed king of all Ireland.

Conn was, the myth says, the progenitor of the Connachta, who seized the Boyne valley in the fourth and fifth centuries. What would this great mythical king think of his name being anglicised as *Constantine* in the nineteenth century?

**CONSTANS** (f) I know of three women named Constance who were given this Gaelic form of their name by their Irish teachers. (Ó Corráin and Maguire point out that *Constans* was in occasional use as a male name in early Christian Ireland, but that it never became popular.) *Constance* is the English and French medieval form of the Late Latin name *Constantia*, which is either a feminine form of *Constantius* or an abstract noun meaning 'constancy'. It was brought to England and Ireland by the Normans. It was the given name of the formidable Constance of Sicily (1158–98), the wife of the Emperor Henry VI. *Constans* seems to me to be a perfectly acceptable form of Constance.

**CORMAC** (m) This is one of the most famous of Irish names, one given to some of the most illustrious, if legendary, ancestors of great Irish septs. Cormac mac Airt was the reputed ancestor of the Uí Néill; Cormac Cas mac Ailella Óluim, the legendary ancestor of the Dál Cais, the O'Briens and Mac Namaras in particular; and Cormac Gelta Gáeth, the legendary ancestor of the Leinstermen. The name is strongly associated with Cashel, Co. Tipperary. Cormac mac Cárthaigh was the king of Munster and the builder of Cormac's chapel in Cashel. Cormac mac Cuilennáin was a famous scholar who wrote with distinction in both Latin and Irish; he was both a king and a bishop. As king he was often embroiled in warfare with his neighbours; as a scholar and churchman he is remembered for *Cormac's Glossary*, a work on the etymology of Irish words, with some essays on the mythology, history and antiquities of Ireland. His political and military career ended in 908 at the battle of Belach Mugna in the south of Kildare, when his forces were defeated by an army consisting of the Leinstermen and the Uí Néill. Cormac was killed in the battle and his decapitated body was buried in the abbey of Díseart Diarmada (now Castledermot), Co. Kildare.

There were some saints who bore the name, including St Cormac, bishop of Trim, remembered on 17 February; and St Cormac of Aran whose feast day is 11 May.

In the seventeenth century this ancient and noble name was changed, even by the MacCarthys, to *Charles*, in deference to Charles I.

Cormac is a combination of *corbb*, thought to be associated with the verb *corbbaid* (defiles) and *macc* (son). It is back in fashion as a given name, but sadly mispronounced by many people.

**CRÍOSTÓIR** (m) The Irish form of the English *Christopher*, from Greek *Khristopheros*, a name made up of the elements *Khristos* (Christ) and *pherein* (to bear). The name was very popular in the early continental Church because the early Christians were metaphorically bearers of Christ in their hearts. A later legend based on this has a saint actually bearing the Christ child over a stream. Hence he is regarded as the patron saint of travellers.

**CRÓNÁN** (m) See *Cuarán*

**CUÁN** (m) This Wexford saint was venerated in Ballybrennan in the parish of Cill Chuáin Mhóir (Kilcowanmore) in the barony of Bantry. John O'Donovan identifies this saint with *Cuán Airbhre*, whose feast day was celebrated on 10 July.

**CUARÁN** (m) This saint was also known as both *Mochuaróg* and *Cronán*. He is honoured in the Wexford parish of Oilgate where there is a well named after him called Cuarán well. He was known to the annalists as *Cuarán an eagna* (Cuarán the wise). *Cronán* was his formal name. *Mochuaróg* was a familial or devotional name for Cuarán; he was referred to as *Mochuaróg na Nóna* (Mochuaróg of the Nones). O'Hanlon's *Lives of the Irish Saints* explains why: 'The saint's zeal for ecclesiastical discipline was so great, he made a regulation directing that a part of the Divine Office which is called None should be recited distinct from a celebration of the Holy Sacrifice of the Mass. It was customary among ancient monks to include the celebration of Mass between the beginning and end of None; and hence it is probable that abuses were found to have occurred with regard to omission of some parts in their office. This our saint wished to correct. On such account he was called Cronan of the Nones.' His feast day is 9 February.

**CUILEANN** (f) This is one of those rare names translated into Irish from a pretty English girl's name, perhaps perceived as

Anglo-Irish here: *Holly*. I have come across a half-dozen or so Cuileanns in recent years.

Cuileann, *Ilex aquifolium*, was thought of by the ancient Irish as being a noble tree and was believed all over Europe to be a protection from evil influences. Pliny thought that the tree, planted near a house, would protect it from lightning and witchcraft. In Brittany the Irish St Rónán had a circle of cuileann bushes around his cell to protect it from evil influences. But there were folk taboos associated with the tree: one should not strike a cow with a holly stick; and in Tyrone people would not plant holly trees near a house for fear the women of the house would be childless. But by and large Cuileann was a lucky tree associated forever with Christmas, its red berries and spiky leaves foretelling Christ's passion.

**CUMMAÍNE** (m) He was a Munster saint who died around 660. His epithet Fata, later Fada, meant 'tall' or 'long'. He is quite famous in Munster legend. According to a short biography written, it is thought, in the ninth century, he was the son of a king of the western section of the royal Eoghanacht sept of Munster, *Fiachna*, a scoundrel if ever there was one. When he was drunk one night Fiachna raped his own daughter, and when the baby was born ordered that he be thrown to a pack of wolves. But instead some kind person put the infant in a milk pail which he hung on the arm of a cross outside a monastery. The abbot found the baby and fostered it, giving it the name Cummaíne, which means 'little pail'. When the child grew up he went to be taught by St Finbarr in Cork. After spending 12 years there he was told by a student that he would die in Cork, so he hit the road and travelled to his father's court in Cashel, where he gave his father some sage advice. Tongues began to wag, he looked so like the king. Eventually he hinted in verse to Fiachna that they were father and son, and in a gesture of remorse the king gave Cummaíne jurisdiction over all the monasteries of Munster. Cummaíne promised heaven to his father for doing so. He was said to have spent his life preaching throughout Ireland and to have died at another

Corcach, in Co. Limerick, thus fulfilling the prophecy of the student at St Finbarr's monastery.

There are other medieval variants of the story. One says that his mother was queen of the Déise in Waterford and was rescued from the River Suir by a friend of St Déaglán (p. 62) and reared by St Íde (p. 104). See also *Comhdhán*.

Cummaíne's feast day is 12 November.

**CÚNLA** earlier **CONNLA, CONDLA** (m) This name is an old one, and was a popular given name down to the eighteenth century, especially in Connacht. There is a saint called Condla whose feast day is 10 May. Cúnla is still given to children in Connemara, where a bawdy song celebrating a man of that name is sung with great gusto in public houses.

**DÁIBHÍ** earlier **DAIBHEAD, DAUÍD** (m) In English *David*. This name became popular in Ireland after the coming of the Anglo-Normans; St David of Wales (Dewi) was a popular object of their devotion. The name was borrowed from the biblical King David, prophet and psalmist whose name in Hebrew, *Dávidh*, meant 'beloved'. The name is often confused nowadays with *Dáithí*. A well-known bearer of the name was the poet Dáibhí Ó Bruadair who died in 1698. His work has been translated by Michael Hartnett.

**DAIMHÍN** (m) Very little is known of this saint, who gave his name to Cill Daimhin (Kildavin) in the parish of Piercestown in Co. Wexford. His feast day is 1 August. There is another place of the same name in Co. Carlow, near Bunclody. His name is not in any of the old martyrologies. It has been anglicised as *Davin*.

**DÁIRE** (m) A mythical personage in the ancient stories. The name means 'the fruitful one', and it is claimed that Dáire was an alternative designation for the Daghda, the great ancestor. He was regarded as a god of fertility, probably a bull-god.

Dáire was the name of the man who owned the great bull Donn Cuailgne in the epic *Táin Bó Cuailnge*. When Medb and her husband Ailill were arguing as to which of them owned the best bull, Medb had to agree that her husband's animal, Findbennach, was the better. So when she was told that there was an even better bull in the province of Ulster, she sent Fergus Mac Róich to the bull's owner, Dáire, to arrange a loan of the bull for a year in exchange for 50 heifers. At first Dáire was inclined to agree, but later changed his mind. This led to the great fight described in the *Táin* between the men of Ulster and the men of Connacht, in which Cú Chulainn played a heroic part. The name is sometimes anglicised as *Darragh*.

**DAIREARCA** earlier **DAR ERCA** (f) This name is still in use. It may mean 'daughter of Erc'. Dar Erca was the mother of St Mel of Longford. There was a legendary Dar Erca who was said to be the mother of 17 bishops; she was reputed to be a sister of St Patrick. There was also Dar Erca, the mother of St Ciarán of Clonmacnoise. She was a Kerrywoman, and is still venerated in south and west Kerry.

**DAIRÍNE** (f) This ancient name, found now mostly in its anglicised form *Darina*, was given by Tuathal Teachtmar, legendary king of Tara, to the younger of his two daughters. His other daughter Fithir had married Eochaidh, king of Leinster. One day Eochaidh arrived at the king's residence at Tara, and when he clapped eyes on the beautiful Dairíne, he had the bright idea of announcing to King Tuathal that the daughter he had married, Fithir, had died. He asked for the hand of Dairíne, to which Tuathal agreed. Some time later Dairíne discovered that the story Eochaidh told her father was a lie, and that her sister was alive and well. The two young women died with shame. Tuathal was not a man to take the news of his girls' death lightly. He marched against Eochaidh and exacted a very heavy tribute. For some reason he did not take Eochaidh's life. The name Dairíne is thought to be derived from *daire* (fertile or fruitful). *Darina* is the given name of the well-known cookery expert.

**DÁITHÍ** (m) He was a king of either the north midlands or of Connacht who died around A.D. 445. His name means 'swiftness' or 'the swift one'. Also called *Naith-Í*, nephew of 'eo' (a yew tree), figuratively, a champion.

Dáithí seems to have been a fierce warrior who did not confine his soldiering to the island of Ireland. He probably raided no further than Scotland, but one medieval text has him raiding into the Alps (the writer of the text was probably influenced by the exploits of the Frankish king Faramund).

Formenus, king of Thrace and a Christian, had, according to the Irish text, raided deep into the Alps and built a tower to the glory of God. Dáithí's army knocked over the tower, and Formenus prayed fervently that the Irish warrior would pay for his misdeed. The king of Thrace got his wish. As Dáithí was inspecting his newly conquered area, a thunderbolt from a furious Alpine storm hit him and killed him. As he was being taken back to Ireland for burial, his army won a further nine battles on the way. He is said to be buried at Cruachan in Co. Roscommon, the royal centre of Connacht.

*Dáith* is a diminutive of the name, which is often rendered as *David*.

**DAMHNAIT** earlier **DAMNAT** (f) *Dymphna* is the anglicised form of this old name which is the feminine diminutive form of *damh* (fawn). Little is known of her. She is associated with Tedavnet, Co. Monaghan, and is commemorated on 13 May. Damnat's enshrined crozier, now in the National Museum, was once used to swear oaths upon.

She is often confused with a *Dympna* or *Dymphna* of Gheel, invoked as the patron saint of the insane on the basis of a spurious legend about her insane father's incestuous love. That she was Irish is also in doubt. Pochin Mould speculates that her name derives from a Germanic name, possibly *Thiemo* or *Dimo*.

There was also a secular Damnat in ancient times, married to Áed Bennan, king of Munster; according to Ó Corráin and Maguire she is considered the ancestress of many families such as the O'Moriartys of Kerry and the O'Cahills, O'Flynns and O'Carrolls.

**DÉAGLÁN** Anglicised *Declan*. He founded the monastery of Ardmore, Co. Waterford. It is said that he was busy Christianising Ireland before St Patrick came, but this is difficult to confirm; some scholars say that he lived in the late fifth and early sixth centuries. His Life, written in Latin and Irish in the twelfth century, is unreliable.

When he grew to manhood, seven men who claimed to have

seen a great ball of fire at his birth became his disciples. They travelled to Rome where he was ordained bishop. When he was saying Mass one day, a little bell dropped down from heaven to him. He gave it to the King of Rome's son, who wanted to return to Ireland with Déaglán, and told him to mind it. When they came to the English Channel on their way back, they failed to find a boat, but miraculously an empty ship appeared which took them home. The king's son left the little black bell on a rock, and when he mentioned this to Déaglán they were well out to sea. Déaglan prayed and the rock floated out to them, and they followed it all the way to Sheep Island. Déaglan struck the rock with his crozier and the rock joined the mainland. Ashore he built his monastery.

The biography mentions many more miracles, and they survive in the folklore of Co. Waterford. Déaglán's feast day is 24 July.

**DEALGNAT** (f) The wife of *Parthalán* (p. 146) bore this name. A story related by Ó hÓgáin has it that when her husband, the leader of a fictitious ancient settlement in Ireland, went out hunting one day, he entrusted the care of the lovely Dealgnat to his servant Topa at Magh-Inis, at the estuary of the Erne. Dealgnat promptly seduced Topa, and afterwards they decided to have a drink from Parthalán's vat of ale. They drank the ale through a tube. When Parthalán returned he too was thirsty; he found the taste of his wife's mouth and the taste of another mouth on the tube, and in a frenzy of rage killed poor Topa. Dealgnat explained her actions thus: 'Honey with a woman, milk with a cat, food with a generous person, meat with a boy, a wright where an edged tool is—one with one, great the risk.' It seems that Parthalán forgave her this, the first adultery ever committed in Ireland.

**DEARCÁN** (m) This is an ancient name from the Déise territory in what is now Co. Waterford. Dearcán is mentioned in the stories told about St Déaglán (Declan). Dearcán was a wealthy local chieftain who, although he admired Déaglán, proved unwilling to take the final step of conversion to Christianity. He hosted a dinner for the austere saint one evening and fed the saint dog meat instead of mutton. Déaglán spotted a dog's claw in the dish and an unholy row ensued. Dearcán was so embarrassed, would you believe, that he converted to Christianity on the spot.

**DEASÚN** earlier **DEASMUMHNACH** (m) The English version, *Desmond*, is now popular in England as well as Ireland, although in the seventies and eighties it was treated as a rather feminine-sounding Irish name by British comedians. Desmond Lynam, the sports presenter, was often the butt of jokes about his name in those days. Desmond is borrowed from the placename *Desmond*, in Irish *Deasmumhan*, which means 'south Munster'. *Deasmumhnach*, which means 'man from Desmond', was rare in late medieval Ireland and unknown in earlier times. *Deasún* is a modern version of *Deasmumhnach*, and is now the usual way of spelling the name.

**DEIRBHILE** earlier **DER BILE** (f) She was a saint who lived in Fál Mór (Falmore), Co. Mayo. She founded a convent there in the sixth century, but nothing more is known about her. Her feast day is 26 October. The English form of the name is *Dervilla*, a name still popular. Dervilla Murphy, the travel writer, is one who bears the name today.

**DEIRDRE** earlier **DERDRIU** (f) Scholars cannot agree about the derivation of this, one of the most beloved of all Irish names. Some say that it may mean 'chatterer'; others have suggested that it may be a reduplicated form of an old word for 'woman'. *Derdriu* was the daughter of Feidlimid, the tragic heroine of the saddest and one of the most beautiful of all Irish stories, the story of the sons of Uisliu. Even before her birth it was prophesied that her life would be tragic because she was heard crying out from her mother's womb, terrifying all who heard her. Cathbad, the magician, said that she was destined to be the most beautiful woman ever seen in Ireland, but that strife and destruction would be the lot of Ulster and its people because of her. When the king of Ulster,

Conchobar mac Nessa (p. 52), heard this dire prophesy, he decided to take action. He ordered Derdriu to be confined in a tower and reared there until she was old enough to be married—to himself. And that was the way it was. She was kept in total isolation, with no company besides a nurse called Leborcham and her foster-parents. One day she watched from her tower as her foster-father skinned a calf below her in the snow that had fallen overnight. She looked on as a raven came and drank the calf's blood. 'I want a man,' she mused, 'with hair as black as the raven's, cheeks the colour of blood, and skin as white as snow.' She asked Leborcham, who was a poetess, if she knew of any man with the attributes she spoke of, and Leborcham replied that she knew of only one such man, Naoise, son of Uisliu. One day as Deirdre looked down from her lonely tower, she saw an extremely handsome young man approach. She knew instantly that it was Naoise. She fell in love with him on the spot and he fell in love with her. They eloped, defying the king's orders. Two of Naoise's brothers went with them to Scotland, and they lived happily there for several years. The jealous old king Conchobar pretended that all was forgiven and invited them to come back to Ireland, sending Fergus mac Róich as his emissary to guarantee their safe return. But when they arrived at Emhain Mhacha, the king's fortress in Co. Armagh, Conchobar separated the couple from Fergus. Naoise was killed treacherously and so were his brothers. Poor Deirdre was then forced to marry the king. Fergus, disgusted at the king's behaviour, went to Connacht and joined the household of Queen Medb. Deirdre lived in misery, pining after Naoise. It was said that she never smiled again. Then one day as the chariot she was in was travelling over the plain, she jumped from it and died as a result of her injuries. Two pine trees grew from her grave and Naoise's and interlocked at the top. Her name is often mispronounced both here and in Britain, where it has achieved popularity. It is not 'Deedree' or 'Deerdree', and there is, alas, an anglicised form, *Deidre*.

**DÉITHÍN** (f) This name was once popular in the west of Co.

Waterford, but is now, alas, seldom given to girls at baptism. She was, it is said, the husband of one Earc Mac Tréin, and her only son was the great *St Déaglán*, anglicised *Declan*, of Ardmore (p. 62). When Déaglán was born to her, without pain, he struck his head on a boulder, making a hole in it. Rain that gathered in the cavity was used by people for centuries in the hope of healing sickness and infirmities.

**DEORÁN** (m) From the Irish surname *Ó Deoráin*, from *Ó* (grandson of) + *Deorán* (exile, wanderer). This male given name, in its anglicised form *Doran*, has gained in popularity in recent years, principally in the counties of the eastern seaboard. I know of no female equivalent. As far as I know neither Deorán nor Doran was given to children before recent times; nor can I account for its growing popularity, unless it be that it is being confused with the English given name *Doron*, apparently a variant spelling of *Dorian*, perhaps influenced by the modern Hebrew name based on a direct borrowing of the Greek *doron* (gift).

**DIARMAID,** earlier **DIARMAIT** (m) Acceptably anglicised as *Dermot*. Also grotesquely anglicised as *Jeremiah*, *Miah* and *Darby*. Diarmuid is a misspelling. Diarmaid is a very old name whose meaning is uncertain. Some scholars have suggested that it is derived from *di-fhormaid*, meaning 'unenvious'; others have their doubts.

The most famous Diarmaid of literature is Diarmaid Ó Duibhne, the great lover of the story *Tóraíocht Dhiarmada agus Ghráinne* (The Pursuit of Diarmaid and Gráinne), which was told by storytellers from the ninth century, although the earliest recension of the story dates from the fifteenth century. Here is a short summary of the great romance.

Fionn Mac Cumhaill, chief of the Fianna, was a widower for a year after the death of his wife Maighnis. On hearing of the beauty of Gráinne, the daughter of the High King Cormac Mac Airt, he asked for her hand. A great betrothal feast was held in Tara. At the feast Gráinne saw the incredibly handsome Diarmaid and fell in love with him. She gave a magic sleeping draught to everybody at the feast except Diarmaid, and then asked him to elope with her. He was reluctant to do so out of loyalty to Fionn, but she threatened him with dire magical consequences if he refused. Off the young couple went, west across the River Shannon, where they rested at a wood called Doire Dá Bhaoth. The following morning Fionn found out about them and set off in pursuit. Fionn's son, Oisín, unwilling to see Diarmaid harmed, sent Fionn's hound Bran to warn him. Diarmaid ignored the warning, and instead enraged Fionn by kissing Gráinne passionately three times in full view of his troops. Aenghus, the god who had fostered Diarmaid, saw the danger they were in and spirited Gráinne away under a magic cloak, while Diarmaid vaulted over Fionn's men and escaped.

They travelled to the southwest and Diarmaid managed to kill a thousand men and their poisonous hounds that had come from the Channel Islands at Fionn's request. The couple went north again and as they crossed a stream, water splashed up Gráinne's thigh. She taunted Diarmaid, saying that the water was bolder than he was. It was then that for the first time they made love. Up to that they had slept with a fish bone between them, as a proof to Fionn that they were not unfaithful to him.

As Fionn's soldiers closed in on them, they took refuge in the forest of an ogre called the Searbhán, who let them use his wood on condition that they did not eat the fruit of a tree special to him. But Gráinne, by this time pregnant, craved for the berries of the tree; in a horrific fight Diarmaid had to kill the ogre to allow her to satisfy her craving.

Fionn and his men had tracked the couple to the wood, and they took refuge in the ogre's tree. The god Aenghus spirited them away once more and went so far as making a truce with Fionn through the intervention of King Cormac. Diarmaid and Gráinne were given lands in his native west Kerry, and in parts of Leinster and Connacht. They lived happily and had several children.

In the meantime the jealous old Fionn was secretly planning his revenge. One night while the couple were residing in what is now Co. Sligo, they were awakened by the baying of hounds. A boar hunt was in progress. This had been planned by Fionn who knew that it was prophesied that Diarmaid would meet his death hunting the great boar of Beann Ghulban (Benbulben). Gráinne begged him not to take part in the hunt, but when he saw that the great beast was killing Fionn's men, his old comrades, he went out to face it. When it charged, Diarmaid jumped on to its back, was thrown off and was gored in the stomach before plunging his sword into the beast's navel and killing it.

As Diarmaid lay dying he begged Fionn twice to bring him a drink of water, and twice Fionn refused, even though water from his hands contained a cure. On Diarmaid's third request Oisín threatened to kill his father if he refused to bring Diarmaid the life-saving water. The old man relented, but before he reached him Diarmaid was dead.

Aenghus brought the great lover's body to his Otherworld dwelling on the banks of the River Boyne, there to join the immortals.

Other Diarmaids of note are Diarmaid Mac Aodha Sláine, High King of Ireland, who reigned with his brother Bláthmac between A.D. 642 and 664, when both died of a plague; Diarmaid mac Cearrbheoil, A.D. 544 to 565, the last great pagan high king of Ireland; and Diarmaid Mac Murchadha, king of Leinster, who invited the Normans to Ireland. Of the many saints who bore the name the most noteworthy are Diarmaid of Inis Clothrann on Lough Ree, whose feast day is 10 January; and Diarmaid of Díseart Dhiarmada (Diarmaid's hermitage), now Castledermot, whose feast day is 21 June.

**DIL** (m) The name of a druid in a story concerning the mythical Munster king, Fiachu Muilleathan. See *Moncha*.

**DOIRE** (m) This name seems to be growing in popularity. I know of three small boys of that name in Co. Waterford. I don't know how old the name is; it has been suggested to me that it is modern. *Doire* means 'a stand of oaks'. I haven't heard of an anglicised version.

**DOIREANN** (f) This lady was the daughter of Midir, the king of the Otherworld. Another Doireann, granddaughter of the

Daghda, the great god, came to seduce Fionn and gave him a magic drink. The name is still in use in Ireland, but unfortunately it has been wrongly translated as *Dorothy*.

**DÓNAL, DOMHNALL** earlier **DOMNALL** (m) The name means, it is thought, 'world-strong'. It is derived from the old Celtic elements *dubno* (world) + *val* (rule). It was very popular in ancient Ireland and was given to five High Kings. One man of this name features among the earliest of our saints. His feast day is 26 April. From the seventeenth century Domhnall has been anglicised as *Daniel*, in other words he has been equated with the biblical character. The two names have no affinity. In Scotland Domhnall has been anglicised *Donald*. The final 'd' of this Scottish form is thought to derive partly from the misinterpretation by English speakers of the Gaelic de-voiced sound, and partly from association with names of Germanic origin such as *Ronald*. The name is very much favoured to this day in the Highlands and Islands, particularly among the clan Macdonald, the medieval lords of the Isles, but it is said to have become rare in other parts of Scotland in recent times, to such an extent that Charles Kennedy, when leader of Britain's Liberal Democrats, and a Scotsman, caused a stir when he named his new baby son *Donald*. One commentator, while admitting that the name was now gaining in popularity in America and England, lamented the fact that many young Scots' lives were blighted by being given the name of a cartoon duck! There is a very beautiful Irish song called 'Domhnall Óg'. It tells of a young woman's grief at being abandoned by a young man of that name in her hour of need. *Domhnall Ó Conaill* (Daniel O'Connell), the Liberator, is the most illustrious Irish bearer of the name.

**DONAT** (m) Known on the continent as Donatus of Fiesole, this Irish saint left Ireland after a Viking raid, possibly on Inis Cealtra on the Shannon, and went on a pilgrimage to Rome about 825. The story has it that on his way back from Rome he was halted at Fiesole near Florence by a great crowd, excited by the election of a new bishop. To make a long story short, the electoral college couldn't come to a decision, and Donat was chosen as a compromise. An unlikely story, you might think, but the crown prince of Italy at the time, Louis II, and his father Lothair I, a strong ruler who had beaten off the Saracens and had fierce tussles with the Viking menace from the north, may have had a say in choosing the Irishman, who held no fear of fighting either enemy. The Vikings had, in the year of Donat's pilgrimage to Rome, sailed up the Arno and destroyed the archives of the bishop. Donat immediately became involved in both the religious and military life of Fiesole, then a more important place than neighbouring Florence. He had a distinguished military career and in 866 helped King Louis in a campaign against the Saracens in southern Italy. As a result he won immunity for the lands of the bishop of Fiesole from royal control, and was given the right to impose taxes and to hold courts. Charles the Bald confirmed these rights in 876.

Donat also put Florence on the map. He was not long in Fiesole when he helped Lothair to establish a university there, and a fine city devoted to learning and the arts grew up. He was very devoted to St Brigid and wrote her biography. He wrote Latin verse in the style of Virgil.

He himself lived not on the hill of Fiesole but in the district known as Badia Fiesolana, not far from Fra Angelico's church. He was, and is, loved by Italians, and many's the Dino is named from him. He wrote his own epitaph, in which he leaves no doubt as to where he hailed from, although he now rests in clay with the worms.

Hic ego Donatus, Scotorum
sanguine cretus,
solus in hoc tumulo, pulvere,
verme, voror . . .

**DONN** (m) The name means either 'brown, dun' or 'lord, king'. He was a mythical figure in literature and may be regarded as the Irish lord of the dead. He was thought to inhabit the island known as Teach Duinn (Donn's house), and a ninth-century text has the eerie lines, 'To me, to my house, you shall all come when you die.' Donn is particularly associated with Cnoc Fírinne (Knockfierna) in

Co. Limerick where, folklore has it, people were brought to visit him when they died; and with the sand dunes of Doonbeg in Co. Clare, where he could often be seen leaving his ghostly abode at night riding a white horse.

According to Ó hÓgáin, some of the stories associated with him seem to have been influenced by Norse lore. He came to a blacksmith one night and asked him to shoe his horse. He tore off one of the horse's legs and handed it to the smith. That poor man, terrified out of his wits, shod the leg, and Donn replaced it perfectly on his steed. We find a similar story in Norse legend about the god Odin and his horse Sleipnir. In Clare he was said to live under the sea and to have drowned people in the sand dunes of Doonbeg.

In medieval times the name Donn was popular among some families. It has gone out of fashion.

**DONNABHÁN** earlier **DONNDUBÁN** (m) from the elements *donn* (brown) + *dubh* (black or dark) + the diminutive suffix *án*. It was a name used in Munster and borne by some princes of that province in early medieval times. It is the origin of the surname *O'Donovan*.

It increased in popularity both in Ireland and abroad in the 1960s in its anglicised form *Donovan*, it has been suggested, through the influence of the rock singer of that name.

**DONNCHA** earlier **DONNCHADH, DONNCHAD** A favourite name among the clans of Munster from the late Middle Ages. Favoured especially by the O'Briens, it was also popular in Ulster in the Scottish form *Duncan* among people of planter stock, and in the form *Donaghy* among nationalists. Anglicised ludicrously as *Dionysius* and *Denis* and as the more acceptable *Donagh* and *Donough*. In the Middle Ages the name was often latinised as *Donat* and *Donatus*, from the Latin 'given.' The name may mean 'brown or dun' or 'king, chieftain'.

The *cumdach* (shrine) of the *Book of Armagh*, written *c.*807, was commissioned by the High King Donnchad in, it is thought, 939, to preserve the precious manuscript book, now in the library of Trinity College, Dublin. It contains the only surviving Early Irish text of the New Testament, and several texts on and by St Patrick.

Another famous bearer of the name was Donnchad, king of Munster from 1014, when his father, Brian Boru, was killed at the Battle of Clontarf. This Donnchad died in Rome in 1064. There is a plea on the shrine of the Stowe missal for prayers for him. That famous manuscript, now in the custody of the Royal Irish Academy, was until recently associated with the monastery of Tallaght, but modern scholars think it was compiled in Lorrha, Co. Tipperary. An inscription on the base of the shrine spells the maker's name as Dunchad ua Taccáin.

A modern Donncha of note is the Munster and Irish international rugby player, Donncha O'Callaghan.

**DUÁN** earlier **DUBHÁN, DUBÁN** (m) This Wexford saint lived at the end of the fifth or the beginning of the sixth century. His name is preserved in the placename Rinn Duáin (Duán's promontory), now absurdly known as Hook Head, from a confusion with the Irish word *duán*, meaning 'a fish hook'. There is a holy well at Churchtown on the Hook promontory called Tobar Dhuáin (Duffin's Well). The saint's feast day is 11 February.

**DUARTACH, DUBHARTACH** (m) The Co. Clare surname *Ó Dubhartaigh*, anglicised *Doorty*, comes from this given name, no longer in use. There is a relic of it in the name of the famous Clare pub Durty Nelly's, near Bunratty Castle. Nelly, whoever she was, was not a dirty person; rather does the pub's name mean that a shebeen on its site once belonged to Nelly's boy Dubhartach, which became corrupted as *Durty*.

**DUBHGHALL** earlier **DUBGALL** (m) This name which means 'black foreigner' was given to the Danes by the Irish, in contrast to fairer Norwegians and Icelanders. The Danes are reported to have come to Dublin in 850; the name quickly became popular among the natives because we find a Dubgall, son of Donnchad and heir to Ailech, slain by a kinsman 20 years later. The Vikings themselves seemed to like the name and one of them, Dubgall, son of Amlaimh, was reported killed at Clontarf in 1014. Anglicised *Dougal*, the name has been made famous by the slow-witted priest in the television series, *Father Ted*. The surname *Ó Dubhghaill* or *Ó Dúill*, anglicised *Doyle*, is derived from it.

**DUBHGHLAS** (m) The name is thought by some to be a compound of *dubh* (black) and *glas* (green), but it could also be from *dubhghlaise* (dark stream). The name is very popular in Scotland in its English form, *Douglas*. Our most famous Dubhghlas was Dubhghlas de hÍde (Douglas Hyde), first President of Ireland, born in Co. Roscommon in 1860 and educated at Trinity College, Dublin. He was a founder member of the Gaelic League in 1893 and its first president. He became the first professor of Irish in University College, Dublin, in 1909. He was a folklorist of note and his books *Beside the Fire* and *The Love Songs of Connacht* had a great influence on the Irish language revival movement and on the interest shown by Lady Gregory, Synge, O'Casey and Yeats in the country's Gaelic heritage. He died in Dublin in 1949.

**ÉADAOIN** earlier **ÉTAÍN** (f) One of the most beautiful of the ancient Irish stories is *Tochmar Étaíne* (The Wooing of Étaín). The name Étaín is very likely related to *et* (jealousy); O'Rahilly and some other scholars thought she may have been a sun goddess. Étaín Echraidhe was the daughter of Ailill, an Ulster king, and she was known throughout the land as being the most beautiful of women, desired by every man in Ireland including a reprobate named Midir, despite the fact of his having a wife of his own, a fiercely jealous woman named Fuamnach. This Midir had made a pact with the god Óengus that he would obtain the beautiful Étaín for him. The deal was that she would join Midir in return for the clearing of 12 plains, the changing of the courses of 12 rivers, and the lady's weight in silver and gold. It goes without saying that Fuamnach was none too happy to see her husband come home with the most beautiful woman in the land. Fuamnach was a sorcerer and she immediately got to work to destroy Étaín. First she turned her into a pool of water. This pool then became a worm, and then a scarlet fly. This fly was no ordinary creature. It was jewel-like, of great beauty, which accompanied Midir everywhere he went and enchanted everybody who looked upon it. For 14 years this poor fly was blown around Ireland by the sorcery of Fuamnach, until one day it fell into a goblet of wine being drunk by the wife of Étar and was swallowed by her. The fly was reborn in the course of time, and when she grew to womanhood became the wife of Echu Áirem, king of Ireland. This was not the end of her troubles. After many more adventures and miraculous happenings, she was eventually restored to Midir.

Another Étaín brought gold and silver as a gift to St Patrick, according to the Fionn stories; and there are a few saints of the name, including Étaín of Tumna, Co. Roscommon, whose feast day is 5 July.

Her name has been anglicised acceptably as *Aideen*, which is better than calling her Étáin or *Aitaun*, as is sometimes done, I'm afraid.

**EALLÓG** (m) A monk at St Fiontan's foundation gave his name to Cill Eallóg, a name since corrupted to Kerlogue, near Wexford town. Little else is known of him.

**EAMHNAT** earlier **EMNAT** (f) Anglicised *Avnit*, which I have seen only once, on a headstone in the ancient churchyard at St Mullins on the banks of the Barrow in south Co. Carlow. Emnat is said to be the mother of the founder of the monastic settlement in the place, St Moling (p. 130).

**ÉAMONN** earlier **ÉMANN** (m) The name is a borrowing from the English *Edmond* (also used in Germany) or *Edmund*, from an Old English personal name composed of the elements *ead* (prosperity, riches, fortune) + *mund* (protector). The English name gained popularity by being that of several well-known people, both royal and saintly, including a ninth-century bishop of East Anglia killed by the invading Danes, supposedly for being a Christian. His martyrdom earned him a cult that spread throughout Europe. The Normans brought the name to Ireland. The name is now used to translate *Edward*, an Old English name from *ead* (riches, fortune) + *weard* (guard).

In the seventeenth century Éamonn was used as a common name for rapparees, Irish irregular soldiers of the time; 'robbers, scoundrels and violent people', according to Fr Dinneen's dictionary. The *Éamonn a' Chnoic* of the song is one such gentleman. Éamonn also gave Irish the term *maide Éamoinn*, a bar across the inside of a door to strengthen it against robbers, and worse.

**ÉANNA** earlier **ÉNNAE** (m) The great saint of Aran is commemorated on 21 March. His name is anglicised as *Enda*. His medieval biographer thought that Énnae meant 'bird-like'.

Énnae's monastery on Inis Mór, the largest of the Aran Islands, was certainly of great importance. His Life is of a late date and cannot be completely trusted. For what it's worth it tells us that young Énnae was trained as a soldier and owed his vocation to the influence of his sister Faenche, a nun, who persuaded him to desist from wooing a student she was teaching and to study for the priesthood. He went to the famous Scottish monastery of Ninian (p. 139), Candida Casa, and when he came home was advised by his influential sister to go to Aran.

Under him Aran became famous as a seat of learning known throughout Europe, and because of the proliferation of ancient churches there, it has become known as Árainn na Naomh (Aran of the Saints).

**EARNÁN** earlier **ERNÁN, ERNÍN, EIRNÍNE** (m, f) There are many saints of this name. Some scholars derive the name from *iarn* (iron). Among these saints is Ernán of Oileán Thoraí (Tory Island), off the Donegal coast. Very little is known of him. His feast day is 17 August. The name is commonly 'translated' as *Ernest*, which is an English name derived from German. The politician and former Abbey Theatre chief Ernest Blythe translated his given name as *Earnán*. The name was sometimes written *Ernín* and earlier *Erníne*. Some were female saints, such as the virgin Erníne Cass (of the curly hair), daughter of Archenn. She is associated with Leighlin in Co. Carlow and her feast day is 28 February.

**EIBHLÍN** (f) Anglicised *Eileen*. This name is a borrowing from the Anglo-Norman personal name *Aveline*, a name of Germanic origin which may represent an Old French diminutive form of *Avila*, a derivative of *Avis*. The element *av-* is found in many Germanic female compound names and is of unknown origin and meaning; *Aveline* was also rendered *Aibhilín* in medieval Ireland. The name may owe its popularity in the Middle Ages to its correspondence in form to the Latin word *avis* (a bird). The combination *bh* in Eibhlín is pronounced *v* but is sometimes dropped, which gives the acceptable anglicisation *Eileen*. Eibhlín was a common name in the eighteenth and nineteenth centuries. Eibhlín Dubh Ní Chonaill, an aunt of Daniel O'Connell, is credited with writing the magnificent eighteenth-century lament for her husband Art Ó Laoghaire (though not all scholars agree that she is the author; some say that this poem was written by a man and put in the young widow's mouth, so to speak). The name *Eibhlín* or *Eileen* became extremely popular in the early twentieth century, probably due to the Gaelic League which taught both the great lament and another poem, 'Eibhlín a Rúin', a love song attributed to Cearbhall Ó Dálaigh. The name has also been anglicised as *Aileen*, *Eily*, *Eveleen* and *Evelyn*.

**ÉIGHNEACHÁN** earlier **ÉICNEACHÁN** (m) This name is a diminutive of the rare ancient northern name *Éicneach*, which may have derived from *écen* (force). The name was commonly anglicised as *Ignatius*, and indeed Ignatius was just as often gaelicised as Éighneachán down to recent times.

**EILEANÓRA, EILEANÓIR** (f) This is the Irish equivalent of the English *Eleanor*. The name was introduced into Ireland by the Anglo-Normans. It derives from an Old French re-spelling of an old Provençal name *Alienor*. It has been said that this name is a variant of *Helen*. However, it is much more likely to be of Germanic origin, the clue lying in the first element *ali* (foreign, strange, other). The reason for the name's popularity among the Normans was its association with *Eleanor of Aquitane* (1122–1204). She was a native of south-west France and became the queen of Henry II. She was followed in the Norman pantheon by *Eleanor of Provence*, the wife of Henry III, and *Eleanor of Castille*, the wife of Edward I.

**EILTÍN** earlier **EILTÍNE** (m) A saint of this name was the patron of Kinsale, Co. Cork. His feast day is 11 December. His name probably comes from the word *eilit*, meaning 'a hind', figuratively 'a sprightly person'. As far as I know he does not figure in the folklore of the district.

**ÉIMHÍN** earlier **ÉMÍNE** (m, f) The name Éimhín is given to boys in honour of the founder of Monasterevin. His name may mean 'ready'. I have seen the name anglicised *Evan*. The saint's feast day is 22 November. The girl's name Éimhín, anglicised *Aiveen*, may come from the same source; opinions on the matter vary.

**EIRNÍN** (m) See *Earnán*

**EIRNÍNE** (m, f) See *Earnán*

**EISIRT** (m) King Fergus Mac Léide's wise man and poet. See *Bébó*.

**EISTIR** (f) The Irish form of *Esther*, the biblical name of a Jewish slave girl who became the wife of King Ahasuerus of Persia. According to the *Book of Esther* she was cunning and persuasive enough to be able to save many Jews from the evil royal adviser Haman. In Hebrew her name was *Hadassah*, which means 'myrtle'. Some scholars think that Esther was a Persian translation of this; others think that it comes from the Persian word *starra* (a star). But the name may well be the Hebrew form of the name of the Persian goddess *Ishtar*. *Eistir*, the Irish form, was used in the Middle Ages and has recently been popularised in Irish schools. Outside of these it is not widely used.

**EITHNE** (f) An illustrious name if the ancient legends are anything to go by: Eithne was the mother of the god *Lug* (p. 114).

A fourteenth-century story tells us that she was the daughter of a retainer of Óengus (p. 8) and was reared with Curcóg, daughter of the sea-god Manannán at Newgrange. She was very beautiful, but because she had been deeply insulted by something a visitor said about her, she refused all food and drink. Óenghus was perplexed and offered her a drink of milk from a dun cow, one of a pair of wondrous cows he and Manannán had purchased in India. She milked the cow herself and said that the milk tasted heavenly, like honey and wine. When Manannán heard the news he sent for Eithne and, because he had the remedy for every sickness under the sun, he offered her a drink of milk from the other cow, a speckled animal. She took it, and the demon angel she suffered as a result of the insult at Newgrange left her and was replaced by a guardian angel. She was no longer a member of the Tuatha Dé Danann but a Christian who would only accept nourishment from the cows of the righteous land of India! So she lived on the milk of the two cows for a long, long time. After a swim in the Boyne one day the magical gift of invisibility, given to her by the Tuatha Dé Danann, left her. She went to a cleric and received instruction from him. Patrick and Óengus came to visit her on the same day and both demanded that the other stay away from her. Patrick told Óengus to go, after he tried and failed to convert him. He did so in great anguish. Eithne was baptised and a fortnight later she died. She was buried with Christian ritual.

An Eithne was also the wife of Conn Cétchathach, he of the hundred battles; another Eithne was the wife of Cormac Mac Airt; and Cú Chulainn also had a wife named Eithne. On the ecclesiastical side St Eithne of Swords and her sister Sodelb were said to have cradled Christ in their arms when he came to them as a baby. Eithne was the name of the mothers of St Aidan of Ferns and of St Colmcille. St Eithne of Tullow, Co. Carlow, is commemorated on 6 July. The name has been anglicised *Edna*, *Ethna* and *Ena*.

**ÉMER** (f) The beloved of the hero Cú Chulainn. His wooing of Émer, described first in a text dating from the eighth century but reworked during the next few hundred years, tells of Cú Chulainn's infatuation. The Ulster hero had outdone all the other warriors in trials of war and they grew jealous of him. Their wives teased them about the extraordinary young man, and this added to their fear and hatred of him. They decided that a wife must be found for him. The king, Conchobar, searched all Ireland for a suitable woman, but none was found. Cú Chulainn himself went searching and saw his beloved on the south bank of the River Boyne in Co. Meath. They spoke in riddles to each other, and the young woman, Émer, said that that he must prove greatness by killing hundreds of men, perform the feat of the leaping salmon, and be able to kill with a sword which would spare men selectively. He also had to have enough stamina as to be able to go without sleep from November until August. He promised to show her that he could perform these feats and off he went. Émer's father was enraged and went to the king in disguise and suggested that young Cú Chulainn should go to Scotland to be trained in arms by an amazon called Scáthach, hoping that he would meet certain death at the hands of some Scottish warrior. A man called Domhnall trained him well in the tricks of walking on live coals and performing great deeds on the point of a spear. As he went to meet Scáthach to further his education, he came to a bouncing bridge over a chasm which knocked off all but the greatest warriors. A frenzy came upon him and he performed the salmon leap to get to the other side. He slept with Scáthach's daughter Uathach, and made the mother give him extra training. War broke out between Scáthach and another female warrior called Aoife. Cú Chulainn beat her in single combat, and slept with her afterwards (see *Conlaoch*). She trained him in the ways of magic. When he returned to Ireland he went to Émer's home and found the place barricaded against him. He laid siege to the fortress for a full year and then charged the place in a chariot with scythed wheels, killing 309 men. He salmon-leaped over the walls, killed nine men on three separate attacks, sparing one man each time. And so, having shown Émer that he had performed all the feats she asked of him, he took her home with him as his wife. She proved that she had the gifts of great women: the gift of loveliness, the gift of a beautiful voice, the gift of needlework, the gift of wisdom and the gift of chastity.

The name, thankfully popular again, is acceptably anglicised *Emer*.

**ÉNÁN** (m) Once a popular name for a boy in north Wexford, in an anglicised form, *Enan*. I know nothing about the saint except that his feast day is 30 January. The name means 'little bird'.

**EOCHAÍ, EOCHAIDH** earlier **EOCHAID** (m) The name is derived from *ech* (later), *each* (a horse). A deity, it has been suggested, could be envisaged both as a master horseman or as one who, like a stallion, possessed great powers of reproduction. Eochaid Airem was a mythical king of Ireland reigning at Tara and the human husband of Étaín (p. 74). Eochaid Éigeas was a poet and sage of the sixth century.

The great Leinster family of poets, *Mac Eochaidh*, trace their origin to him, rather fancifully, it is thought. They anglicised their name *Keogh* and *Kehoe*. Eochaid Feidhlech was a fictional king of Ireland. His name means 'Eochaidh-who-yokes', and the medieval text says that the yoke was first introduced in his reign. That reign was a golden age in Ireland, a time of peace and prosperity, and all because, it was said, in the third year of his reign Jesus Christ was born. Eochaid Mac Luchta was a fictional king of either Connacht or Munster, depending on which medieval text you are reading; Ó hÓgáin calls him a character invented from the debris of the cult of the deity. For a story about another king called Eochaid, Eochaid mac Maolughra, see *Ruán*.

**EOGHAN** earlier **EÓGAN** (m) The name means 'bred from the yew'. It was one of the most popular names in ancient Ireland. An Eógan was the reputed ancestor of Cinél Eógan, enshrined in the name of the territory Tír Eoghain (Tyrone); Eógan Brecc was the reputed ancestor of the Déise; yet another Eógan was the ancestor of the Eoganacht, the kings of Munster. There are many saints of the name. Notable are Eógan of Moville whose feast day is 31 May; and Eógan of Ardstraw, Co. Tyrone, whose feast day is 23 August.

The Ardstraw Eógan was studying at Clones when he was captured by raiders from Britain. He managed to escape, or so the story goes, and continued his studies at the famous monastery of Candida Casa in Galloway. From there he made his way home in due course and founded the monastery of Kilnamanagh, near Tallaght, where he may have met Caoimhín of Glendalough (p. 33) who was a student there, before eventually settling down in his new foundation at Ardstraw. His name was given to countless generations of the O'Donnells and MacSweeneys of Donegal. Before 700 the name Eógan was latinised as

*Eugenius*, a Greek name which meant 'well bred'. In fact the two names have no connection with one another. In southern Ireland the name is anglicised as *Eugene* or *Gene*.

**EOLANN** earlier **EOLANG** (m) In the nineteenth century the name, anglicised as *Olan* and *Oling*, was known in north Co. Wexford where there is a village, Cam Eolaing, known in English as Camolin, scene of a battle in the 1798 Rebellion in which the insurgent army was famously successful.

**EÓRANN** (f) This lovely name is still given to children in Co. Antrim, anglicised as *Oran*. She was the wife of Suibhne, mythical seventh-century king of Dál nAraide, whose story is told in the medieval text *Buile Shuibhne*, which has been translated by Seamus Heaney. Hearing the bell of St Rónán (p. 151), who had the temerity to build a church in his territory, Suibhne rushed to expel the saint. His queen, Eórann, tried to stop him and grabbed him by the cloak, and he ran naked to attack the saint, throwing his psalter into the lake. An otter restored the book to the saint, who cursed Suibhne and prayed that he would fly naked through Ireland and die pierced by a spear. Suibhne became deranged and in his wanderings through Ireland he met his wife Eórann, who by then was living with another man. Suibhne forgave her and advised her to live with her lover. After many adventures he met Moling, the saint of St Mullins in Co. Carlow, and in that lovely place by the banks of the Barrow he died, having been pierced by a spear thrown by a jealous husband of a woman who fed him regularly by giving him milk poured into holes she made in pats of cow dung. Moling heard his confession and anointed him before he expired at the door of his church.

# F

**FACHTNA** (m, f) This name, still popular among the people of west Cork, may mean 'hostile, vicious'. The name was once common all over Ireland and there were female Fachtnas as well as males. This is no longer the case.

According to one legend a Fachtna was the father of Conchobhar Mac Nessa, the legendary king of Ulster. There was a saint called Fachtna who lived near Lough Foyle; and another saint, a bishop, of whom nothing else is known except his feast day, 19 January.

The west Cork Fachtna mac Mongaig is the patron of the diocese of Ross. He was the founder of the monastery of Ros Ailithir, now called Roscarbery. He lived in the sixth century but precious little else is known about him with any certainty. Óengus in his Martyrology calls him 'son of the wright'. We cannot know where exactly he was born, but it was somewhere near the sea according to tradition. Ros Ailithir was a famous school which became known for a metrical geography of the world written by a monk named Airbertach, who died in 1016. The work is a compilation of classical material and it contains references to tigers, elephants, oil wells, Indian magnets and asbestos. The monastery and school founded by Fachtna was destroyed in a Viking raid.

**FAND** (f) This lovely lady was the daughter of Áed Abrat and the wife of the sea-god Mannanán mac Lir. Ó Corráin and Maguire suggest that the name may be connected with the Old Irish word *fand* (a tear).

**FEARDORCHA** earlier **FERDORCHA** (m) The name is still in use, particularly in

Donegal. It was common in Munster from the sixteenth century to the end of the eighteenth. It has been anglicised as *Frederick*, *Ferdinand* and *Freddie*, names with which it has no connection. The 'Fear Ó Laoghaire an leanbh', the baby mentioned in *Caoineadh Airt Uí Laoghaire* may, I think, be a pet name for Feardorcha.

**FEARGHAL** earlier **FERGAL** (m) This ancient name means 'valorous'. This was the given name of Mac Maele Dúin, ancestor of the O'Neills, who died in 722 in battle against the Leinstermen. The battle was known as Cath Almaine and is the subject of a story written in the tenth century and rewritten some time later. Fergal and the king of Munster, Cathal Mac Fionghuine, were old enemies but made peace. Fergal invaded Leinster to collect tribute. In his large army there was a boy called Donn Bó, a widow's son, who was allowed to go with the king if he pledged the young lad's safety. He was a great singer, storyteller and reciter of poetry, which was why Fergal wanted him in his company. The weather proved terrible that winter and Fergal's army went astray in the snow. To keep himself alive Fergal took a leper's only cow and burned his house. The leper vowed vengeance. Donn Bó, disgusted at Fergal's actions, refused to sing or recite any poetry. In the battle against the Leinstermen at Almaine (Allen, in Kildare), both Fergal and Donn Bó were killed. At a feast that night the Leinstermen could hear a sweet singer lamenting outside. They sent out men to bring the singer in. It was Donn Bó. They put his severed head on a pedestal and bade it sing. It did so and all the company wept for the dead boy. The head was taken out and reunited with the body, whereupon Donn Bó miraculously came to life and returned safe and sound to his mother. Fergal's head was brought to his old adversary, Cathal, who lived in Glanworth, Co. Cork. Angered at Fergal's slaying, Cathal honoured the head, which blushed and thanked the king for his courtesy. Cathal brought the head of Fergal back to the Uí Néill, Fergal's royal sept.

Fergal of Salzburg, also known as *Virgil* and *Virgilius*. An Irish monk of the name, possibly of Aghaboe, arrived in

Salzburg around 720 and became abbot of a monastery there. A cantankerous man, he drew the fire of St Boniface at Mainz, who twice reported him to Rome. On the first occasion the Pope, St Zachary, took sides with Fergal; the second time round the Pope seemed to be incensed at Fergal's strange views on cosmology. Fergal was a learned man and an inspired missionary, and ultimately was consecrated bishop of Salzburg. He took a great interest in the province of Carinthia, where he is still venerated. He died at Salzburg in 784. The cathedral there, a stone's throw from Mozart's house, is dedicated to him.

**FEICHÍN** earlier **FECHÍNE** (m) Anglicised *Festus* and *Festie*. A common name in ancient Ireland, it meant literally 'little raven'. Feichíne was a name given to five Irish saints, one of whom is Feichíne of Fore, Co. Westmeath, whose pet name was Mo Enna. One Latin account of his life and two Irish ones survive. It was said that his birth was foretold by Colmcille. He was well bred. His father Caolcharna was of the royal Uí Néill of Tara, and his mother Lasair was of the royal Eoghanacht sept of Munster. It was said that he was given his name by his mother when she saw him gnawing a bone when he was an infant. 'Look at my little raven,' she is reputed to have said.

He was destined to become a saint, according to the old stories. When he was a baby and sleeping between his parents, he would be found in the morning lying on the ground, his arms stretched out in the form of a cross, and a flock of angels hovering over him to protect him.

He was educated by St Naithí (p. 136) at Achonry in what is now Co. Sligo, and there he was ordered by an angel to go to Omey Island off the Galway coast and found a monastery there.

He was an astute politician. He had various dealings with the joint High Kings Diarmaid and Bláthmac, and had to resort at times to drastic measures to have his way. He caused the latter's fortress to burst into flames in a row over hostages; and on another occasion when he was refused entry to Diarmaid's fortress, he caused a man who opposed him to drop dead. He brought him back to life when the king released the hostage he sought. He was a friend of King Guaire of Connacht, but for a while there was enmity between him and King Ailill of Naas. On a journey to seek the release of a hostage from Ailill, one of his chariot horses died and the saint replaced him with a fairy horse from a river pool. He proceeded to cause an earthquake that shook the king's palace to its foundations, and in the panic that ensued Ailill dropped dead. He was, of course, brought back to life by Feichíne when all the hostages were released. Folklore concerning the saint persists in Fore. His feast day is 20 January.

**FEIDHLIM, FEIDHLIMIDH** earlier **FEDELMID** (m, f) One famous bearer of this name was *Fedelmid Mac Criomhthain* (770–847), king of Munster, who was also a warrior cleric who fought the kings of Leinster, Connacht and Ulster in his day. The Munster stories have him as a sort of Irish Charlemagne and he was even regarded as a saint. But his bloody battles were remembered outside his province, and the Annals say that when he returned from destroying Clonmacnoise in 846 he had a terrible dream in which he was visited by St Ciarán, who stuck his crozier in his belly. As a result Fedelmid was afflicted with a wasting disease which killed him a year later. The name is very popular still in Ulster and generations of schoolchildren have enjoyed the little song 'Báidín Fheidhlimidh' which was sunk off Tory Island. The name has been anglicised as *Phelim*, *Felimy* and *Felix*. There were some saints of the name, notably St Fedelmid of Aghalurchar, Co. Fermanagh, remembered on 23 December; and a saint of the diocese of Kilmore, whose feast day is 3 August. *Fedelmid* was very occasionally given to girls in olden times.

**FERDIA** earlier **FER DÉA, FER DEODA, FER DEADH, FER DIADH** (m) There are many variants of the name in medieval literature. all of which associate him with divinity or fire. A fictional warrior in the Ulster Cycle, in the *Táin Bó Cuailnge* his epic fight with his friend Cú Chulainn at the ford is described with great drama.

In some recensions of the tale they beseech each other to stop fighting and recall their past friendship. They embrace and give one another healing herbs, food and drink. But on the third evening they break all contact with one another and resume mortal combat, using all the tricks they know. Cú Chulainn's charioteer sends his spear, the *ga bolga*, downstream to him, and flinging it from between his toes wounds Fer Diadh in the anus. He lowers his shield, and Cú Chulainn pierces him through the heart. He dies in the arms of his old friend. *Ferdia* is still given to children in the area connected with the *Táin*, the town of Ardee in Co. Louth, in Irish Áth Fhir Diadh (the ford of Fer Diadh).

**FIACHA** earlier **FIACHU** (m) Fiachu was the given name of many warriors of old, and the supposed ancestors of famous dynasties. The O'Byrnes of Wicklow spelled it Fiacha and this was the name given to Fiacha Mac Aodha Ó Broin. His name was anglicised as *Feagh Mac Hugh O'Byrne*. *Festus* was the anglicised form bestowed by the National Schools.

**FIACHNA** (m) His was a popular name in ancient Ireland. The name is another diminutive of *fiach* (a raven). Some kings and warriors bore the name. The most celebrated of them was Fiachna mac Baodáin, the powerful king of the Dál nAraidhe (south Antrim and north Down). One legend concerning him is interesting. It tells how Fiachna sailed to Scotland to aid his ally Aodán mac Gabhráin against the Saxons. While he was away from his fortress at Moylinny in Antrim, a handsome stranger came to visit his wife. He gave her a choice: she could either sleep with him in return for his protection of her husband who was in mortal danger; or she could refuse and suffer the consequences of her husband's death. She slept with him, and the stranger saved her husband in battle, having come between the two armies and slain the principal warrior of the Saxons. Fiachna and his allies took heart and routed the Saxon army. The stranger explained what had happened at home to Fiachna, who seems to have accepted matters when he heard that the seducer of his wife was none other than Manannán, the god of the sea. A child was born of the union and named Mongán. The root of this name, *moing* (mane), was a poetic kenning for the sea. Scholars such as Ó hÓgáin have pointed out that this story has been influenced by the motif of a childless queen fertilised by a sea-spirit, which was the origin of the legend of the foundation of the Merovingian dynasty of the Franks.

**FIACHRA** (m) Two important saints bore this name, which may have meant 'battle king'. One was Fiacre of Breuil, the object of devotion in France, who settled in Breuil and lived there until his death *c.*670.

He was said to be a horticulturist of note and has become the patron saint of French gardeners. He was also, it was said, a man who could cure syphilis. A picture of the saint formed the sign of an inn from which hackney carriages were first used and gave French a new word, *fiacre*, which travelled to Germany and Austria with Napoleon's armies and entered German as *fiaker*. In Vienna some of the horse-drawn fiakers which one may hire at St Stephen's great cathedral have medals attached to the bridle bearing the image of the Irish saint. There is an Austrian dish, *fiaker goulash*, once fed to the hackney drivers by their wives. The dish is popular in many Tyrolean alpine resorts. Where Fiachra came from in Ireland is not known. His feast day is 30 August.

A different St Fiachra lived at Ullard, near Graiguenamanagh, Co. Kilkenny. He was the confessor of St Comgall of Bangor (p. 49). His feast day is 8 February. His holy well used to be visited by many seeking a cure for cancer, among other diseases.

There used to be a great devotion to a St Fiachra in Scotland. Perhaps because of the traditional historical links with France, this was Fiachra of Breuil. There was a St Fiachra's well at Nigg in Kincardine which caused endless trouble after the Reformation. In 1630, 'Margrat Davidson, spous to Andre Adam, was adjuget in any unlaw of five poundis to be payed to the collector for directing hir nowriss with her bairne to Sanct Fiackres Well, and weshing the bairne tharin for recoverie of hir health; and the said Margrat and hir nowriss were ordainit to acknowledge their offence before the Session for their fault, and for leaveing ane offering in the well.'

**FÍNÍN** earlier **FÍNGHIN, FÍNGIN** (m) This ancient name could be translated as 'wine-birth'. It is a favourite name to this day in Munster, as it has long been associated with the great families of that province, the MacCarthys, O'Mahonys, O'Driscolls and O'Sullivans. One of the earliest Fíngins of note was Fíngin mac Aeda, king of Munster, who died in 619. There is a saint of the name whose feast day is 5 February. One placename derived from the saint's name is Doire Fínín (Fínín's oak wood) near Ballingeary in west Cork.

The scholar and antiquary Fíngin Mac Cárthaigh Mór, who died in 1640, 'translated' his name as *Florence*, but in fairness to the man this equation of Fíngin with Florence was in vogue as early as the latter part of the thirteenth century. *Florence* is still a popular name in west Cork, where the diminutives are *Florry*, *Florrie* and of course *Flurry*, the name given by Somerville and Ross to their famous foxhunter and rogue in their stories about the Irish RM, Mr Flurry Knox.

**FINNIAN** earlier **FINNÉN** (m) Two very important saints, Finnian of Clonard in Meath, and Finnian of Moville in Co. Down, bear this name, which is derived from *finn* (fair, pale-coloured) plus, according to Ó Corráin and Maguire, the British ending *-iaw*.

Finnén of Clonard went to Wales and there became acquainted with the monastic life before coming home and setting up a series of monastic houses, including Cluain Iráird (Iráird's meadow), Clonard, situated in the heart of Ireland and one of the most vital religious and scholastic centres in the country. A century and a half ago the site was marked by ruined churches and a round tower; all have since disappeared, alas. In Finnén's time there were 3,000 students accommodated here, according to the early Lives; allowing for the exaggerations of these works, it is clear that Clonard was a very important place indeed in the history of the early Irish Church. Finnén's name seems to have been at one stage written *Uindio* or *Uennio*; hence the *Vennianus* written about by Columbán in his correspondence with Gregory the Great, and regarded as the author of the first Irish Penitential, a handbook for confessors.

Finnén lived frugally on barley bread and water, but on Sundays he allowed himself a cup of mead or ale and a slice of salmon. Finnén, 'teacher of Ireland, treasure of Clonard', as an Anglo-Norman antiphon describes him in the late thirteenth century, died in 549, according to the Annals of Ulster.

Finnén or Finnian of Moville, *Maigh Bhile* (plain of the great tree), was one of the most famous scholars of ancient Ireland. He went to Scotland and studied at the monastery of St Ninian at Candida Casa at Whithorn in Galloway, an establishment which, it is claimed, was modelled on continental houses and may have had women students. He came back to Ireland to found Moville on Strangford Lough. The late stories of Colmcille being a student there and of miracles performed there by him may be regarded as fanciful, although Colmcille and Finnian were certainly lifelong friends. The famous story of Colmcille copying Finian's manuscript, which led to the copyright judgment of the high king, 'To every cow its calf, to every book its copy', is also thought to be fanciful by many scholars. Finnian of Moville died in 576 according to the *Annals of Inisfallen*; in 579 according to the *Annals of Ulster*.

**FÍONA** earlier **FÍNE** (f) Fíne was abbess of St Brigid's great foundation at Kildare. She died in the year 805. Sometimes anglicised *Feena*, the name is more often than not mispronounced Fióna in Ireland. This is not a genuine Irish name at all, but one invented by the nineteenth-century Scottish novelist William Sharpe for one of his characters, Fiona McLeod. If he thought that this name was a feminine form of Finn or Fionn he was sadly mistaken; no such form exists in Irish, early or modern.

**FÍONÁN** earlier **FÍNÁN** (m) There were many Irish saints of this name, of which the most widely known were Fíonán Cam of Kinnitty and Fíonán Lobhar of Swords and Ardfinnan. *Fionn* and *Fin* mean 'white', referring to hair colour; *án* is a diminutive.

Fíonán Cam seems to have been a Kerryman from Corca Dhuibhne in the west of the county. His nickname *Cam* (crooked), may have referred to a squint. He was, it is said, educated by Brendan of Clonfert, who advised him to start his own monastic establishment at Kinnitty, in what is now Co. Offaly. His life seems to have been hopelessly confused with Fíonán of Swords, Fíonán Lobhar, but it is fairly certain that he was connected with Church Island on Lough Currane in Kerry, which has a Romanesque church, a series of crosses and a big beehive cell which has been identified by archaeologist Françoise Henry as a kiln for drying grain. Some scholars have tended to discard the stories of this saint's connection with Inisfallen, Lough Leane and Skellig Michael. His feast day is 7 April.

Fíonán Lobhar was no leper. Lobhar really meant 'ill, infirm'; in the past leprosy was used to describe many skin diseases such as eczema. Although nowadays Kerry people confuse this saint with Fíonán Cam, Fíonán Lobhar was born in Leinster and was connected with Colmcille's Swords in north Dublin. That saint's Life says: 'A church was built there by Colmcille. And Colmcille left a good man of his household to succeed him there, Fíonán Lobhar. And there he left the missal that he himself had copied.'

If the story of his connection to Swords is true, it could account for Fíonán's popularity in Scotland. The *Martyrology of Aberdeen* gives his feast day as 18 March. (In Ireland it is 16 March.) In 1643 the Presbytery of Inverness burned at the market cross 'ane Idolotrous image called Saint Finane, keepit in a private house obscurely'. Eilean Fhionain in Lough Sheil commemorates the Irish saint; as does the placename at the head of the lough, Glenfinnane, where Bonny Prince Charlie raised his standard in the '45.

**FIONN** earlier **FINN** (m) Mythical leader of the Fianna, a word used to describe young warrior-hunters. Stories concerning this band have been popular for over a thousand years. Finn's youth is depicted in the medieval text *Macgnímartha Find* (The Boyhood Deeds of Finn). In one famous story he is called Demne, and meets a sage called Finnéigeas on the banks of the Boyne. Demne is only seven and is fascinated when the old man tells him of his attempts to land the Salmon of Knowledge from the river. He has been seven years trying to catch the fish and has just succeeded. He allows the boy to tend the fire over which the fish is being cooked, but warns him not to eat any of it. As the boy turns the fish on a spit he burns his thumb, and putting it in his mouth to relieve the pain, he is thereby given the salmon's gift of wisdom and knowledge. Finnéigeas, whose name means 'Finn the Seer', can do nothing about the boy's new-found gift, but decrees that in future he should be called not Demne but Finn, which means 'blond, fair, brilliant'. He is actually the Celtic god *Vindos*. When he comes of age he is made leader of the Fianna, a sort of royal bodyguard as well as a hunting band, by the High King Cormac mac Airt, as a reward for destroying a demon who had taken over his fortress. The stories and lays concerning him are beautiful for the most part, containing wonderful descriptions of life in the outdoors as well as robust adventures full of magic, sorcery and hunting. The tales of Finn and his men were as popular in Scotland as they were in Ireland. See *Diarmaid, Oisín, Oscar, Gráinne, Conán.*

**FIONNBHARRA** earlier **FINNBARR** (m) The name means 'fair-head', and it was the name of the man reputed to be the founder of the early monastery of Cork, and now patron of the diocese. He died around 633 and his feast day is 25 September. There are half a dozen versions of his Life in Latin and two in Irish. Interestingly, no mention is made in the Latin Lives of his supposed foundation of Gougán Barra, that beautiful place at the source of the River Lee, and the scene of pilgrimages, public and private, for countless generations.

Finnbarr was, it was said, the son of Amhairgin, the illegitimate son of a nobleman and chief metalworker to the local king or chieftain. He fell in love with a bondswoman of the chieftain Tighearnach of Raithleann. Unfortunately so did the chieftain, who would have slain the lady but for a miracle. Amhairgin and his woman had a child who was called Finnbarr because of his shock of blond hair. His name was shortened in Irish to Barre and Bairre not long after this time. He was venerated in the Hebrides as well as on the Scottish mainland. The island of Barra in the Outer Hebrides is named after him. An account written in 1695 tells of a pilgrimage on Barra in honour of the saint. It mentions 'St Barr's wooden image standing on the altar, covered with linen in the form of a shirt. All the islanders observe the anniversary of St Barr; it is performed riding on horseback, and the solemnity is concluded by three turns round St Barr's church.' Perhaps Finnbarr visited the place himself; however, it is just as likely that the devotion was brought there by pious Cork monks.

Whether Finnbarr was ever in Gougán Barra or not, and one distinguished modern scholar has his doubts, he will forever be associated with a foundation which may have stood where the Church of Ireland cathedral, named from him, now stands in Cork city.

There is a famous Cork city hurling club named after him. The name has been anglicised *Finbar*, *Finnbar*, *Finbarr* and *Barry*.

**FIONNCHÚ** earlier **FINNCHÚ** (m) A saint of the name who died around 664 was the founder of a monastery at Brí Gobann, Mitchelstown, Co. Cork. Finnchú means 'fair warrior or fair hound'. Stories about him still survive in the folklore of the Mitchelstown area, where his name has been anglicised as *Fanahan*.

A fanciful medieval biography of Finnchú depicts him as more a warrior than a saint. His father Findlugh was supposedly banished after rising against the high king. This Findlugh got a girl pregnant. The king of Munster gave her shelter and she did little errands for the royal household. Once when she was sent to a brewer to fetch some ale, she was refused; the child she was carrying spoke from her womb and caused all the ale vats to burst. The child was baptised Finnchú by St Ailbhe and was taken north for schooling at Bangor by St Comhghall. He was given the task of keeping animals out of the monastery meadow, and when the king of Ulster grazed his horses there when he came to visit Comhghall, the child turned them into stone and caused the king to sink to his knees in the field. Finnchú was a warrior-saint who fought many battles, but was noted for his self-mortification. He used to suspend himself from hooks in the presence of dead people being waked in his church in order to keep the devil away from them. A strange saint indeed, if we were to believe the medieval stories. His feast day is 25 November.

**FIONNUALA, NUALA** earlier **FINNGUALA** (f) The name means 'fair shouldered' and was very popular in Ireland in the later Middle Ages. One lady of the name, an O'Brien, built with her husband Aodh Rua O'Donnell the monastery of Donegal town and gave it to the Franciscans; the couple are buried there. She may be responsible for the great popularity of the name in Co. Donegal to this day. The name is also popular in other parts of Ireland, particularly in its shortened form *Nuala*, which was being used as far back as the thirteenth century. It was latinised as *Filorcia* and *Fenollina*, and has been transmuted into a variety of foreign names when Irish names went out of fashion at different times during our history, particularly in the eighteenth and nineteenth centuries: *Flora*, *Penelope*, *Penny* and *Nappy* among them. Sir Walter Scott is probably responsible for the popularity of the Scottish form *Fenella*. *Finola* is now popular in Ireland.

**FIONNÚIR** earlier **FINNABAIR** (f) Daughter of Ailill and Medb of Connacht. She fell in love with Fraoch (p. 98). The name may mean 'white spirit or ghost'. She has a Welsh equivalent, *Gwenhwyvar*, the wife of King Arthur. I have seen the name anglicised *Fennure*.

**FIONTAN** earlier **FINTAN** (m) There were two important early Irish saints of that name. One was Fintan of Clonenagh, Co. Laois, a pupil of St Colmán of

Terryglass, Co. Tipperary. He died in 603. His feast day is 17 February.

Another Fintan was founder of the monasteries of Taghmon, Co. Wexford, and Taughmon, Co. Westmeath. These place-names mean 'Munnu's house', Mo Fhinniu or Munnu being the saint's pet name. This Fintan died in 635; his feast day is 21 October. He was a well-travelled man, having studied at St Comhghall's house at Bangor and at Iona. Fintan was possibly from Irish *fin* (fair). Other scholars have suggested that the name could mean 'white old one' or 'white fire' or from a Celtic compound *Vindo-senos* (old Find).

Whatever its origin, Fintan was a seer of Irish mythology long before our saints' days, which suggested to Ó hÓgain that Fintan was a variant in ancient lore of the mythical seer Find. He is said to have come to Ireland with a woman called Cessair and her followers of three men and 50 women, some 40 years before the biblical Deluge. When the other two men died, the other women made advances to poor Fintan, and he ran away from them and hid in a hole near the River Shannon, close to Portroe, Co. Tipperary. He stayed there until the waters subsided.

There is a vast store of lore about him. He lived for thousands of years. At the time of the Crucifixion, a stranger came to him and persuaded him to become a Christian. From this stranger he got knowledge of the ancient past of Ireland.

Other lore has him travelling about as a one-eyed salmon, an eagle, and a falcon, before resuming his human form again. It was said that his body was mysteriously carried off to a secret place to await the Last Trump.

**FÍTHEAL** earlier **FÍTHEL** (m) This ancient name may mean 'fairy' or 'goblin'. He was the chief judge at the court of the High King Cormac Mac Airt. The seventeenth-century historian Seathrún Céitinn (Geoffrey Keating) retells an ancient story about Fítheal. As the great and wise judge lay seriously ill, he called his son Flaithrí to his bedside and gave him four pieces of advice: not to bring up a king's son; not to entrust a secret to his wife; not to help the son of a slave to rise to importance in the world; and not to give his sister control over the dispersal of his wealth. Fítheal died and his son decided to test the wisdom of the old judge's advice. So he promoted the son of a servant of his and saw that the man grew very rich. He asked his sister to look after some of his money. He then took on the job of tutoring a son of King Cormac. The boy he caused to be taken out into a wood to live for a while with a trustworthy swineherd; he promised to take him back shortly. When he returned home he pretended to be very distressed, and told his wife that the cause of his misery was that he had killed the king's son. He pleaded with her not to tell a soul about the matter and to stand by him. Constant she was, but yet a woman, and she babbled about what her husband had told her. The high king soon heard the story and Flaithrí was arrested. The slave he had promoted was one of those who swore false evidence against him. Languishing in prison he asked his sister to go bail for him, but she denied having ever been entrusted with any of his money. In dire straits now, he asked for an interview with Cormac and was granted one. He told the king that his son was not dead, but was enjoying life under the greenwood trees in the care of a swineherd. He directed the king's men to the man's little house, and they brought home the prince to his father. Flaithrí then explained to Cormac that he was testing the advice he got from his father, and found it, to his cost, to be excellent.

**FLANN** (m, f) This ancient name was very popular in medieval times. One Flann Mac Lonáin was called Chief Poet of Ireland—by himself, it is true. He died around 920. He was called Flann Aidhne. Aidhne is a district in north Clare and south Galway. A story from not long after his time tells of Flann and some companions sitting alone in an empty house, famished with hunger. Enter a giant leading a bullock. In return for the promise of a milch cow, the giant kills the bullock for the poet and departs. The following year the giant returns and demands the milch cow, or else! Flann recites a poem for him, and the giant, who is really the god Aengus (p. 8), tells him that the poem is the cow he demanded. Another story says that when he was murdered and buried near Terryglas in north Tipperary, he rose from the dead to recite a poem he had composed about himself and some other people who were buried with him.

There were many saints of the name, including Flann, bishop of Finglas, whose feast day is 21 January; and Flann, abbot of Lismore, Emly and Cork, whose feast day is 14 January. The diminutives are *Flannán* and *Flannacán* (below).

Some distinguished women also bore the name *Flann* in ancient times. Among them are Flann, daughter of Donnchad, and queen of Aileach, who died about 940. The name has been ludicrously anglicised as *Florence*.

**FLANNACÁN, FLANNAGÁN** (m) This is a diminutive of *Flann* (p. 96). One notable man of this name was Flannacán mac Cellaig, who died about 896. He was a poet and king of Brega (Meath). From this first name came the surname *Ó Flannagáin* (O'Flanagan). I have never heard of this diminutive being given to a child in recent times.

**FLANNÁN** (m) Diminutive of *Flann* (p. 96). This seventh-century saint was abbot of Cill Dá Lua (Killaloe), Co. Clare. The name means 'red'. His twelfth-century Latin biography says that he was the son of a king of a Dál gCais sept and was famous for his miraculous powers. When he succeeded Dálua, founder of the monastery, he travelled on a sea rock to Rome to be consecrated. When he returned, his father gave up his kingship and became a monk. Flannán, according to his biographer, was adept at foiling robbers and other miscreants. Once he turned meat they were cooking on a spit putrid before their eyes; on another occasion he turned some men who were mocking him to stone. While he was abbot, his lands and his people flourished, the River Shannon teemed with fish, the land was rich in fruit and crops, and the poor prospered. His name is anglicised *Flannan*. His feast day is 18 December.

**FLIDAIS** (f) This sexy mythical lady's name was probably

connected with deer; the word *oss* is contained in her name and means 'a deer'. She may have been an animal goddess. Because of her association with animals she was associated with Fergus mac Róich and became his woman. He was a man of voracious sexual appetite and Flidais, alone of all the women of Ireland, could satisfy him. When for one reason or another she didn't share his bed, she was replaced by no fewer than seven women. One of the tales of the Ulster Cycle tells of the couple's wooing.

She was, when he first saw her, the wife of Ailill Finn, king of the Gamhanra sept in what is now Co. Mayo. The satiric poet Bricriú brought them together at the court of Queen Medb. No sooner had he done so than they fell madly in love and immediately began to plot the demise of poor Ailill. At a feast given by Flidais at her fortress, Ailill, becoming suspicious that dark deeds were afoot, made captives of Fergus and his retinue. Flidais got her husband very drunk and, not quite knowing what he was doing, Ailill released Fergus and his men at her request. They immediately joined Medb and her forces against him. Ailill, completely outmanned, fought with great bravery and when all his men had fallen, he asked a smith named Ceartan to allow him to escape with him in his boat. Ceartan refused, and Ailill beheaded him with a slingshot. Ailill fought on, refusing to surrender until he was slain. And so Flidais went off with her beloved Fergus, taking with her her famous herd of cattle, among them her prized cow called the *Maol*, the hornless one, whose milk of an evening could feed 300 men and their families. They may not have deserved to do so, but the story goes that Flidais and Fergus lived very happily until she died in his arms many years later in his fortress in Ulster.

**FRAOCH** (m) This man was a mythical hero of the Ulster Cycle, his mother being a woman of the Otherworld called Bé Find, a sister of Bóinn. *Fraoch* means 'heather'. An eighth-century text called *Táin Bó Fraoich* tells two long stories about him. A fourteenth-century poem retells the first story. Medb, queen of Connacht, fell in love with Fraoch. But he preferred her beautiful daughter Finnabair, which caused Medb to plan to do away with him. There was a pool in the river where she used to bathe, and it was protected by a water monster. Medb asked the young man to bring her some branches from a rowan tree which grew by the pool. As he approached the tree he was attacked by the monster. He was unarmed, but Finnabair threw him a knife. In the fight Fraoch succeeded in killing the monster, but he himself died from his wounds. Poor Finnabair died from grief shortly afterwards. The story passed into the folklore of Scotland and it was told and retold there for centuries. The English girl's name *Heather* has been gaelicised as *Fraoch* in some schools.

**FURSA** (m) Fursa was an important Irish saint of the seventh century. His birthplace is unknown, but medieval biographies say that he was the son of a Munster prince, and his mother a daughter of the king of Breifne, Áed Finn. Another tradition says his mother was named Gelgéis (bright swan). After schooling in a Lough Corrib monastery founded by St Brendan, he went to Headford, Co. Galway. From there he travelled to see his father in Munster and while in his father's house he had his famous vision during a bout of illness. Angels brought him to a hilltop, and looking down he saw four fires impending over the world: the fires of lies, greed, discord and cruelty. The fires became one, and a legion of demons attacked Fursa. He was thrown into the arms of a man who had given him his clothes before he died, and for accepting a sinner's clothes Fursa's face and shoulder were scorched. The scars remained with him when he recovered from his sickness.

He travelled to Britain, settling in the territory of Sigebert, king of the East Saxons, and when that king, his patron, was killed in battle with the Mercians, Fursa crossed over to the continent and settled at Lagny on the Marne. He was supported by the Frankish king Clovis II. He died when travelling in Gaul and his body was transferred to Peronne, *Peronna Scottorum* (Peronne of the Irish), which became a centre of devotion to the saint as well as a famous monastery and centre of learning.

Bede was impressed with the story of Fursa's vision and related it; it became widely known on the continent. Some have said that Dante sourced the *Divina Comedia* from it. The date of his death is given as 16 January 649 or 650; 16 January is his feast day. His name has been anglicised *Fursey. The Unfortúnate Fursey* is a very amusing novel by Mervyn Wall.

# G

**GARBHÁN** earlier **GARBÁN** (m) The name comes from *garb* (rough). There were five saints called Garbán and very little is known of any of them. The best known of them is Garbán of Cenn Sáile, not the Cork town but a place near Swords, Co. Dublin. His feast day is 9 July. There was an early king of Munster who bore this name, which in our day has been anglicised *Garvin* and *Garvan*.

**GEARALT** (m) Irish form of *Garret* or *Garrett*, said to have been introduced into Mayo by an Anglo-Saxon monk named *Garalt* in the eighth century and reintroduced by the Normans.

**GEARÓID** (m) Irish form of both *Gerald* and *Gerard*, names introduced by the Normans. These names are of Germanic origin. *Gerald* is composed of the elements *gar*, *ger* (spear) and *wald* (rule). *Gerard* is composed of *gar*, *ger* (spear) and *hard* (brave, strong). *Gearóid* is from Old French *Geraud*. Gearóid Iarla (Gerald, the Earl) was a famous late medieval poet of the Fitzgerald family.

**GEARÓIDÍN** (f) The diminutive female form of *Gearóid*. The English form *Geraldine* was, it appears, invented by the Earl of Surrey in a praise-poem for Lady Fitzgerald.

**GOBNAIT** (f) Possibly a feminine form of *Gobán*, a derivative of the name of the Irish god of arts and crafts, *Goibniu*. She is the saint of Baile Bhuirne (Ballyvourney) in west Cork, and of Kilgobnet across the county border in Kerry. She is associated with beekeeping and her feast day, 11 February, is considered to be the ideal day for planting potatoes. A prayer to her, still said by pilgrims seeking a cure at her shrine, goes: Go mbeannaí Dia dhuit, a Ghobnait naofa / Go mbeannaí Muire dhuit is beannaím féin duit, / Is chugatsa a thánag ag gearán mo scéil leat / Is ad iarraidh mo leighis ar son Dé ort. (May God greet you, holy Gobnait / May Mary greet you, as I do / To you I come to complain of my sorrows / And to ask you for a cure, in the name of God.) The saint's name has regrettably been anglicised as *Abigail*, *Abina* and *Abbey*, even in her own district in west Cork.

**GORMÁN** (m, f) The name means 'dark complexioned'. There is a saint of the name commemorated in the placename Cill Ghormáin in the parish of Gorey, Co. Wexford. His feast day is 25 October. The name was also given to girls. It has been anglicised as *Gorman*.

**GORMLAITH** (f) This beautiful and very popular name in ancient times comes from a combination of *gorm* (illustrious) and *flaith* (sovereignty). Perhaps the most illustrious Gormlaith was the daughter of the king of Leinster who married Brian Boru and was the mother of Sitric, king of Dublin. The name has regained popularity in Donegal where, since the decline of Irish in the nineteenth century, it had been anglicised as *Barbara*, of all things.

**GRIAN** (f) I have never, thankfully, heard an anglicisation of this ancient name which means either 'sun' or 'sun-goddess'. The goddess had her home, or at least one of her homes, at Pailís Gréine (now Pallasgreen) in Co. Limerick. Above Old Pallas a lush hill rises, and there *Grian*, the sun-goddess, held court. In legend she is said to be a daughter of Finn. The name was once common in that part of Limerick; it used to be found too in the vicinity of Cashel, Co. Tipperary, and in north Waterford. Loch Gréine, mentioned in Brian Merriman's bawdy romp, *Cúirt an Mheón Oíche* (The Midnight Court), is named from her.

**GUAIRE** (m) King of Connacht from *c.*655 to *c.*666, Guaire was known for his generosity. One anecdote concerning him, still common in the folklore of east Galway and north Clare, tells of him enjoying a sumptuous meal in his fortress, while further south his bishop St Colmán mac Duach was fasting with a lone cleric in the wilderness of the Burren. On Easter Sunday, weak from fasting, Colmán found that he had no food. At the same time Guaire, with a fine meal before him, thought that some holy man should have such food to eat on Easter Day. Immediately the bowl Guaire was eating from rose in the air and was miraculously transported to Colmán. Guaire followed the bowl, and finding Colmán and his clerk, brought them back after they had eaten to his fortress and presented them with a herd of milch cows. The road between the king's fortress at Dúrlas and the Burren was afterwards known as *Bóthar na Mias* (the road of the dishes).

Guaire performed his final act of charity after his death. As he was being taken to Clonmacnoise for burial, his bier was approached by a beggar. Guaire stretched out his dead hand and threw a fistful of sand at the poor man. The sand turned to gold. See also *Aonna*.

# I

**IARLA** earlier **IARLAITH** (m) Very little is now known about this sixth-century saint, patron of the archdiocese of Tuam. He established his first monastic house at Cluain Fois (now Cloonfush), a few miles from Tuam, and later transferred to Tuam itself. He was said to be a great teacher; tradition has it that he had Brendan of Clonfert and Colmán of Cloyne among his pupils.

No evidence remains of his foundation at Tuam except for a restored High Cross. Until its loss in 1830 a beautiful silver shrine associated with the saint was kept at Teampall na Scríne, Tuam. A pilgrimage to his Holy Well not far from the town was famous all over Connacht until its suppression in the 1840s.

The name took the form *Jarlath* in the National School rolls and in parish baptismal registers after 1831. It is still quite common in this form. The saint's feast day is 26 December.

**ÍDE** earlier **ÍTE** (f) This saint is the patroness of Kileedy, Co. Limerick. Her feast day, still celebrated with fervour, is 15 January. Legend had it that she was none other than the foster-mother of Jesus. The name, which may derive from Old Irish *itu* (thirst), is anglicised as *Ita* and is often confused with *Ida*, a Norman name of Germanic origin derived from *id* (work). It is generally accepted that she was a native of the Déise area of Waterford, the daughter of a nobleman called Ceannfhaolaidh, and that another nobleman wanted to marry her. Her father did not want her to be a nun and kept pestering her until an angel told him in a vision to mend his ways. It was then that she headed for west Limerick. It is claimed that her first name was actually Deirdre and that Íte was a pet name given to her because of her *íota* (thirst) for holiness.

Legends about her still abound in folklore. A farmer whose crop was being devastated by sparrows came to her for help. She banished the birds to a nearby pond until the crop was harvested. A whitethorn tree at Killeedy is said to have grown from a thorn which she plucked from her donkey's hoof; the thorns were perfectly harmless because they grew downwards on the tree. She is also the folk heroine of a story told of Brigit of Kildare as well, in that she cured a man born with the ears of a horse (p. 108).

**IOBHAR** earlier **IBAR** (m) He was one of the early saints of the south-east and had his foundation on a little island in Wexford Harbour called Begerin, now part of the reclaimed lands of the Wexford North Slob. Ibar was latinised as *Iberius.* Mícheál Ó Cléirigh mentions an ancient vellum book, *seanleabhar ró-aosta meamraim*, which likened the life and character of Ibar to John the Baptist. Tradition places him as a pre-Patrician saint. Ó Cléirigh has the following reference: 'Iobar, epscop. As i a cheall Becc-ere .i. inis fil for muir amuigh le hUibh Cheinsealaigh a Laignibh' (Iobar, bishop. His church is Beag-Éire, an island in the sea off Uí Cionsealaigh in Leinster). His name is sometimes anglicised as *Ivor.* The name may mean 'yew'. He died about 500 and his feast day is 23 April.

**ÍOMHAR** earlier **ÍMAR** (m) This is an imported name introduced by the Vikings. The Old Norse personal name was *Ívarr* and it was very popular among those who settled in the coastal towns of Arklow, Wicklow, Wexford, Waterford and Limerick. It proved quite popular among the Irish as well. The Old Norse name is composed of the elements *yr* (yew, bow) and *herr* (army, warrior). A king of Northumbria and of Dublin bore the name, and a *St Ímar* who taught St Malachy at Armagh had no Norse blood in his veins. The name has been anglicised as *Ivor.* The name became popular in Ireland, especially in Limerick and Clare, where the surname *Ó hÍomhair*, anglicised as *Howard*, grew from it.

**IRIAL** earlier **IRÉL** (m) The legendary Ulster warrior Conall Cearnach had a son bearing this name. The name was popular among many families in the later Middle Ages and is still given occasionally to male children today.

**ISIBÉAL** (f) See *Sibéal*, of which it is a variant.

**IUBHDÁN** (m) King of Fairyland. See *Bébó*.

**KERRY** (m, f) This name, popular among Irish-Americans, seems to be derived from the name of the southern county. There is no Irish equivalent; I know of no *Ciarraí*, alive or dead. There is a story told of a witty Irish broadcaster who, when interviewing the New York GAA boss John Kerry O'Donnell, asked where he got his second name, and was told that it was given to him to honour his relatives who came from Co. Kerry. 'How nice,' said his interviewer. 'Isn't it lucky for you that they didn't come from Hackballscross.'

# L

**LABHRAIDH** earlier **LABRAID** (m) This mythical king was the supposed ancestor of the people of Leinster. He was known as Labhraidh Loingseach (exiled person), Labhraidh Moen (dumb) and Labhraidh Lorc (fierce.) Part of his legend still lives in folklore and is believed to echo the first coming of the Leinstermen to Ireland in the second century B.C.

The seventeenth-century historian, or pseudo-historian, Seathrún Céitinn (Geoffrey Keating), retold the story, still found in an expanded version in folklore, of 'Labhraidh and the Horse's Ears'. Twentieth-century versions have, with a complete disregard for timescale, brought Leinster's great mythical king into contact with Leinster's principal saint, Brigit of Kildare. In Brigit's medieval biographies we are told that she was visited by a flat-faced man, and that by a miracle she gave him eyes with which to see the world. The storytellers expanded this in the story of King Labhraidh's terrible affliction: he was born with the ears of a horse. He came to the saint of Kildare for consolation and in a state of depression laid his royal head on her lap. 'I don't know what blemish you speak of,' she said to him, after she had blessed him. When Labraid got off his knees and felt his head, the horse's ears were gone, replaced by ordinary human ones.

The name Labraid also appears among the lists of early clerics. A Labraid, abbot of Slane, died in 845.

The name Labhraidh has been anglicised as *Lowry*.

**LABHRÁS** (m) The name means 'laurel bush'. Flanagan was of the opinion that this name would be a better equivalent for Laurence than *Lorcán* (p. 113), and points out that in the notice of the death of St Laurence O'Toole he is described as Labhrás, not Lorcán.

**LAISREÁN** earlier **LAISRÉN** (m) From *lassar* 'flame'. This is an exclusively male name. It is anglicised *Laserian.* He is the saint of Devenish Island in Lough Erne. Known affectionately as *Molaisse*, he was educated by St Finian of Clonard. Little is known of his life except what is related in the unreliable medieval miracle stories surrounding him. According to one of these, he brought a shipload of soil to Devenish from Rome, to sanctify the place, along with various relics of Sts Peter, Paul, Stephen and Clement, a lock of the Blessed Virgin's hair and an ankle bone of St Martin of Tours. His feast day is 12 September.

**LAOGHAIRE** earlier **LÁEGAIRE** (m) A very common early name which was given to some distinguished men, including Láegaire, High King of Ireland when St Patrick came to Ireland as a missionary. The saint's seventh-century biographer Muirchú's account of the king's capture of Patrick, when he had lit a paschal fire at Slane while Láegaire was about to light one at Tara in honour of the sun god, and of the king's subsequent conversion, is regarded as fanciful. It is more likely that the saint's other seventh-century biographer, Tíreachan, is correct in stating that Láegaire was not converted.

There were other famous fictional characters who bore this name. One could be considered the champion of poets. His name was Láegaire Buadhach and he was one of the important men at the court of Conchobar mac Nessa in the days of the Red Branch. There is an interesting eleventh-century text which describes his death.

Mughain, wife of King Conchobar, was unfaithful to him. Her lover, the poet Áed, was caught *in flagrante* and was sentenced to death. He asked that he be executed by drowning. The king agreed. The poet was taken to lake after lake and they all dried up after he sang a spell. Finally he was taken to a lake directly in front of the warrior Láegaire's house. The spell wouldn't work there.

Furious that they should try to kill a poet in this manner, Láegaire rushed out of the house to fight the poet's abductors. He struck his head against the lintel of the door in his hurry. His blood and brains were spattered over his cloak. Nevertheless, he managed to kill 30 of Áed's executioners before he himself died. The poet was allowed to go free.

A medieval romance, dated by some as from the fourteenth century, concerns a young handsome prince called Laoghaire. He was the son of the Connacht king Criomhann Cas. At his father's assembly by the shores of Enloch (Lough Nen), near Athlone, a stranger was seen approaching out of the mist. He was dressed in expensive clothes and he introduced himself as Fiachna from the Otherworld. His wife had been abducted, he said. He managed to kill that abductor, Eochaidh, but she was then taken by Eochaidh's nephew Goll who lived at a fairy palace at Magh Meall. He was looking for recruits who would help him get his wife back. Laoghaire and 50 of his young warriors agreed to help. They dived into the lake after Fiachna and soon reached the Otherworld. They slaughtered Goll's men and Fiachna was reunited with his wife. Fiachna's daughter married Laoghaire, whose men got 50 beautiful Otherworld women for their valour. At the end of a year, Laoghaire wanted to go home to explain things to his father. Fiachna consented but warned him and his men to ride horses there and not to dismount. When they emerged from the lake the king asked them to stay. Unlike Oisín (p. 141), he refused to dismount, and having told the king that they were blissfully happy in the Otherworld, they galloped back into the lake and were never seen again.

**LAOISE** (f) This seems to be a female equivalent of *Laoiseach*. It has been anglicised as *Lucy*, a name of a totally different origin.

**LAOISEACH** earlier **LAIGSECH** (m) Some say this name derives from the sun-god *Lugh*; others that it is the more prosaic 'man of Laois'. Certainly it was a favourite name among the chiefs of Laois, the O'Mores. It was anglicised in the National

Schools as *Louis*, *Lewis* and *Lucius*, names with which it has no connection whatever; and *Lysagh*, which is only slightly more acceptable.

**LASAIR** earlier **LASSAR** (f) A beautiful name from the Middle Ages, it means 'flame'. Lassar of the royal Eoghanachta sept of Munster was the mother of St Feichíne of Fore (p. 85), Co. Westmeath. There was a Lassar, daughter of Laeghaire Mac Néill, king of Tara; St Lassar of Co. Meath was the mother of St Ibar of Wexford (p. 105); and a saintly nun of that name from somewhere near Macroom, Co. Cork, was said to have been taught by St Finbarr of Cork. The patron date of St Lassar of Meath is given as 18 February.

**LASAIRFHÍONA** (f) I know of a lovely dark-haired singer of Irish songs from Inis Oirr in the Aran Islands who bears this name, which means 'flame of wine'. It was a common name in the Connacht of the Middle Ages, a favourite name among the Mac Dermott and O'Connor clans, among others. Lasairfhíona was the daughter of King Cathal Crobhdearg, 'Cathal Mór of the Wine-red hand'. She was known as the foremost among the women of the northern half of Ireland, and she died in 1282. This beautiful name has been anglicised as *Lasrina* and *Lassrina*.

**LÍADAIN** (f) She was a seventh-century poetess. Four centuries later a great love story, which reminds one of the story of Abelard and Heloise, was written about her love of Cuirithir. She met him while on a circuit of Connacht and he followed her to her home in Munster. She was at this time a nun under the guidance of St Cumaine Fada, who forbade the lovers to sleep together. He relented and cruelly agreed that they might sleep together just once—but with a clerical student lying between them. Cuirithir was banished by Cumaine and he became a monk who travelled to the far off territory of the Déise in Co. Waterford. When Líadain heard this, she followed him, but her lover went to sea in a little boat before she could reach him. The Déise people pointed out to her a flagstone on which he used to pray, and Líadain made it her bed until she died of grief. They buried her beneath the stone.

St Ciarán of Seir's mother was also called Líadain. The ancient legend has it that while she was asleep she turned her open mouth towards heaven and a star fell into it; in this miraculous way her son was conceived. Another Líadain is a patron saint of the Dál Cais.

**LIAM** (m) This is the modern version of a name introduced here by the Anglo-Normans, the old Germanic name *Willahelm*. Very popular among the Burkes and Butlers as *Uilliam*, it was also favoured by many old Gaelic families, and not even the odium surrounding William of Orange affected its popularity.

**LIAMHAIN** earlier **LIAMUIN** (f) The legend has it that a woman of this name was a sister of St Patrick.

**LÍ BAN** (f) The name means 'loveliness of women' and it was borne by a beautiful mermaid in the twelfth or thirteenth century. She was the daughter of a man named Eochaidh who, together with all his people, was drowned when the waters of Lough Neagh rose and flooded the land. Lí Ban, immured in her tall bower, escaped. Disconsolate, she prayed to be turned into a salmon, and this was granted her. Her little dog was transformed into an otter. For 300 years they swam in the seas until one day a monk called Beoán, sailing to Rome at the request of St Comgall of Bangor, heard her sing among the waves. He drew near to her and she told him her sorrowful story. She promised to meet him a year from that time on the sea at Larne, in what is now Co. Antrim. She had evolved into a mermaid and was caught in a net by another monk called Fergus. When Beoán returned from his pilgrimage to Rome, a dispute arose with Fergus concerning the ownership of Lí Ban; at length, after both had prayed and fasted, it was decided, on the advice of an angel, that two stags from her sister's grave should be yoked to her chariot and that the stags be allowed to take her where they would. They stopped at a little church where the monks took her in and gave her the choice of either dying on the spot and going directly to heaven, or staying alive for another 300 years. She chose to die. She was baptised by Comgall and christened *Muirghein* by him. The name means 'sea birth'. She then went to God.

**LOCHLAINN** (m) The northern clans brought this name, which means 'Viking', into prominence in early medieval times. It is still in use. It has been anglicised as *Loughlin* and *Loughlan*, with the pet-form *Locky*. The Scottish form is *Lachlan*.

**LOMÁN** (m) The name derives from *lomm* (bare). The most important saint of this name is Lomán of Trim, Co. Meath, whose feast day is 11 October. According to tradition this Lomán was a British disciple of St Patrick, a cousin according to some. The chieftain of the district around Trim, Feilim, son of King Laoghaire of Tara, gave the lands around Trim to Patrick and Lomán. Patrick built a church there and in time this acquired a monastic character, with Lomán's successors combining the duties of abbot and bishop. For some generations only Feilim's successors could aspire to these ecclesiastical offices. The name Lomán is anglicised as *Loman*.

**LONÁN** (m) A medieval name now no longer used, except in its anglicised form *Lonan*. The name comes from *lon* (a blackbird) plus the diminutive suffix *-án*. There was a St Lonán Finn who used to be commemorated on 22 January. Nothing is known of him. There was also a saint called *Lon*, commemorated on 24 June. Yet another saint whose life is hidden in antiquity is Lonán of Trevnet in Meath, whose feast day is 1 November.

**LONNÓG** (f) The name is probably the diminutive of *lonn* which means 'headstrong'. We meet this woman in the medieval story of *Suibhne Geilt* (Mad Sweeney), the king who died in the arms of St Moling after spending years as a bird, doomed to fly about Ireland due to a clerical curse. She befriended the friendless Suibhne. See *Rónán* and *Eorann*.

**LORCÁN** (m) Anglicised quite acceptably *Lorcan* and, unfortunately, *Laurence*, a name with which it has no connection whatever, Lorcán was a very common name in the early Middle Ages. The grandfather of Brian Boru bore the name. The most famous Lorcán was St Lorcán Ó Tuathail (1228–80), patron of the archdiocese of Dublin, known in English as Laurence O'Toole. He was abbot of Glendalough and was appointed archbishop of Dublin. When Henry II came to Ireland with papal approval, Lorcán submitted to him; he had previously resisted the conquest. His relationship with the king was a fraught one. When Henry went to Normandy, Lorcán followed him to discuss some papal bulls concerning Irish matters to which the king took exception, but before the pair met Lorcán died at the Augustine monastery at Eu on 14 November 1180, now his feast day. He was canonised in 1226.

**LÚCÁS** (m) This Irish version of the name of the author of the third gospel of the New Testament has been in vogue since the late Middle Ages, when it was a favourite name among the members of the learned MacEgan family. *Lucas* was the Latin form of Middle English *Luke*; the name's origin is the post-classical Greek name *Loukas* (man from Lucania). Lúcás was a physician, a gentile, and a convert of St Paul.

**LÚGADÁN** (m) This saint is a shadowy figure in the early Irish Church. He gave his name to the placename Templeudigan, a few miles from New Ross, Co. Wexford. He was believed to be St Patrick's nephew. There is a holy well in the area dedicated to St Patrick, and patterns used to be held there on 17 March until 1820. No trace of any legend, or indeed of any devotion, to *St Lúgadán* survives. Perhaps he never existed, or perhaps he was a cleric of such little significance that the idea of making him a relation of St Patrick arose to give him some stature. The name is no longer given to children in the district; one local source suggested that its falling from popularity may have something to do with its phonetic proximity to the word *liúdramán* (a lanky, lazy lout).

**LUGH** earlier **LUG** (m) This mythical hero was originally a Celtic god. His Welsh name was *Lleu*, his mother the beautiful Eithne. His name possibly means 'brightness, light'. Julius Caesar mentions that the Gauls worshipped a god whom he equated with the Roman Mercury: 'They say he invented all the arts, he is their guide on every road and journey, and they consider him to have the greatest influence on money-making and commercial transactions.' Lug is the god in question; of that there is no doubt. He is also known in Ireland as *Samildánach* (master of every art). The Irish added the sobriquet Lámhfhada (long-armed) to his name. Lug was also the focus of a harvest festival cult; one harvest fair was held in his honour at Lyon, a place named after him, on 1 August, according to classical writers. The same type of celebration has been held in Ireland since ancient times, and is called Lughnasa.

The fullest account of Lugh is to be found in *Cath Maige Tuiread* (the Battle of Moyturra), which dates from the eleventh century but has material written down many centuries earlier. In this account a demonic people called the Fomorians were pitted against the Tuatha Dé Danann, a divine race. Balor of the Fomorians (p. 12) gave his daughter Eithne to a prince of the Tuatha Dé Danann, and they had a son, Lug. Now the Tuatha Dé Danann king, Nuadhu, had to relinquish the throne because of losing an arm in battle. He was replaced by the tyrant Fomorian Breas. His reign of terror ended when the Tuatha Dé Danann gave Nuadhu a silver arm and restored him to the throne. Breas gathered an immense army from the northern zones of the globe to invade Ireland. Nuadhu was at Tara attempting to frame a battle plan when a most handsome stranger approached the fort and asked to gain entry. He was refused at first, but when he proclaimed that he had all the arts the king would require to win the war, he was allowed into Nuadhu's presence. He showed the king his great strength by flinging a huge flagstone a great distance, and he followed this by playing magic music on a harp. The king was so impressed that he was named commander of the army. At Moyturra (in Co. Sligo) Lugh slipped away from the fighting armies and circled the battlefield while he chanted a spell. In the course of the battle, which was the bloodiest ever seen, Lugh came face to face with his Fomorian grandfather, Balor. This man had an eye which he never opened except in battle. The army on which it would gaze would be destroyed on the spot. It took four men to open it. But as soon as the evil eye was opened, Lugh cast a slingshot at it and drove it through Balor's head. Balor fell dead. The battle ended with a rout of the Fomorians, but Lugh spared the life of Breas in exchange for advice about ploughing, sowing and harvesting.

Folklore about Lugh survives to this day, particularly in Co. Donegal where much has been collected.

**LUGHACH** (f) This ancient girl's name probably derives from *Lugh* (above). In *Laoithe na Féinne*, the great ballad lore of the Fianna, *Lughach* is the daughter of Fionn.

**LÚÍ** earlier **LUGHAIDH, LUGAID** (m) This is another name derived from *Lugh* (above). It is a very old name and popular in ancient Ireland. Various Lugaids are said to be ancestors of some of the great families of Ireland. One was the reputed ancestor of the Munster family of O'Driscoll; another of the O'Mores; another still of the Dál Cais. Lugaid mac Con was a renowned Munster warrior. There are quite a few saints of the name. Perhaps the most famous is Lugaid moccu Ochnae, who is better known as *St Molua* of Clonfertmulloe, Co. Laois. He is also associated with Druim Sneachta (Drumsnat), Co. Monaghan. He was born around 554 and died in the early years of the next century.

His three Lives tell us that he was a Munster man, the youngest of three sons, and that he was the boy who herded the family's cows. He attracted the attention of St Comgall (p. 49) who, after Molua's ordination, told him to go to Druim Sneachta and found a monastery there. He afterwards came south to Clonfertmulloe and made it his principal foundation.

His rule was said to have been approved by Gregory the Great. He insisted on the importance of frequent confession, and a story retold in the Lives tells of a lay visitor to his foundation who refused to go to confession. One day as the pair went for a walk, the visitor was surprised when Molua knelt by a roadside cross and asked God to forgive him for not going to confession that day. The visitor asked Molua was it not sufficient to ask God for forgiveness. Molua replied, saying he felt that daily confession was necessary for him. Just as the floor should be swept daily to keep it clean, so should one's soul be cleaned by frequent confession.

Some of the stories told in the Lives about the saint's boyhood and early manhood are charming. One of these which tells of a minor miracle performed during his life with Comgall is amusing. He fell asleep holding his lighted candle during Matins and let it fall into the holy water font. He plucked it out before Comgall turned around and, of course. it was still burning brightly.

The name has been rendered *Lewis* and *Louis* in English.

**LUÍSEACH** earlier **LUIGSECH** (f) It appears to mean 'bright girl'. *St Luigsech* was one of the early virgin saints. She is commemorated on 22 May.

**MÁBLA** (f) This name seems to be a gaelicisation of *Mabel*, itself from the now rare English name *Amabel*, from the Latin *amabilis* (lovable). It was once a very common name in the Donegal highlands but seems to have gone out of fashion in recent years. There is a pleasant eighteenth-century song about a girl called *Mábla Shéimh Ní Cheallaigh*, which could, I suppose, be translated as 'Gentle Mabel Kelly'.

**MAC CÁIRTHINN** (m) The name means 'son of the mountain ash'. It is now quite popular in the northern counties in its English manifestation, the quite acceptable *Macartan*, who is the patron saint of the diocese of Clogher. He is reputed to have been placed in that diocese by St Patrick. Fragmentary medieval Lives of the saint give little information about him. O'Hanlon has written that his grave at Clogher was long pointed out and venerated and that people used to come there on his feast day, 24 March, and take soil from the grave as a relic. The Great Shrine of St Mac Cárthinn, intended to contain relics including a fragment of the True Cross, is probably the still extant *Domnach Airgid*. This seems to have been no more than a simple wooden box. It was covered with metal plates as early as the seventh or eighth century, further decorations being added later, when it contained only a gospel book. Other relics connected with Mac Cáirthinn's foundation in Co. Tyrone are two high crosses and the thirteenth-century processional Cross of Clogher.

**MAC DARA** (m) A common name in Connemara, St Mac Dara is regarded as the patron of local fishermen. The name means 'son of the oak'. His feast day, 16 July, is celebrated in an annual pilgrimage to St Mac Dara's Island.

**MACHA** (f) This Otherworld lady of the Ulster Cycle seems to have been a goddess of the land, as her name means 'pasture'. She certainly represented sovereignty in Ulster myth and the chief fortress of the Ulstermen, Eamhain Mhacha, now called Navan Fort in Co. Armagh, is named from her, as is the town of Ard Mhacha (Armagh).

A medieval account of this formidable woman says that once upon a time in Ireland there were three kings, Dithorba, Aodh and Ciombaoth, who decided to rule the country between them, each of them in turn serving as king for seven years. When they had served three terms each Aodh died and his daughter Macha, which meant 'Red-head', demanded his share of the sovereignty. When she was refused, she won her term by force of arms. When Dithorba died she refused to recognise his five sons, defeated them in battle and married the remaining king, Ciombaoth. Off she went to Connacht to encounter the fled sons of Dithorba. She found them in a wood cooking a boar. They had a feast, and afterwards each in turn invited her to sleep with him. She tied each of them up and forced them to return to Ulster with her, where she put them to building her a fine fortress. To mark out the site of this fortress she used a clasp which she wore around her neck. *Eo* means 'clasp' and *muin* means 'neck'; the fortress was therefore named Eamhain.

Ó hÓgáin tells of another medieval story which has a man named Crunnchú seduced by a beautiful woman who entered his house and became his housekeeper and consort. She became pregnant. Crunnchú set off to the court of King Conchobar mac Nessa, and his woman, Macha, told him that on no account was he to mention her presence in his house. But at a feast Crunnchú spilled the beans and said that he had a woman at home who could out-run the king's unbeaten racehorses. Crunnchú was arrested and the woman sent for. She told the king that she was pregnant, but was told that if she didn't race and win, her husband would be killed. She won the race, collapsed, and died after giving birth to twins. Hence the place got the name Eamhain Mhacha (the Twins of Macha) according to this particular etymologist. Before she drew her last breath Macha cursed the Ulstermen. The debility they subsequently suffered in times of great stress was known as the *cess noidhen* (the debility of childbirth); it affected them badly in the saga of *Táin Bó Cuailgne.*

Macha was always associated with horses, and it is significant that Cú Chulainn's great horse was called the Grey of Macha.

**MAINCHÍN** (m) The are two well-known saints called Mainchín, which means 'little monk': Mainchín the Wise of Laois, remembered on 2 January; and Mainchín of Limerick, a patron saint of Dál Cais. The name has been anglicised as *Mannix* and *Munchin.* Mainchín Seoighe (Mannix Joyce), the contemporary Limerick historian and antiquarian, is one who bears the name. A story is told in the twelfth-century text *Aislinge meic Conglinne* about a monk called Mainchín. The scholar Anére mac Con Glinne of Roscommon thought it a good idea to go on a circuit of Munster because he had heard that there was full and plenty wherever the gluttonous king Cathal Mac Fionghuine was. He came to the monastery at Cork, where Mainchín was abbot, and was very disappointed with the welcome he got. The guest house was a miserable hut open to the elements, the bedclothes crawling with vermin. He expected a servant to attend to his wishes, but found nobody. So he took out his psalm book and began to sing. Then he began to satirise the monastery, and Mainchín had him flogged and thrown into the Lee. The following morning the scholar was sentenced to be crucified. All the way to the place of execution he satirised the monks and delayed his end by various ruses such as drinking water from a well from the top of a pin. The monks begged Mainchín to put off the execution for a day and he agreed. Tied naked to a pillar, an angel came and recited a vision, after which the scholar composed another satire describing the king's genealogy through a list of food names, describing a journey through sumptuous food and ending with a description of the king's residence, which was composed entirely of delicious exotic dishes. Mainchín allowed the scholar to visit the king because he had heard that only by a vision could the king's demon of gluttony be expelled. After a series of adventures, including setting the house on fire, Mac Con Glinne expelled the demon from the king and was handsomely rewarded.

**MÁIRE** (f) This is a borrowing from the Latin *Maria*, a backformation from the early Christian name *Mariam*, an indeclinable Aramaic alternative form of the Hebrew name *Miriam*. In the early Church Máire was not used as a given name in deference to the Blessed Virgin. In late medieval times compounds such as *Mael Muire* (devotee of Mary) were reserved for the Virgin, while Máire was used as an ordinary given name. The diminutive of the name, *Máirín*, has given the English *Maureen*. Other anglicised forms are *Maura* and *Moira*.

**MÁIRÉAD** earlier **MÁRGRÉG** (f) The Irish form of *Margaret*, French *Marguerite*, German *Margerethe* and *Grete*; but which of them gave us our name? One possible answer is the lady called *Marina* in the Eastern churches, thought to be a virgin saint in the reign of Diocletian. This Margaret of Antioch was one of the most popular saints of western Europe in the Middle Ages, but in fact nothing is known about her except her name; her apochryphal Lives are pure fictitious romances. The story goes that she was a daughter of a pagan priest of Antioch and that when she became a Christian she declined to marry a prefect called Olybrius, who thereupon denounced her. She was put through terrible tortures. Apart from those, it was said that she was swallowed alive by Satan who visited her in the form of a dragon. She survived that ordeal because the story says that finally she was beheaded. This fable was written, it was said, by Theotimus, the lady's friend and attendant, who claimed to have been an eyewitness. Her emblem is the dragon. She is the patron of women in childbirth. A daughter of Henry III was christened Margaret because the saint's name was invoked during her birth.

The name is a borrowing from the Latin *margarita*, from a Greek word for 'a pearl'. Another Margaret, thought by some to be responsible for the popularity of the name in Ireland since the Middle Ages, is St Margaret of Scotland, wife of King Malcolm III, who died in 1093. Her name may be due to her Hungarian connections; she would have been known there as Margit.

**MÁIRTÍN, MÁRTAN** (m) The English, French and German form of the name is *Martin*, from Latin *Martinus*. This was derived from *Mars*, the god of war and earlier of fertility. The name became popular in the Middle Ages because of St Martin of Tours. Born in Upper Pannonia, an outpost of the Roman empire in Hungary, he was the son of a Roman officer. He became a leading figure in the fourth-century Church, but is now chiefly remembered for his charity in dividing his cloak in two and giving one half to a beggar.

Martin, Máirtín and Mártan are popular names in Ireland, and he is an important figure in Irish folklore. Sulpicius Severus wrote his biography, which left its mark on several early Irish and Hiberno-Latin texts. He was reputed to be the maternal uncle of St Patrick.

He is remembered on 11 November, and in many countries in western Europe it was customary to slaughter an animal on the eve of his feastday. Up to very recently Irish people used to kill a fowl on Martinmas Eve and sprinkle the blood on the door and around the kitchen while prayers were said to the saint for protection during the coming year. It was believed that no wheel should be turned on his feastday and that mills should close down. In the old days this prohibition extended to travel by any wheeled carriage and even to spinning. This was so because it was believed that Martin was crushed to death by his own mill wheel. In Wexford some fishermen still refuse to go fishing on his feastday. It is said that he can be sometimes seen riding a white horse on the sea on Martinmas Eve as a warning to men not to put to sea.

**MÁNAS** earlier **MAGHNUS, MAGNUS** (m) Originally a Latin byname meaning 'great', it was taken from the name Charlemagne, known in Latin chronicles as Carolus Magnus. The Scandinavian peoples used Magnus as a given name and that it became very popular may be seen from the fact that seven medieval kings of Norway bore it. There are also some Scandinavian saints of the name, notably Magnus, Earl of Orkney, who died in 1116. The name reached Ireland, probably from Scotland, in the Middle Ages and is still very popular in Donegal.

**MAODHÓG** earlier **MÁEDÓC** (m) Better known as *Aédán* or *Aidan*, this important saint was the first bishop of Ferns. His father's name was Setna, who was married to Eithne, a woman of royal Connacht blood. They were for many years childless, and gave alms frequently at a religious foundation at Dromlane in the present Co. Cavan in the hope that God would bless them with a family. The story goes that God answered their prayers and that Eithne had a son on an island called Inis Breachmhaí (Breaghwy) in a lake in east Breifne at a place now called Templeport, Co. Cavan. Eithne christened her boy *Áed*, Aodh in modern Irish. Add the diminutive suffix *án* and you have *Aédán*, anglicised as *Aidan*, *Aiden*, *Aedan* and *Eden*. By adding the prefix *mo* and the diminutive *óc* you have Old Irish *Máedóc*, the name by which our saint was universally known. This gave the acceptable anglicisation *Mogue*, a name common in Wexford until very recently, and the ludicrous *Moses*. The child was given to the High King Ainmhire as a hostage. He grew in sanctity and in time went to Wales where he studied under St David, bishop of Mynyw (Minevia). He landed on the coast of the present Co. Wexford on his return. Culleton in his *Celtic and Early Christian Wexford* says that he was given land at Ferns (Fearna) by a man named Brecc, a cousin of Brandubh, king of Leinster, and was later given more land by Brandubh himself for curing him of a terrible sickness. He is said to have established 30 religious foundations in his diocese. He is also venerated in his native Breifne, and in his *Settlements of Celtic Saints in Wales*, E.G. Bower writes: 'St

Aidan of Ferns had dedications in Wales at Llawhaden, Nolton West, and Solfach in Pembrokeshire; at Llanmadog in Gower, and at Capelmadog in Radnorshire, if we allow that his name might occur as *Madog*, from the form Mo-Aed-Og.'

*Maodhóg*, *St Aidan* of Ferns, died around 624 and was buried in his church at Ferns, although some Cavan historians say that he was laid to rest in his native Breifne. At any rate he is commemorated in both Wexford and Breifne on 31 January, the day of his death.

**MAOLÁN** earlier **MAELÁN** (m) The modern surname Ó Maoláin, anglicised as *Mullins*, *Mullan* and *Moylan*, derives from this name which originally meant 'warrior'. Maelán was a lector at the great monastery of Kells, Co. Meath. He died in 1050.

**MAOLCHOLUIM** earlier **MÁEL COLUIM** (m) Anglicised *Malcolm*, it means 'devotee of St Columba', who played a leading part in the conversion of Scotland and northern England to Christianity. The name in its anglicised form is not unknown in the north of Ireland, and there is a well-known southern rugby international named Malcolm O'Kelly.

**MAEL-, GIOLLA-, GILLA-** In the Middle Ages these prefixes were used before saints' names because it was considered presumptuous to name children directly after saints. Hence we get names prefixed by Mael (devotee of) in such as Máel Coluim. Gille (servant of) serves the same purpose.

**MAOL EOIN** earlier **MÁEL EOIN** (m) The name means 'devotee of St John'. A saint of the name was given the feast day 20 October. The surname *Ó Maoil Eoin*, anglicised *Malone*, derives from this given name.

**MAOL ÍOSA** earlier **MAEL ÍSU** This ancient name has survived along the border counties among families such as the Maguires, O'Hagans and O'Hanlons. The name means 'devotee of Jesus'. The best-known man of this name was the poet Mael Ísu Ó Brolcháin who died in 1086. A fine poet, some of his verses have been translated by Frank O'Connor and others.

**MAOL MHÓRDHA** earlier **MAEL MÓRDA** (m) A common name this in medieval Leinster and still popular there in its anglicised form, *Myles*. The name comes from *mórdha* (proud, self-important).

**MAOL MHUADH** earlier **MAEL MUAD** (m) The name derives, it is thought, from *muad* (proud, noble). It was much in favour among the O'Mahony clan of which Mael Muad, King of Desmond, was considered the founder. He lived in the latter part of the tenth century. The name gave the surname *Mulloy*.

**MAOL MHUIRE** earlier **MÁEL MUIRE** (m, f) The name means 'devotee of Mary'. A favourite name in the Middle Ages, Máel Muire ua Gormáin compiled an early martyrology of Irish saints. The males who bore the name anglicised it as *Milo*, *Myles* and *Myler*. Maol Mhuire was a very popular girl's name in parts of Ulster down to the middle of the nineteenth century. A woman of that name was the mother of the high king Niall Glúndubh who died in 966. Another lady who bore the name was a daughter of Amlaib, king of Dublin, who became the wife of Mael Sechnaill II, the high king. The name is still given to girls.

**MAOLMHAODHÓG** earlier **MÁEL MÁEDÓC** (m) The name means 'devotee of St Máedóc', but he is now universally known by a 'translation' of his name: *Malachy*.

Malachy, Máel Máedóc ua Morgair (1094–1148), was a reformer of the Church and had St Bernard of Clairvaux as his biographer.

Pochin Mould's account of him says that he was born in Armagh where his father was a celebrated scholar. He had a brother called Gilla Críst (servant of Christ) and a sister who was so far from being pious that Máel Máedóc broke off relations with her. St Bernard says that after her death she appeared to Máel Máedóc appealing to him to keep saying Masses for her soul until she was released from purgatory. Gilla Críst became bishop of Clogher. Taken under his wing by Cellach, bishop and abbot of Armagh, Máel Máedóc set out to reform the Irish Church in the troublesome area of marriage, in which there were conflicts between the Church's law and early Irish law on the contract. The sacraments of Penance and Confirmation were also ignored to a great degree. In a sojourn at Lismore, Máel Máedóc came into contact with the Benedictines, for the abbot at the great Waterford monastery was an Irishman who had been trained at Winchester. Cellach brought him back to the North and consecrated him bishop of Bangor. Eventually, and after much turmoil, Cellach made him bishop of Armagh and successor to St Patrick. He resigned after a time and ruled the diocese of Down. He went to Rome in the cause of reform and met Bernard at Clairvaux. On his return from Rome he met Bernard again and left some of his monks behind him. He wanted to bring Ireland more into the stream of continental religious life, and out of his meetings with Bernard came the introduction of the Cistercians into Ireland. He also called at Arrouaise and was responsible for introducing the Augustinian Canons into Ireland as well. Ireland would eventually have 26 cathedral churches in the care of these Canons Regular.

*Malachy*, as he has come to be known, died in the arms of St Bernard on his way to meet Pope Eugene III to ask him to create two archbishoprics. Four were eventually granted at the 1152 Synod of Kells. Of Malachy, Bernard wrote that when you saw him plunged into Church affairs, 'you thought he was born only for his country; if you had seen him alone, living on his own, you would have thought he had lived only in God and for Him.' The great reformer's feast day is 3 November.

It has been suggested that the very English Woodhousian given name *Marmaduke*, common only in a small area of north Yorkshire, is derived from Máel Máedóc.

**MAON** earlier **MAEN** (f) The name means 'silent'. The name was that of deities in early mythologies and was usually a female name in the legends. Maen was the daughter of Conn Cétchathach (Conn of the Hundred Battles) (p. 54). Another Maen was the mother of the legendary judge, Morann (p. 133).

**MARCAS** (m) The English *Mark*, from Latin *Marcus*, the

second evangelist and patron of Venice, where *Marco* is a very common name. The name was introduced into Ireland by the Anglo-Normans but was never very common here.

**MARGO** (f) I once heard of an enterprising teacher who translated as *Margo* the name *Margot*, a pet form of *Marguerite* found in England, Germany, France and many eastern European countries. *Margo*, queen of the fairy mound, was the mother of the lovely *Étaín* (p. 74). The origin of the Irish name is not known.

**MATHÚIN** earlier **MATHGHAMHAIN, MATHGAMAIN** (m) This was once a favourite name in Munster. Brian Boru had a brother of the name who became king of Cashel. The name means 'bear cub'. The Mahonys and the Mac Mahons have taken their names from Mathúin. It has been acceptably anglicised as *Mahon*.

**MÉABH** earlier **MEADHBH, MEDB** (f) Now acceptably anglicised *Maeve*. The word means 'intoxicating, capable of making men drunk' (by her looks, one supposes). Medb Lethderg, goddess of Tara, who upheld its sovereignty, was the first great Medb of mythology; Medb of Cruachan (Rathcroghan), Co. Roscommon, was another. This formidable queen of Connacht in the epic *Táin Bó Cuailgne* had many of the attributes of Medb Leathderg, 'strength and power over men, shrewd and wise, fierce and merciless', according to one text. The two Medbs were really one and the same person. The Connacht Medb, like the goddess of Tara, had many husbands, the first being Conchobhar mac Neasa and the last, Ailill Mac Máta of the *Táin*, who was reared from childhood in his fortress and, when he grew up to be a fine champion, was chosen by the queen to be her husband. Medb's confrontations with Cú Chulainn are the stuff of high drama; she also figures in a background role in several other stories of the Ulster Cycle. The story of the *Táin* is widely available; Thomas Kinsella's translation is still in print.

The name of the fabled queen was regrettably 'translated' in the nineteenth century, especially in Ulster, into *Madge*,

*Marjory* and *Mabel* among others. *Meidhbhín* is a pretty diminutive which may be acceptably anglicised *Maeveen*. Shakespeare's Queen Mab, the fairy's midwife of *Romeo and Juliet*, may owe her name to the legendary queen of Connacht.

**MEL** (m) Bishop and patron of Ardagh, whose feast day is 6 February, died in 487. Legend has it that his mother Dar Erca (p. 61) was a sister of St Patrick. Scandalous gossip had it that he had an affair with Lupita, another sister of Patrick and his own aunt, while he was bishop of Ardagh. This was found to be untrue, but Patrick insisted from then on that consecrated people should live in separate communities.

**MELL, MELLA** (f) This ancient name may come from an old word for 'lightning'. Mell was, according to legend, the sister of St Kevin of Glendalough, and Mella was the mother of St Manchán of Lemanaghan.

**MIS** (f) This young lady was the heroine of a literary romance. According to the medieval Dindsenchas (place-lore), she got her name from the mountain called Sliabh Mis in Co. Kerry, south-west of the town of Tralee; her husband gave her the mountain as a bride-price. This story wasn't considered good enough for some later storyteller who, probably in the sixteenth century, wove a more romantic tale around her name. A later tale, probably a retelling of this now lost text, is very interesting. It was written in the eighteenth century.

*Mis* was the daughter of Dáire Donn, the chief of some invaders who were annihilated by the Fianna at Fionntrá (Ventry). Poor Mis came upon her father's corpse on the battlefield, drank his blood and became demented as a result. She was the only one of the invaders left alive; she fled to Sliabh Mis and killed everybody who came near her hideaway. The king of Munster offered a reward to anybody who could bring her to him alive. Many tried and paid the penalty. Eventually the king's harper, a man called Dubh Rois, went in search of her. He tried to lure her from her hiding place by playing beautiful music on his harp, and succeeded. Instead of killing him, she recalled to him that her father once played such an instrument. She also noticed the purse of gold and silver he was carrying, and commented that her father had such coins. As Dubh Rois was sunbathing, she examined his private parts with interest and said that she remembered her father having such. Dubh Rois explained to her what his member was for and, intrigued, she consented to have intercourse with him. She became quite tame after prolonged bouts of lovemaking and soon she allowed him to clean her. Afterwards he taught her how to cook. She eventually became mentally stable once again and was transformed into the beautiful woman she once was. She went home with him and they married. When Dubh Rois was later killed, she lamented him in verse.

**MOBHEOC** (m) See *Beoc*

**MOCHAOI** earlier **MOCHOE** (m) This saint lived sometime in the sixth century; there are no known biographies of the man who was abbot of Nendrum on the island of Inish Mahee, Co. Down.

A lovely story about him is related in a medieval text edited by Stokes. The saintly man went into a forest to fell trees to build a church, and while he was there a bird sang three songs for him. He thought that each song lasted only a short time, but in fact each lasted for 50 years. When he came back to his monastery nobody knew him, but a little church had been erected there in his memory.

**MOCHAOMHÓG** earlier **MO CHÁEMMOC** (n) This is a pet form of *Cáemgen*. There is a long list of saints who bore this name, but the best known is probably a saint still prayed to in Leamakevogue and its environs near Borris in Ossory, Co. Tipperary, better known for its hurlers than for its sanctity!

**MOCHUARÓG** (m) See *Cuarán*

**MOCHUDA** (m) See *Carthach*

**MOIBHÍ** earlier **MO BÍ** (m) This saint, associated with Glasnevin in Dublin, may, it seems, have been christened Berchán; Mo Bí was a pet name. He was a student of the great teacher Finian of Clonard

(p. 89) before setting up his own monastery at Glasnevin. He is reputed to have had over fifty students there, including Colmcille (p. 46). We don't know very much about his life. He had the reputation of being given to writing poetry, but none of his work survives. When the bubonic plague struck, Mo Bí ordered his students to disperse; he himself stayed on, caught the plague and died. There is a holy well at Grange, Glasnevin, dedicated to him, but for a long time no rounds or other devotions have taken place there. It was, until recently at least, visited by people who took away the well's waters to cure various blemishes such as warts, and also to relieve toothache and sore throats.

The *Liber Hymnorum* of the early Church has a reference to Mo Bí's girdle or belt. Such articles were worn as a protection sometimes; it has also been suggested that they were worn to ensure chastity. Mo Bí's cowl was also regarded as a protection. An early *lorica* prayer called a *crios* (belt) contains an allusion to Mo Bí's *cochall* (cowl). Saints' cowls were believed to give protection against plague; his didn't do anything for poor Mo Bí, who died of it in 544, according to the *Annals of Inisfallen*. His feast day is 12 October.

**MOLAISSE** (m) See *Laisreán*

**MOLING** earlier **MO LING** (m) This is one of the great saints of seventh-century Ireland. He is the founder of St Mullins on the Barrow about eight miles from New Ross. He died in either 692 or 697. Like most of the early saints, his Lives tell little of his true history, but the legends abound. He was the son of a carpenter who lived near the sea in Co. Wexford; his mother was named Emnat, the sister of his father Faelán's wife. She decided to kill the baby as soon as it was born, but a dove flew in her face every time she reached to grab the child, and she was unable to commit the infanticide. Some monks luckily arrived on the scene and they took the baby with them and reared him, naming him Dairchell or Tarchell. He gained his nickname from his athletic prowess. A story has it that an old woman, watching him jump across a stream, gave him the pet name

*Mo Ling* saying, 'Well has the scholar Mo Ling jumped in Luachair.' Interestingly, it is said in present-day St Mullins that the saint, even as an old man, could leap across the wide Barrow where the tidal race ends, using two stepping stones at low tide: a magnificent triple jump indeed.

At beautiful St Mullins, Mo Ling cut his own mill stream for his mill. He worked day and night, refusing to drink from the stream or wash in it until he was finished. The mill stream may still be seen, and wading up against the current was always part of the traditional pilgrimage on the saint's feast day, 17 June. There are tales of miraculous floods cutting down timber for the building of Mo Ling's foundation; tales of his great kindness to animals, particularly foxes; and there is the tale of the woman who brought her dead child to the saint, only to be told by the saint he could do nothing for her, as he did not want to interfere with God's prerogative of raising the dead to life. The woman flung the child at Moling who ducked, allowing the child to fall into the Barrow. The saint rescued him, and miraculously he came to life.

Another legend tells that Mo Ling brought an end to the hated *borama* (tribute). An amusing retelling of this story was recorded in the 1880s by Patrick O'Leary, a Graiguenamanagh historian. A man had listened to the argument between the king and the saint. Then, 'He upped an' asked the king did he know what he was after promising that little grey-headed ould man. "Begor, I'm not rightly sure," says the king, "for he had such quare ould Irish I could hardly understand him." "Well," says the courtier, "you're after promising him not to ask the tax until the day after the day of judgment."'

Moling is said to have studied at Ferns and to have gone later to Glendalough; he then returned to Ferns where he became bishop. His book, now known as *The Book of Mulling*, is in the library of Trinity College, Dublin, having been for centuries in the possession of the Kavanagh family. It is said to be in Mo Ling's own hand.

In a Benedictine library in Carinthia in Austria, I saw an ancient manuscript poem which mentions in its title *Suibhne Geilt*, the mad birdman, who, cursed by St Rónán (p. 151), was destined to fly naked around Ireland and who died in Mo Ling's arms by the Barrow and was there laid to rest by him.

**MONCHA** (f) This lady plays a tragic part in the story of the important mythical King of Munster, Fiachu Muilleathan. Texts from the eighth century onwards say that he was the son of Eoghan, son of Ailill Ólam, and that he was born posthumously. Before the battle of Magh Mucramha in which he died, Eoghan was told by a druid called Dil at a place called Druim Dil (now Drumdeel), near Clonmel, Co. Tipperary, that he would be slain. The druid had a daughter called Moncha and he arranged that Eoghan would sleep with her in the hope that future monarchs of Munster would descend from himself. Eoghan perished in the battle, and when Moncha's time came to have her baby, her father took her to the banks of the Siúir at Knockgraffon, telling her that if she had the baby that day he would one day become the chief jester of Ireland, but that if she could delay the birth until the sun rose the following morning he would become the most powerful king in the country. She went into the Siúir and sat on a stone all night to delay the birth until morning had come. But she died of her travail. The baby was born with his head widened because of its contact with the stone on which his mother had sat, and so he was called Muinleathan or Muilleathan (broad crowned).

**MÓR** (f) This byname meaning 'great, tall' was one of the commonest female names of the Middle Ages. It is still in use, as is its diminutive *Móirín*, anglicised *Moreen*. The most famous Mór was probably Mór Mumhan (Mór of Munster), a mythical woman representing the land goddess.

Ó hÓgain has written about her continuing place in Munster folklore. A Kerry tradition has Mór marrying a man named Donnchad who lived in the centre of Ireland. She henpecked the poor man so badly that he left her and went south as far away from her as possible. Their three sons and a daughter went with Mór, but were so overcome with misery that their plight became proverbial: *íde chlainne Moire* (the misfortune of Mór's children). The two eldest boys went abroad to seek their fortunes and became famous warriors who slew giants for their king. The youngest lad set off to find them and the king agreed to let them come home on holiday. They stayed too long and the king sent a ship to find them and bring them back. But there was nobody on board the strange ship; all the brothers could see was a black cat walking the deck. Naturally, they went on board to examine the ship, at which the black cat hoisted sail; and off they went, never to return. The cat was the king in magical disguise. The poor daughter married a lout who beat her unmercifully, and Mór began to regret that she herself had ever separated from Donnchad. She set out to find him. She reached the top of a local hill and was astounded at the length of the land she had to travel. She urinated on top of the hill and created the streams which run down to this day from Mám. As Ó hÓgain says, such humorous aetiological lore has not lost the aura of myth, and several local proverbial sayings refer to her doings as if she embodied the human state generally. *Leaghadh mhúin Mhóire* (the evaporation of Mór's pee) refers to the impermanence of things; and ostentation is censured by the phrase *cailín aige Mór agus Mór ag iarraidh déirce* (Mór having a servant girl while she herself begs).

**MORANN** (m) This mythical judge was famed for his great wisdom, and is the hero of some fanciful medieval stories. He was said to be born with a caul, part of which remained like a necklace adorning his neck, and the stories, some of which are ancient, tell of the caul, the *iodh* (sin) of Morann. Being human, Morann was occasionally unsure of the correctness of his judgment, but in the event that the judgment he was about to give was unsound, the caul would tighten about his neck. Later stories say that the judge would place his caul around the neck of a prisoner charged with a capital crime; if guilty the caul would choke him, and if innocent it would loosen and the prisoner would walk free.

Ó hÓgáin writes that the caul figures prominently in the pseudo-historical writings about Morann, who was said to be the son of Cairbre Catcheann, a king who came to the throne by banishing his rivals from Ireland. Cairbre had two sons who were born with cauls on their heads, but the crazed king had them killed, thinking their births to be monstrous. Morann too was born with a caul, and when he was thrown into the sea on his father's orders, a huge wave broke over him, dislodging the caul. The infant then spoke to the soldiers who had tried to drown him, saying that the sea was rough and asked them to lift him out. As much out of fright as out of pity, they took him from the sea and asked a local smith to look after him. Later Cairbre came to the house of the smith to take part in an ale-feast, and the child jumped from his cradle on to the king's lap as soon as he saw him. Cairbre's soldiers asked him how much was the child worth to him, and the king replied that he was worth his weight in gold and silver. The soldiers then told him who the child actually was. He was brought up by the king and eventually became chief judge of Ireland.

**MÓRNA** (f) This name was once common in Co. Clare. I can find no saint of the name mentioned in the lists. Perhaps her name derived from *Mór* (p. 132).

**MUIRCHEARTACH** (m) This given name gave the GAA commentator Mícheál Ó Muircheartaigh and the jockey Johnny Murtagh their surnames. It probably means 'seaman' or 'mariner'. The name was very common in early and medieval Ireland; the legendary High King Muirchertach mac Erca was one distinguished early bearer of the name. Muircheartach was said by Seathrún Céitinn, the unreliable seventeenth-century historian, to have removed the Lia Fáil (the Stone of Destiny) from Tara to Scotland, from whence it was taken by the English King Edward I to Westminster to be used as the coronation stone. Not likely. The ancient stone pointed out at Tara is more likely the real Lia Fáil.

**MUIREANN** earlier **MUIRENN** (f) The probable meaning of this name is 'white like the sea' or 'lovely like the sea'. In the tales of Finn we find a Muirenn who is Oisín's wife. Another Muirenn is the daughter of Derg and foster-mother of the hero Cael. Four abbesses of Kildare were called Muirenn, and the name, under the guise of *Myrun*, is found in the *Landnáma bók* of Iceland. She was an Irish princess. The lovely name Muireann is still popular.

**MUIRÍOS** earlier **MUIRGHEAS** This was a much-favoured Connacht name and it was given to at least one Connacht king in the early medieval period. Subsequently it became popular among some of the major Connacht clans such as the MacDonaghs and Mac Dermotts. It was also adopted in Kerry by the O'Connells of Uibh Ráthach, who anglicised it as *Maurice*.

**MUIRIS** (m) Borrowed through English and French from the Latin name *Mauricius*, a derivative of *Maurus*, a byname meaning 'Moor' or 'swarthy, dark-skinned'. Introduced into Ireland by the Anglo-Normans, it was more popular among the nobility than among the ordinary folk; it was a favourite name of, for example, the FitzGeralds. Gradually the native Irish grew accustomed to it and it became widespread, especially in Munster.

**MURCHÚ** (m) Not to be confused with *Murchad/Murchadh*, this very early Irish name seems to be gaining in popularity. It means 'hound of the sea'. The earliest Murchú we know of is the one who wrote a Life of St Patrick. His feast day is 8 June.

# N

**NÁBLA** earlier **ANÁBLA, ANNÁBLA** (f) The name Nábla, common still among some Donegal families, notably the MacGinleys, comes from *Annabel* or *Annabella*, a name popular once in Scotland. The Anglo-Normans brought the name to Ireland. It was anglicised as *Mabel* in the nineteenth-century purge of native names. Funnily enough *Mabel* is a form of *Amabel*, from which the Scottish *Annabel* and *Annabella* probably evolved.

**NAITHÍ** earlier **NATH-Í** (m) This name was common in ancient times. One man of the name was a grandson of Niall Naígiallach (Niall of the Nine Hostages) (p. 138).There are a few saints of the name, notably Nathí of Achonry, teacher of Feichín of Fore (p. 85).

**NAOISE** (m) The lover of Deirdre (p. 64).

**NEACHTAN** earlier **NECHTAN** (m) This name, according to Ó Corráin and Maguire, is cognate with the name of the Roman god Neptune and means 'descendant of the waters'. He was the husband of Bóinn. He was the guardian of the well of knowledge and of the sacred hazel wood that grew close to it. Nechtan told his wife not to eat the hazel nuts from the tree, but she disobeyed him. The well's water burst forth in a fit of anger and chased the fleeing Bóinn, which turned into the river we know as the Boyne.

There are some saints of the name, notably Nechtan of Dungiven, whose feast day is 8 January. The O'Donnells of Donegal were fond of the name and from it came the surname *Ó Neachtain* and its anglicised version, *Naughton*.

**NEASÁN** earlier **NESSÁN** (m) This name has undergone a

revival in recent years in the south of Ireland, particularly in its anglicised form *Nessan*.

There are five saints of the name but the best known is probably St Nessán, known as 'Nessán the deacon', founder of the famous monastery at Mungairit (Mungret), Co. Limerick. He is thought to have died in 551. Unfortunately, nothing more is known about him. His feast day is 25 July. It has been suggested that Nessán is a male form of *Nessa* (below).

**NÉIDHE** earlier **NÉDE** (m) Fictional poet of ancient Ireland. His uncle was Caier, king of Connacht, and an early text describes an altercation between them. Caeir had no son of his own and he had adopted his nephew, caring for him and educating him in the noble arts. Little thanks he got for it. Néde plotted with the king's unfaithful wife to bring him down. She told him that there was a *geis* (a magical prohibition) on the king, not to give to any other a special knife he carried on his person. Néde asked him for the knife one night, and when he was refused he made up a vicious satire shaming Caier. Three hideous blisters arose from the blushes on his face; he was decreed deformed and consequently had to relinquish his kingship. He fled south to a fort near Kinsale, Dún Chearmna, to hide his shame. Néde became king of Connacht in his place, but after a year he began to feel ashamed of what he had done and followed the rightful king south to offer his apologies. When poor Caier saw him he fell dead. But the fates were not finished with the usurper. The slab of stone on which the rightful king lay grew red-hot and burst into flames; a splinter of the stone flew up and pierced the ursurper in the eye, killing him.

**NESSA, NEASA** earlier **NESS** (f) The name Nessa or Neasa has undergone a revival in recent years, particularly in Munster. The name is of uncertain origin. In the ancient legends about the saints Ness is the daughter of a man called Faelán, the mother of St Mo Cháemmoc (p. 129) and the sister of St Íte. The sagas mention Ness as the daughter of Echú Sálbuide, wife of Fachtna, king of Ulster, and the mother of the great king of Ulster, Conchobar mac Nessa, by Cathbad, a magician, according to one story. When Nessa's husband died, he was succeeded by Fergus mac Róich, his half-brother. Fergus was in love with Ness and did all in his power to persuade her to marry him. She agreed on one condition: that her son Conchobar be allowed to rule for a year instead of him. At the end of the year even Fergus had to admit that Conchobar made a great king. The country prospered under his wise rule, which was largely directed by Ness. For some reason Fergus went off to Connacht and placed his army at the disposal of Ailill and Medb. So it was that he fought the men of Ulster when the war described in the epic *Táin Bó Cuailnge* broke out.

**NIALL** (m) Scholars have long debated the origin of this famous name. One suggested *nel* (a cloud) as its origin; another traced it to a root meaning 'passionate, vehement'. Some distinguished bearers of the name led to its popularity. Niall Naígiallach (Niall of the Nine Hostages) was the ancestor of the O'Neills of Ulster. He, it is said, brought St Patrick to Ireland as a slave. Niall Frasach, who died in 778, was High King of Ireland. According to the Annals a famine had ravished the land just as he came to power, but he prayed with seven of his bishops and, miraculously, three showers fell from heaven, one of silver, one of honey, and one of wheat which covered all his fields. His epithet *fras* means 'shower'. This illustrious name has been anglicised as *Neil* and is common now all over the English-speaking world. It has a modern female form *Neila*. *Niall* is often mispronounced *Nyall*. See *Caireann* and *Torna*.

**NIAMH** earlier **NIAM** (f) It is good to note that this ancient name is becoming very popular again. It means 'brightness, radiance' and was the name of the beautiful woman who was Oisín's (p. 141) lover and who brought him to Tír na nÓg (the Land of Youth) in the later Fenian stories. Niam, Ó Corrain and Maguire suggest, may have been the name of a goddess, and may have been the early name of the Munster Blackwater.

There were other Niams famous in legend and saga. One was loved by the great hero Cú Chulainn; she was one of the wives of the Ulster warrior Conall Cearnach. The daughter of Óengus Tírech, legendary king of Munster, was also named Niam. She was another of Oisín's women, and went off hunting with him for six months in Ulster. But another story has it that this Niam was the daughter of the king of Ulster, Áed Donn, and that she talked him into fighting his first ever battle over her.

Niamh up to recently was often, alas, written *Nieve.* I am glad that this trend has recently been reversed, and that even RTÉ announcers are now beginning to pronounce the name properly.

**NINIAN** (m) The name of this saint is still in use in parts of Munster. He helped spread Christianity in Scotland, but it is not at all certain where he came from. He is described as Irish by some sources, as Scots by others; some Welsh authorities also claim him; and since he is still remembered in Brittany under the names *Ninian* and *Ninn,* that part of France also claims him as one of their own.

**NÓINE** (m) Nóine is a wonder-child who is described in medieval stories. One account relates how a king named Dáire was told by his druid that if his daughter had a son, he himself would die. The king watched his daughter like a hawk, but he was not to know that Mac ind Óc, otherwise known as the god Óenghus, had his eye on her. She became pregnant by the god, and the pregnancy lasted nine years. She gave birth to a son who, when he emerged into this world, had a curly beard and long flowing hair. He spoke immediately and his first utterance consisted of nine sayings. When he had finished, the king, Dáire, died. Ó hÓgáin points out that this plot derives from the Lugh myth of a prophesied wonder-child who will kill its tyrant grandfather.

Another version of the story has it that the girl in question, whose name was Finghile, was playing on the beach when an apparition came in from the sea and made love to her. She became pregnant and when her baby was born the king, Dáire, died. The child gave nine commands to its mother, and then he himself died, 'for it is illegal for a son to argue with his mother'.

Many scholars have pointed out that the child Nóine was originally identical with Finn.

**NUALA** (f) See *Fionnuala*

**NUALLÁN** (m) This old personal name is now rarely used except in its anglicised form, *Nolan*, which has become quite popular in England and particularly in Australia. The old personal name is thought to be a byname representing a diminutive of *nuall* (champion, chariot fighter).

**OILIBHÉAR, OILIFÉAR** (m) These are the Irish forms of *Oliver*, a popular name in the England of the Middle Ages. It is of Norman and hence ultimately Germanic origin. *Olivier* was the name of one of Charlemagne's retainers who became famous as the prudent friend and companion of the headstrong Roland in the *Chanson de Roland*. Long thought to be derived from Late Latin *olivarius* (olive tree), most scholars now agree with Hanks and Hodges that as Charlemagne's other paladins all bear solid Germanic names, it is more likely an altered form of a Germanic name, perhaps a version of *Olaf*. The Scots Gaelic forms are *Olghar* and *Oilbhreis*. The name has survived the odium attached to Oliver Cromwell; St Oliver Plunkett is probably responsible for many of the Olivers christened today. *Oiliféar* was the common form of the name in the Déise, particularly in Kilkenny, where the last native speakers of Irish survived until the 1940s.

**OISÍN** (m, f) The name was a common one in early Ireland; it means 'little fawn'. Although the name is applied to women as well as men, the most famous Oisín was the son of Fionn Mac Cumhaill. By the ninth century he was part of the Fianna lore.

In the early Middle Ages a story was told about Oisín's birth. His mother used to visit the Fianna in the form of a doe. Later storytellers discarded this plot and had Oisín's mother, a beautiful woman, marrying Fionn. But he didn't watch over her properly, and when he was absent hunting one day, a malicious wizard turned her into a doe. Fionn searched for her but to no avail. She gave birth to Oisín while she was still in the form of a doe. Some years later, when Fionn had given up all hope of finding her, he came on a handsome boy in a forest clearing. The child related to Fionn that he had been brought up by a deer, and Fionn knew immediately that he was speaking to his son.

A twelfth-century text called *Agallamh na Seanórach* (the Colloquy of the Old Men) tells how Oisín and Caoilte survived the rest of the Fianna and lived to meet St Patrick himself. From that time on until the middle of the eighteenth century, additional lore was added to the conversations between the saint and Oisín as both held forth on the theme of the relative blessings of the monastic life and the outdoor life of the great hunter-warriors.

There is a beautiful story which tells of Oisín hunting one day and being visited by a beautiful fairy woman from Tír na nÓg (the Land of Youth). He went with her to her homeland and after a while wished to visit Ireland again to see his people. She let him go after warning him not to set foot on the soil of Ireland. He did not realise that 300 years had passed and that all his Fianna comrades were dead. He travelled on horseback, and watched while some puny-looking men had difficulty moving a boulder. When he bent from the saddle to help, his surcingle broke and he fell to the ground. He immediately grew ancient and lost his beautiful woman, called *Niamh Cinn Óir* (Niamh of the Golden Head), for ever.

**OISTÍN** (m) See *Aibhistín*

**ONÓRA** (f) We can thank the Anglo-Normans for this name, which is derived from their *Honora*, thought to be from the Latin *honor* (beauty, reputation). Ó Corráin and Maguire have pointed out that the Irish form may be a reflection of the form commonly used in England from the twelfth to the fourteenth century, *Annora*. Among the forms also current in Ireland are *Nora*, *Nóirín* and *Nóinín*.

**ÓRÁN, ODHRÁN** earlier **ODRÁN** (m) This name is said to have been rare in ancient Ireland, but there are nevertheless more than twenty saints of the name recorded. Opinions differ as to the origin of the name. Some have suggested that it may derive from a word for 'an otter'; others that it is from *odhar* (brownish, sallow). St Odrán of Latteragh, Co. Tipperary, is possibly the most famous of these early saints. Another one worth remembering is Odrán, St Patrick's charioteer. Some might see him as a martyr. The legend has it that while St Patrick was travelling to Munster, a local chief called Failge Berraide decided to kill him. He lay in ambush for the saint's chariot. Sensing the plot, Odrán swapped places with the saint, allowing Patrick to take over the reins of the chariot, pleading that he was unwell. At the place of the ambush the assassin, mistaking the charioteer for the saint, killed Odrán with his spear. Notwithstanding the dying Odrán's pleas, the assassin was killed in retaliation by the saint's followers.

The word has been anglicised as *Oran* and *Odran*.

**ÓRNAIT** earlier **ÓRNAT** (f) Now anglicised *Orna*, this is the female version of *Odrán*, and so it may mean 'sallow complexioned' or it may be derived from an Irish word for 'an otter'. There is a saint of this name whose feast day is 13 November. Unfortunately, nothing whatever is known of her life. The wife of the great Guaire, king of Connacht, was named Órnat, and Cuan, king of Munster who died in 641, had a daughter bearing the name.

**OSCAR** (m) A grandson of Fionn Mac Cumhaill, his name contains the element *os* (fawn). A great warrior, his name has spread from Ireland thanks to the popularity of James Macpherson's versions of the Fenian lays in the eighteenth century. Later the name became very common in Scandinavia, and spread further due to Napoleon's love of Macpherson's work: he insisted that the name Oscar be given to his godson Oscar Bernadotte, who later became King Oscar I of Sweden. The most famous of our own Oscars is undoubtedly the brilliant Oscar Wilde, poet, novelist and playwright (1854–1900).

**OSNAIT** earlier **OSSNAT** (f) This lovely old name has long fallen into disuse, although it was common enough in the early period. The most famous *Ossnat*, a feminine form of *Ossán*, was a saint whose feast day is 6 January, a sister of St Mo Laisse of Devonish.

**PÁDRAIG** (m) The patron saint of Ireland lived between *c.*389 and 461. He was a Briton and was captured in his youth and brought as a slave to Ireland. He managed to escape and went to Gaul. He spent years studying at Auxerre before returning as a missionary to Ireland. He converted many at the court of the high king at Tara before travelling around the island on his mission of conversion. He established his principal see at Árd Mhacha (Armagh) around 445. By the time he died he had succeeded in converting almost the entire island. He codified the laws and cleverly did not break up the social structure of Ireland. Instead he grafted Christianity on to it. He wrote his autobiography in Latin in which he refers to himself as Patricius (patrician), which seems to place him in the Roman noble class. It has been suggested, however, that the name may really represent a latinised form of some lost Celtic name that once existed among the Britons. The Patrician scholar, Liam de Paor, suggested that the saint's burial place may be close to the eighteenth green of Enniscrone golf club in Co. Sligo.

The form *Patrice* is very popular in France. The early Irish neglected the name; it came to prominence in the time of the Anglo-Normans when the native Irish called it *Pádraigín*. The ninteenth-century scholar John O'Donovan wrote that he did not believe that 'Patrick' as the name of a man 'is a hundred and fifty years in use'. The English form *Patricia* is an eighteenth-century Scots invention. The Irish female form *Pádraigín* is an even later one. *Pádraic* and *Páraic* are regional Irish variants and there are a host of diminutives, *Páid*, *Peaití*, *Páidín* and *Páidí* among them. The anglicised variants *Padge* and *Pauge* are found in Leinster.

**PARTHALÁN** (m) This is an Irish version of *Bartholomaeus*, a name explained by St Jerome as 'son of him who stays the waters'. Isodorus of Seville repeated this in the seventh century, and both men contributed to the adoption by Irish pseudo-historians of Parthalán as a figure who settled in Ireland with his followers after the Deluge. A text of the pseudo-historical *Lebor Gabála* (the Book of Invasions) states that Parthalán fled Greece after murdering his father and brother in an attempt to gain the kingship. He lost an eye in his attempt, and worse was to follow his great crime of kin-slaying. He reached Ireland after a seven year odyssey, with his wife Dealgnat (p. 63), his three sons and their wives, and some followers. One of these followers, Beoil, opened the first hostel in Ireland; Bréa gave us the art of cooking; and Malaliach instituted the first brewery, making ale from ferns. They settled in the only unforested place they could find, the plain on which Dublin city now stands. Curiously, the accounts admit that the Fomorians, a demonic race, were already in Ireland; Parthalán had to fight them, and he won a famous battle on a plain in south Donegal in which nobody was killed 'because it was a magic battle'.

After 30 years in Ireland Parthalán died on the Dublin plain, Sean-Mhagh Nealta. His people lived here for another 525 years and then died of a plague between two Mondays in May.

**PEADAR** (m) A common name nowadays, it is a borrowing of the English *Peter*. It is relatively new. *Piaras* (below) was the medieval form.

**PEIG** (f) The Irish equivalent of English *Peg*, shortened form of *Peggy*, itself a pet form of *Margaret* or obsolete *Meggie*. Peig Sayers, the Blasket Islands storyteller, is our best-known lady bearing the name.

**PIARAS** (m) Introduced into Ireland as *Piers* by the Norman French. It was the Middle English form of *Peter* and will be known to students from the title of Langland's great poem

'Piers Plowman' (1367–86). It survived as *Pierce* until the eighteenth century as a popular English name, and to this day as *Piaras* in Ireland. Piaras Feirtéir, the Kerry poet of Anglo-Norman lineage, was one who bore the name.

**PILIB** (m) Borrowed from English *Philip*, itself from Greek *Phillipos*, which is made up of the elements *philein* (to love) and *hippos* (horse). It was brought to Ireland by the Anglo-Normans among whom it was a very popular name. The native Irish adopted it quickly as *Pilib*, and it became popular among some northern clans such as the Maguires of Fermanagh and the O'Gallaghers of Donegal before it achieved widespread acceptance.

**PÓILÍN** (f) A feminine diminutive form of *Pól* (see below). The English *Pauline* is from the French *Paulina*. *Póilín* is a newish coinage which has gained favour in recent times.

**PÓL** (m) Irish form of the English, French and German form of *Paulus*, a Latin family name, once a nickname meaning 'small', and in the post-classical period used as a given name. The name of the saint who is regarded with Peter as the co-founder of the Christian Church, his epistles form part of the New Testament. He was beheaded in Rome about A.D. 65. The Irish name, and indeed the English form *Paul*, were rarely used here until quite recent times.

**PROINSIAS, PROINSÉAS** (m, f) Borrowings of the English name *Francis* which became popular with the rise of the cult of St Francis of Assisi (1181–1226). *Francesco* was a nickname given to the saint because of his rich father's business dealings in France; he was baptised *Giovanni*. The name *Francis* was not popular in England until the fifteenth century. It may have taken another century for the name to be assimilated into Irish.

**RAGHALLACH** (m) An old Irish name of unknown origin. A Raghallach was king of Connacht between 622 and 649. A story about him was written in the Middle Ages, probably to discredit the O'Connors who were descended from Raghallach. It goes like this: Raghallach had a nephew, and became very jealous of him because he was afraid that the young man was plotting to overcome him and take his crown. Pretending to be very ill he sent word to his nephew that he would like to see him before he died. The young man, who is not named in the story, didn't trust his uncle and took a troop of warriors with him. Raghallach pretended to be deeply insulted that his nephew, whom he wished would succeed him as king, would come to visit him with an armed escort. The nephew foolishly told his men to withdraw and the young man was slain on the spot. Deeply upset, the king's wife Muireann consulted her druid as to the king's future and was told that as he had killed all his own relatives, he would himself be killed by one of his own children. So when the queen in time had a baby, the king ordered that it be taken out and given to a swineherd to kill. The swineherd could not bring himself to kill the infant, and unknown to anybody left it near a church. A holy woman took the baby and brought it up.

When the baby girl grew up, her beauty became the talk of Connacht, and the king, of course, heard about her. He ordered that she be brought to him. Neither he nor his queen knew who the girl really was. Muireann got insanely jealous of the young woman, and swam across the Shannon away from her husband to the man who had once fostered her, the High King Diarmait mac Aodha Sláine. St Feichíne heard about Raghallach's infatuation with the young woman and came with a deputation of other holy men to upbraid him for his wife's desertion. They got the cold shoulder. So the holy men fasted and prayed and cursed him, hoping that he would die before the feast of Bealtaine, the great May feast. As that time of year approached, Raghallach was injured as he chased a stag on an island. The stag escaped by swimming and the king followed it in a boat, alone. When he reached land he saw that the stag had been killed by three wild men who were busy devouring it. The king claimed the beast and the men killed him with spades they were carrying.

It is impossible to know if the given name *Reilly*, so common in Australia and England, originated in the Irish name; there is a suggestion that *Reilly* originates in an English place-name composed of the Old English elements *ryge* (rye) + *leah* (a clearing, meadow). At any rate *Raghallach* gave the surname *Ó Raghallaigh*, anglicised *O'Reilly*.

**RAGHNAILT, RAGNAILT** (f) This was a feminine form of *Raghnall* (below) and was as popular as its male counterpart in the late Middle Ages—perhaps even more so. One lady bearing the name was the wife of Domhnall Mór Ó Briain, king of Thomond. Unfortunately, it was latinised in medieval documents as *Regina*.

**RAGHNALL, RAGNALL** (m) The name came via the Viking invaders from the Old Norse *Rögnvalder*, from the elements *regin* (advice—possibly from the gods) and *vaaldr* (ruler). It is sometimes anglicised *Ronald*, *Randal* or *Ranald*. The Irish borrowed the name early and it became popular particularly among the MacDonnells of Antrim who liked the form *Randal*, and pronounced it *Ranal*. But there were many famous Raghnalls in the south. One was the king of Waterford who died in 1018. Another was Raghnall Ua Dálaigh, poet of Desmond, who died in 1161. The surname *Mac Raghnaill*, nowadays *Reynolds*, derives from the Norse given name.

**RATHNAIT** earlier **RATHNAT** (f) This name, rare nowadays, represents a diminutive feminine form of *rath* (prosperity). It used to be a common name until the nineteenth century in the Glens of Antrim. There was a saint, Rathnat, associated with the ancient foundation Kilraghts, Co. Antrim, who is commemorated on 5 August. She used to be invoked in cases of female infertility. Rathnait has been anglicised as *Ronit*, a name with which it has no association whatever, as *Ronit* is a modern Hebrew name meaning 'song'.

**RÉAMONN** (m) This is thought to be derived from an Old English name composed of *raed* (counsel) and *mund* (protector). This explanation would justify the anglicisation *Redmond*, very common in Ireland, especially among the northern families of MacArdle, McCann and O'Hanlon. The name was introduced by the Anglo-Normans. Perhaps the most famous Réamonn or Redmond was the raparee Redmond O'Hanlon who roamed the roads of Ulster and north Leinster for years before being treacherously killed in 1681. He referred to himself as 'chief ranger of the mountains, surveyor general of the high roads, lord examiner of all travellers and high protector of his benefactors and contributors'. His fame was such that the French newspapers of the time referred to him as Count O'Hanlon. The folklore concerning him is extensive.

**RÉILTÍN** (f) This is a translation of the English name *Stella*, Latin for 'star', and seems to be of recent origin. Stella was not used as a first name before the sixteenth century, when Sir Philip Sidney coined it for the beautifully crafted sonnets addressed to the lady Stella by Astrophel.

**RÍONACH** earlier **RÍOGHNACH** (f) This name, now fairly popular, is an old one and means 'queenly'. It was the name of the wife of Niall of the Nine Hostages, and she gave to the world some powerful sons, two of whom gave their names to the northern counties of Tír Eoghain and Tír Chonaill. There were two Ríoghnachs among the saints of the early Church.

One of them is commemorated on 18 December; the other on 9 February. The name has been both latinised and anglicised as *Regina*. *Ríona* is a simplified form of the name, but it is also used as a simple form of *Caitríona*, with which Ríonach has no connection.

**RISTEARD, RISTERD, RIOCARD, RICARD** (m) Various forms of an enduring Germanic personal name, in English *Richard*, and introduced here by the Anglo-Normans. It is made up of the elements *ric* (power) + *hardy* (brave, strong). The Scots Gaelic form is *Ruiseart*, the Welsh *Rhisiart*. It is difficult to say why it has endured in Ireland outside the Anglo-Norman families. It is doubtful if Richard I, Coeur de Lion, had as much influence on popular imagination here as he had in England. *Risterd* was a favoured name among the Butlers of Ormond and is still used in Co. Waterford. The Wexford surname *Rackard* evolved from the form *Ricard*.

**ROIBEÁRD** (m) In Scots Gaelic, *Raibeart*, which gave the byname *Rab*, common in Northern Ireland. The English, of course, is *Robert* and is one of the French names of Germanic origin introduced here by the Anglo-Normans. The name is made up from the elements *hrod* (fame) and *berth* (bright, famous). It was the name of two eleventh-century dukes of Normandy: the father of William the Conqueror, and his son. It gained popularity in Ireland because of the admired Robert the Bruce (1224–1328) who fought to free Scotland from English rule.

**RÓNÁN** (m) A popular name in ancient Ireland, *Rónán* has again gained popularity in our days. The easily pronounced anglicised version *Ronan* has no doubt helped. There were ten saints of the name, the most interesting perhaps being Rónán Finn of Magheralin, who appears in the medieval story *Suibhne Geilt* as the man who cursed Suibhne who went insane at the battle of Moira. Poor Suibhne, who had gone flying like a bird around Ireland stark naked, was caught out on a fearful wet and stormy night, and such was the shock he sustained in his misery that his sanity was restored to him. So he set off on his long journey home to Dál nAraidhe. His adventures were revealed to St Rónán, who became fearful that Suibhne would revert to his old ways and would persecute the Church again. So he prayed hard and long, and it seems that his prayers were answered, because as Suibhne passed Sliabh Fuaid, now the Fews in Co. Armagh, he was tormented by phantoms who kept up an incessant roaring at him, telling him that he was a lunatic and that he would shortly return to that state. He went on his way delirious. This unforgiving saint died in 664 and his feast day is 22 May. Other saints of the name are Rónán of Lough Derg whose feast day is 13 January; Rónán of Lismore who died in 763 and whose feast day is 9 February; and Rónán of Dromiskin, Co. Louth, who is remembered on 18 November. The name derived from *rón* (a seal). Ronan O'Gara, the Irish rugby international does honour to his ancient name.

**RÓS, RÓISE, RÓIS** (f) This name, common among the Ulster families from the sixteenth century, is now popular throughout Ireland. It was brought to Ireland by the Anglo-Normans but did not gain favour here until some centuries after their arrival. The diminutive *Róisín* is probably more widespread now, due perhaps to the traditional song 'Róisín Dubh', translated by James Clarence Mangan (1803–49) as 'Dark Rosaleen' and to Seán Ó Riada, whose treatment of the air gained a deserved reputation as background music to a short film on Ireland's War of Independence. *Róisín* is a figurative name for Ireland.

Ostensibly from the Latin *rosa*, the name of the flower. But this is now disputed because girls' names derived from flowers are generally of nineteenth-century origin. It could be, of course, that *Róis* is an exception, referring to the flower as a symbol of the Blessed Virgin Mary, but to some authorities it seems likely that the name is Germanic in origin, its first element being from *hrod* (fame). *Hros* (horse) has also been suggested by Hanks and Hodges and by Ó Corráin and Maguire.

**RUAIRÍ, RUAIDHRÍ, RUAIDRÍ** (m) The name may mean 'red

king' or 'great king'. It was a common given name in the Middle Ages, favoured especially by the Connacht and midland families of O'Shaughnessy, O'Connor and O'More. The last High King of Ireland who died in 1198 was Ruaidrí Ó Conchobair. The name was also very popular in Ulster; indeed it still is. It was anglicised as *Roderick* in Connacht, and in Ulster as *Roger* and *Roddy*. The most popular anglicised form in use today is *Rory*.

**RUÁN** earlier **RUADHÁN, RUADÁN** (m) The name means 'little red one'. The greatest saint of this name was Ruadán who founded the monastery of Lorrha and whose feast day is 15 April. He died in 584. His name has been anglicised in Britain as *Rowan*, as in Rowan Atkinson. The saint was educated by St Finnian of Clonard, Co. Meath. The legends concerning him are numerous. He had, it was said, a wonderful tree at Lorrha; its sap provided food and drink for all who tasted it. The High King Diarmait mac Cearrbheoil took a hostage from Ruadán and returned him in exchange for 30 dark-grey horses. They were magical animals which had come to Lorrha from a river, and the king's horses proved no match for them at racing. To the king's annoyance they raced away from him one fine day and galloped all the way to the sea, where they disappeared for ever among the waves. Ruadán was a miracle worker, according to the old stories, famous for his healing touch. In a late medieval tale we read that the Munster king, Eochaid mac Maolughra, plucked out his eye to satisfy a Scots druid called Labhán. Ruadhán prayed that the druid's two eyes be given to the king, which was done miraculously, and so the king was given the nickname Súil Labháin (Labháin's eye); from this, it was said, the Munster family named Ó Súilleabháin derived. This is very much anachronistic, as Ruadhán lived in the sixth century, while the king, Eochaid mac Maolughra, lived in the ninth. The name Súildubhán actually meant 'dark-eyed'; the explanation that Súilleabháin meant 'one-eyed' is nonsense, a folk etymology.

# S

**SABIA** (f) This is a latinised form of *Sadhbh* (below). It was fairly common in medieval times and one hears it occasionally today in some Munster counties.

**SADHBH** earlier **SADB** (m, f) One of the most popular names in late medieval Ireland, the name may mean 'sweet'. Sadb was the daughter of Conn Cétchathach (Conn of the Hundred Battles). According to legend she became the wife of Ailill Ólum, the great king of Munster. Ailill and Medb of Connacht had a daughter known as Sadb Sulbair (Sive of the pleasant speech). Brian Boru too had a daughter called Sadb. *Sábha* and *Sadhbha* are found in Connacht. The most acceptable anglicised form is *Sive*, the heroine of John B. Keane's popular play.

**SAOIRSE** (m, f) The name means 'freedom' and it is a comparatively new coinage, given mainly to girls, although some boys have also been called Saoirse. It seems to have first made its appearance in Northern Ireland early in the twentieth century and made its way south.

**SAORLA** earlier **SAORLAITH, SAERLAITH** (f) The distinguished historian Donnchadh Ó Corráin and his wife Fidelma have a daughter bearing this name. It means 'noble princess'. It is an ancient name, once given to the mother of an early abbot of Armagh.

**SÁRÁN** (m) The origin of this name, borne by three saints of the early Irish Church, is uncertain, but it may be from *sár*, the superlative (best, noblest). Ó Corráin and Maguire suggest the rare early noun *sár*, which means 'chief, ruler'. *Sárán* was until comparatively recent times a common given name in Offaly, the location of the foundation of St Sárán of Tisaran. This saint's feast day is 20 January. There is also a St Sárán associated with Great Island in Cork Harbour, whose feast day is 15 May; and another saint of the name associated with Cluain Crema, Clooncraff, whose feast day is 8 January.

**SÁRNAIT** earlier **SÁRNAT** (f) These are feminine forms of *Sárán* (above). One saint of the name is mentioned in the ancient tracts. This Sárnat, like Sárán of Tisaran, is associated with Co. Offaly.

**SCIATH** (f) This was once a favoured name for a girl in the Muscraí district of west Cork but seems to have gone out of fashion. There was a saint of that name who was invoked against pulmonary illness down to the beginning of the twentieth century, possibly because *sciath* means 'a shield'. Sciath's feast day is 6 September.

**SEALBHACH** earlier **SELBACH** (m) This name, associated with the family of Ó Donnchadha an Ghleanna, the poetic O'Donoghues of Kerry, was, according to the stories told about Fionn Mac Cumhaill and his band of Fianna warriors, the name chosen by Diarmaid Ó Duibhne (p. 66) for a son of his. The modern surname *Ó Sealbhaigh*, anglicised *Shally*, *Shaloo* and *Shallow*, derives from it.

**SÉAMAS** (m) Irish versions of *James*, itself borrowed from the New Testament Latin name *Jacobus*. It was a name much in favour among the Anglo-Norman settlers; the Earls of Desmond were particularly fond of it. *Séamas* is now the accepted 'official' spelling of the name, but it appears that *Séamus* is the more popular. It is, of course, how the Nobel literature laureate from Bellaghy, Co. Derry, spells his name, and for that reason alone may be accepted again as the norm. It is pronounced *Shamus* in Co. Waterford. In Kilkenny a common diminutive is *Shem*.

**SEÁN** (m) The name is borrowed from the French *Jehan*, itself from the Latin *Johannes*. It first appeared in Ireland as *John*, a favourite among English families from the twelfth century onwards and brought to Ireland by the Anglo-Normans. It was quickly adopted by the Irish where it appeared first as *Seón*, *Seónag* and *Seinicin*, adaptations of *Jenkin* or *Jonkin* (little John).

The name has, unfortunately, been rendered *Shaun* and *Shawn*, but the tendency to use those phonetic renderings has been reversed since Sean Connery's first name was seen to pose no problems for international audiences. *Shane* echoes the northern pronunciation of the name.

**SEANACH** earlier **SENACH** (m) The Old Irish word *sen* means 'ancient'. It was, according to O'Rahilly, the name of a god. *St Senach* was a holy man who lived on an island in Lough Erne. He is remembered on 11 May.

**SEANÁN** earlier **SENÁN** (m) Anglicised *Senan*, this was a saint of Co. Clare who founded a monastery on Inis Cathaigh (Scattery Island) at the mouth of the River Shannon. *Senán* was probably a nickname: it means 'little old one'. It was said that St Patrick foretold the birth of the saint and that a wise man from Clare identified him as being carried in her womb by a girl called Geirgreann. When the child was born his mother was clutching a stick cut from a rowan tree; the stick burst into foliage and bloom. Planted, it grew to be a famous tree.

Senán is associated with St Martin of Tours, but the accounts we have of his life are untrustworthy. We have the conventional miracles such as people who have died in accidents being restored to life. There is a charming story of a girl called Canair walking over the Shannon waves to Scattery Island, and insisting that Senán allow women as well as men to follow the monastic life there. Senán gave way after a long argument. Indeed, when his time came to die, he insisted that his body be taken to the convent on Scattery to rest. St Martin was said to be transported miraculously from France to Senán's deathbed to administer the last rites, as had been arranged many years before. Senán's feast day is 8 March.

**SEANCHÁN** earlier **SENCHÁN** (m) The name of a pet form of

*Seanach* (p. 156). Among the saints bearing this name is one Senchán, an abbot of the great Munster foundation of Emly, who died, it is thought, in 781. The most famous of the Senchán
s was a poet and genealogist named Senchán Toirpéist. Nobody knows what his sobriquet means.

Senchán Toirpéist lived around the end of the sixth and the beginning of the seventh century. His best-known work was the *Cocangab Mór* (Great Anthology), but little of it survives except some verses on the genealogy of the Leinstermen. We have, however, a late tract which may be based on it.

The first mention of Seanchán himself in literature dates from the ninth century. In it we learn of a poetess from east Limerick who went missing on a tour of this country, Scotland and the Isle of Man. As chance would have it, Seanchán and a retinue of 50 went to Man at this time. As they prepared to sail, a hideously ugly man asked him if he could go with them. This creature had a bulge on his head from which pus flowed; his rags were alive with lice. His appeal to Seanchán for pity, during which he said that he would be better company than the poets in the boat, amused Seanchán, and he told him to come on board. When they made landfall on Man they saw an old woman on the strand. They introduced themselves. She laid down a challenge, to finish a half-quatrain of verse. Seanchán and his fellow poets failed the challenge, but not so the stranger they had taken with them. Twice more he took up the old hag's challenge and succeeded. Seanchán realised that the hag was none other that the missing Limerick poetess. They took her back to Ireland with them. On the journey home the filthy stranger was transformed into a handsome young man. On reaching land he disappeared. He was the Spirit of Poetry.

**SEÁRLAIT** (f) Gaelic form of *Charlotte*, a French and English feminine diminutive of *Charles*, which became popular in the sixteenth century and even more so subsequently due to the influence of Queen Charlotte, wife of George III (1744–1818), and later due to the popularity of the novelist Charlotte Brönte (1816–1855). The Irish version of the name is rarely used.

Its cognates are *Carlotta* (Italian), *Karlotte* (German), and *Charlotta* (Scandinavian).

**SÉIMÍ** (m) A form found in Ulster of the Scottish male name *Jamie*, common among the Lowland Scots as a pet form of *James*. The Highland counterpart is *Hamish*. See *Séamas*.

**SEOIRSE** (m) The English *George*, which is from Old French, from Latin *eorgius*, from Greek *Georgios*, from *georgos* (farmer), a compound of *ge* (earth) and *ergein* (work), the name of several saints of old. Among them is the man who is now regarded as the patron of England, Germany and Portugal. He probably never existed, but some sources say that if he did he may have been one of Diocletian's martyrs killed in Palestine in the fourth century. The legend of Seoirse slaying the dragon was invented in Italy in medieval times. In Scotland he is known as *Seoras* and *Deorsa*. Our best-known Seoirse is the composer and musicologist Seoirse Bodley.

**SEOSAIMHÍN** (f) The female form of *Seosamh* (below), from the French *Josephine*, adopted by the English-speaking world.

**SEOSAMH** (m) The modern variant of *Ioseph*, the name used by pre-Norman clerics for the biblical *Joseph*, the English and French form of the Hebrew *Yosef*, meaning 'God shall add (another son)'.

**SETANTA** (m) The literature tells us that before he became famous, Cú Chulainn, the great hero of the Ulster Cycle, was known as *Setanta*, which corresponds to the name of a Celtic tribe which settled in Britain, the Setantii. He was born and reared in the territory of Muirtheimhne in present-day Co. Louth. The story of his slaying the hound of Culann, the smith, is well known; it is told in the biography of his youth inserted into the *Táin*. Culann had a monstrous hound which he released only at night. Setanta came late to a feast, playing tricks with his ball and hurley, and was confronted by the ferocious beast. He seized the hound by the back and throat and dashed its head against a pillar stone. Culann accepted the boy's offer to guard his fortress until another hound could be found and trained. Thus he came to be known as Cú Chulainn.

The only modern-day Setanta I know of is Setanta Ó hAilpin, the Cork hurler. Perhaps other Setantas will follow.

**SIBÉAL** (f) The medieval French form of this name was *Isabel*. It was very popular among the Anglo-Normans who introduced it here. Anglicised as *Bella* and *Elizabeth*. The latter name actually gave the French *Isabel* in the first instance. See *Isibéal*.

**SÍLE** (f) The name derives from *Cecily*, the English form of the Latin name of the second or third-century virgin martyr *St Cecilia*, regarded as the patron saint of music, although why this is so is not clear. However, she has inspired works such as Henry Purcell's *Ode on St Cecilia's Day*. The Anglo-Normans brought the name to Ireland and in time it became *Síle*. In the eighteenth century the name became synonymous with Jacobite Ireland in the Munster counties. 'Síle Ní Ghadhra' and 'Síle Bheag Ní Chonalláin' are songs from that time which come to mind. This very popular name suffered from anglicisation in the nineteenth century when it became, especially in Munster, *Julia*, *Sabina* and *Sally*. The forms *Sheela*, *Sheelagh* and *Shelagh* are much more acceptable and have attained great popularity in England, and in Australia where *Sheila* has become a universal slang word for a girl.

**SÍNE** (f) An Irish form of *Jane*, derived from Anglo-Norman *Jeanne*. Anglicised as *Sheena*.

**SINÉAD** (f) The Irish form of *Janet*, derived from the Anglo-Norman *Jeanette*. There is a diminutive form *Sinéidín*. The chanteuse Sinead O'Connor is the best-known bearer of the name.

**SIOBHÁN** (f) The name is derived from the Anglo-Norman disyllabic form *Jehanne*, a form of *Jane* now widely known wherever English is spoken, thanks to the fame of the Irish actress Siobhán McKenna (1923–86). The name is anglicised sometimes as *Shevaun* and *Chevonne*.

**SÍODA** (m) This was once a common name among some Munster families. The MacNamaras of Co. Clare were particularly fond of it. It seems as if the name derived from the Irish word for silk (*síoda*). It is, I believe, no longer in use except in its anglicised form, *Sheedy*.

**SÍOMÓN** (m) The Irish form of *Simon*, the common English form of *Simeon*. The Hebrew from which it derives means 'hearkening'. *Síomón/Simon/Simeon* became popular because it was the name of the man who first blessed the infant Jesus, and the name of the man who helped Jesus carry his cross to Calvary.

**SIONAINN** earlier **SINANN** (f) The corresponding male form is *Shannon*. Neither of the Irish forms is, to my knowledge, now used as a first name. *Shannon* has become popular among Irish Americans and has spread to Ireland. The name comes from the river, and here is one of four versions of how the river got its name, taken from the medieval mythical geography of Ireland, the *Dindshenchas*: At the bottom of the ocean there is Connla's well. Six streams rise upwards from it; the seventh is Sinann. The nine hazel trees of the sage Crimall drop their fruits where the waters from the well break the surface; the hazels stand by the power of magic spells, under a dark mist of magic. All grow in mysterious fashion their leaves and fruit; a wonder too is that they all ripen together. When the nuts are ripe they fall down into the well; they scatter below at the bottom and the salmon feed on them. From the juice of the nuts are formed magic bubbles; these are the bubbles that flow down the green-flowing streams.

There was a golden-haired girl of the Tuatha Dé Danann, the lively Sinann, bright of face, the daughter of Lodán Luachairglan. One night the girl thought, that lovely red-lipped, sweet-voiced girl, that she had every kind of fame at her command except one, the knowledge of the mystic art. That lovely girl came to the river one day and saw the magic bubbles. Out she ventured after them into the green-flowing, fast-flowing water. She was drowned; and from her Sinann is named.

**SOMHAIRLE** (m) This name was common in the north of Ireland, particularly among the Mac Donnells of Antrim. It fell victim to the anglicisation trends of the nineteenth century both in Ireland and in Scotland where it was also very popular. It was borrowed into Irish from the Old Norse *Summorlieth* (traveller in summer) meaning 'Viking'. It is often acceptably anglicised as *Sorley*.

**SORCHA** (f) The name means 'bright' or 'shining'. Sorcha was a common name from the Middle Ages until the nineteenth century when the decline of the language under the National School system and its clerical managers led to so many of the ancient names being transmuted. Sorcha was then rendered as *Sally* and *Sarah*. Sorcha Cusack, the actress, is a well-known bearer of the name and is probably responsible for its growing popularity in England.

**STIABHNA** (m) See *Stiana*

**STIANA, STIABHNA, STIOFÁN** (m) Versions of the Irish name of *Stephen*, the first Christian martyr, whose feast day is 26 December. The name is from the Greek *stephanos* (a crown or garland).

**SUIBHNE** (m) Apart from the famous Suibhne Geilt, the bird-man of the great medieval story (see *Rónán*), mention might be made of Suibhne Meann, High King of Ireland from 615 to 628. His father Fiachna, although related to the great Niall of the Nine Hostages, had no interest in politics until, so the story goes, his wife, in bed one night, told him that he should be ashamed of himself. He roused himself after that and collected an army by beating them all in single combat. The name could be anglicised *Sweeney*.

# T

**TADHG** earlier **TADC** (m) This name, originally meaning 'poet', has been popular since very early times, and is still common. Indeed Tadhg agus Síle could be said to be the equivalent of Jack and Jill in English, and Tadhg is found in such phrases as *Tadhg na Sráide* (Tadg in the Street), meaning both the common man and man-about-town; *Tadhg-an-dá thaobh* (Tadhg who plays the two sides), an untrustworthy boyo; and *Tadhg na Scuab* (Tadhg of the Brushes) is the Man in the Moon. Brian Boru had a son called Tadc who died in 1023. In the nineteenth century Tadhg was anglicised in some bewildering forms: *Thaddeus*, *Theophilus*, *Theodosius* and *Timothy*, and in the north *Teague*, a name applied to Catholics in general by loyalist bigots. The surname *Mac Thaidhg* has been anglicised as *McTeague*, and worse, *Montague*.

**TASSACH** (m) This early name borne by St Patrick's craftsman probably means 'easy-going'. He was, according to the stories surrounding the early saints, a bishop, and it was he who heard St Patrick's last confession and anointed him before he died.

**TEAMHAIR** earlier **TEMAIR** (f) The name is used nowadays only in its anglicised form, *Tara*. The old word meant either 'eminence' or 'spectacle'. Temair is central to most of the great dramas in early Irish literature. In Irish mythology Temair was the name of the beautiful woman who gave her name to the royal seat. It was also the name of the wife of the High King Diarmait Ruanait, who died in 665. A saint of the name is mentioned. Whether she ever existed or not is a moot point.

**TIARNÁN** earlier **TIGEARNÁN** (m) This name is nowadays

anglicised acceptably as *Tiernan*. The name derives from *tigern*, which means 'lord or chieftain'. There is one saint of the name, now forgotten. There were, naturally, given the name's origin, many medieval rulers who bore the name, the most notorious being Tigearnán ua Ruairc, king of Breifne. This man was embroiled all his life in intrigues of all kinds. First of all he opposed the ambitions of Turlough O'Connor, king of Connacht, and then when it suited him, submitted to him and joined forces with him. In 1132 he changed his mind about Turlough and broke off the alliance, but six years later he felt the wind had changed and he made peace with O'Connor again. In 1142 he got a large portion of east Meath as a reward for his services, but when he lost this newly acquired land two years later he changed his coat again but had to pay tribute to Muirchertach mac Lochlainn, king of Cinél Eoghain, who was staking a claim to the High Kingship of Ireland. Nobody could trust him, and by 1152 he had been deprived by his former allies of all his newly won territories, including his castle at Dangan. His greatest embarrassment, however, was the humiliating loss of his wife Dervorguilla, to Diarmait mac Murchadh, the gentleman who had invited the Anglo-Normans to Ireland. Tigearnán was assassinated by the Anglo-Normans in 1172.

**TIARNMHAS** earlier **TIGHEARNMHAS** (m) This ancient name means 'noble' or 'lordly'. The man who bore this name was a fictional prehistoric king of Ireland. It was said that during his reign the first gold mine in Ireland was discovered somewhere near Naas, Co. Kildare. He was somewhat of an arbiter of taste, and it was claimed that due to him the first gold and silver ornaments, the first gold and silver drinking utensils, and the first clothes using the colours purple, blue and green were designed. He it was who ordered that coloured garments must be worn according to social status: one colour for bondsmen, two for peasants, three for soldiers, four for under-lords, five for chieftains, six for learned men, and seven for royalty. He came to a sad end, according to the legend. He was said to have originated the cult of the idol Crom Cruach at Magh Sléacht, the plain of Tullyhaw in Co. Cavan. He went there to celebrate the festival of Samhain accompanied by an immense retinue. They were struck down by an unspecified illness, possibly the plague, and three-quarters of his followers died with him.

Tighearnmhas is the invention of medieval writers, and although they placed his reign in the pagan era, his sudden death, as Ó hÓgain says, was meant to signify the wrath of God against the sin of idolotry.

**TÍREACHÁN** earlier **TÍRECHÁN** (m) This name means 'man whose possessions are great'. The best-known bearer of this name is Tírechán, the biographer of St Patrick.

**TOMALTACH** (m) This old given name which gave the Ulster surnames *Tomelty* and *Tumelty* seems to have died out in Ulster in the nineteenth century. It was once in favour among some of the clans of Connacht, especially among the MacDonaghs. It was anglicised *Timothy* and *Thomas* after the introduction of the National Schools in the early nineteenth century and quickly went out of favour among the O'Beirnes, Geraghtys and the northern MacDermotts, among whom it was common during the Middle Ages.

**TOMÁS** (m) From the biblical name *Thomas*, in Aramaic 'a twin'. Common among the Anglo-Saxons, it was confined among them, and among the Irish in the early medieval period to clerics. There was a Tomás, abbot and scribe of Bangor, who died around 794, and Tomás, bishop of Linn Duachaill, who died about 808. Possibly out of respect for St Thomas Becket, the name in its Irish form grew popular among the Anglo-Normans. It has once more grown in popularity in recent times. Tomás Ó Criomhthain, the author of *An tOileánach*, the great account of life in the Blaskets, and Tomás Mulcahy, the Cork hurler, are well-known bearers of the name.

**TRAOLACH, TÁRLACH** earlier **TOIRDHEALBHACH, TAIRDELBACH** (m) This name, which Ó Corráin and

Maguire say means 'instigator, abettor', was very popular in the Middle Ages and has retained its popularity, especially in some of its anglicised forms such as *Terence*, *Terry* and *Turlough*. Some famous kings bore the name in the eleventh and twelfth centuries: Tairdelbach Ó Briain, king of Munster, who claimed the kingship of Ireland and who died in 1086; and Tairdelbach Ó Conchobair (Turlough O'Connor), king of Connacht and king of Ireland, who died in 1156. *Traolach* is popular in Munster; *Tárlach* in the northern counties, especially in Donegal.

**TREASA** (f) This is the Irish equivalent of *Theresa*, and it came into being from Irish devotion to the saint of Avila and later Thérèse of Lisieux. It is said that the name originated in Spain, and that the first Teresa was the wife of St Paulinus of Nola, who was given her name because she was born on the Greek island of Thera. Most scholars now either dismiss that theory out of hand or consider it unreliable.

**TUATHAL** (m) This name was given to many of the warriors and kings of old. The most famous is Tuathal Techtmar, later called Tuathal Teachtmhar. Some scholars say that he was a mythic king and leader of the Goidelic invasion; others claim that he may have been historic, reigning in the second century A.D. The name Tuathal is the Irish version of a postulated Celtic *Teutovalos*, which means 'leader or ruler of the people'. Techtmar may mean simply 'wealthy, possessing riches'. The name Tuathal survived in Ulster until the middle of the nineteenth century; indeed in Co. Donegal it was given to children until the beginning of the twentieth century, when it suddenly became obsolete. During the Middle Ages it was favoured among members of the bardic family Ó hUiginn (O'Higgins). The literature surrounding Tuathal Techtmar is extensive, but there is no trace of him to be found in the folklore of Ireland. Tuathal has been anglicised *Tully* and *Toal*, while the Wicklow surname *Ó Tuathail* has been anglicised as *O'Toole*.

# U

**UAINE** (f) This lovely ancient name was given to a Clare baby I know by her parents who mistakenly thought that it meant 'a lamb'. They were happy when they were told that the eminent scholar Whitley Stokes thought that Uaine was an old word for 'a lady or a queen'. Others have said that it means 'green' and that the lady may have been a goddess of the land. Uaine from a fairy fort near Tonn Chlíona (p. 45) had as her companions the birds of the Land of Promise, according to the Fianna stories. She was a wonderful musician.

**UAITÉAR** earlier **UATÉR** (m) This name came with the Normans. Its origin is an old Germanic personal name composed of *wald* (rule) and *heri, hari* (army). The name *Wealdhere* was common in England before the Norman invasion but was replaced after 1066 by continental forms of the name. The Irish forms are borrowed directly from the medieval English forms *Water* and *Wauter*.

**UILLIAM** (m) See *Liam*

**ULTÁN** (m) This is a favourite Ulster name, and is actually a diminutive form of *Ultach* (Ulsterman). There were many Ultáns among the early saints, but the most famous and certainly the best loved was Ultán moccu Conchobair of Arbraccan, Co. Meath, who lived in the sixth century; his dates are uncertain. He became bishop and abbot of the monastery founded by St Breccan, which subsequently bore the name Tiobraid Ultáin. One of the reasons put forward to account for this name was that the *tiobraid* (well) close by was a place where Ultán used to bathe in even the most inclement weather as a penance. But it was his devotion to children that made his name revered. He was said to have supported every orphan he could find throughout Ireland, and there were many of these due to their parents being carried off by the plague. He was also a scholar of no mean ability and a poet who wrote a memorable poem in Irish in honour of St Brigit, as well as Latin verses in her honour and, it was said, her Life. Tíreachán, the man who wrote St Patrick's biography, was a friend and pupil of his. Ultán may be regarded as the patron saint of orphans. His feast day is 4 September. His name has been acceptably anglicised as, simply, *Ultan*.

**ÚNA** (f) This has been a very popular name in Ireland since medieval times. Úna Olchrothach was, according to the old story, the daughter of the king of Lochlann and became the mother of the famous Conn Cétchathach (Conn of the Hundred Battles). There is a beautiful Connacht song, 'Úna Bhán', which tells of the love of Úna MacDermott for Tomás Láidir Costello. In the nineteenth century the name suffered from the fashion for Anglicisation, becoming *Oona* and *Oonagh*. It is now popular in these forms in Britain and Australia. But the nineteenth century brought a worse fate: it was also rendered *Agnes* and *Unity*.

**VAUK** (m) See *Beoc*

**VOGUE** (m) *See Beoc*

# PRINCIPAL SOURCES

*Annals of Ulster*, ed. W.M. Hennessy and B. MacCarthy (Dublin 1887). *Annals of Inisfallen*, ed. Seán Mac Airt (Dublin 1951). *Chronicum Scottorum*, ed. W.M. Hennessy (London 1886). *Annals of the Four Masters*, ed. J. O'Donovan (Dublin 1848–51). *Annals of Loch Cé*, ed. W.M. Hennessy (London 1871). *Annals of Clonmacnoise*, ed. E. Murphy (Dublin 1896).

*Corpus Genealogiarum Hiberniae*, ed. M.A. O'Brien (Dublin 1962). *Corpus Genealogiarum Sanctorum Hiberniae* (Dublin 1985). *Vitae Sanctorum Hiberniae*, Charles Plummer (Oxford 1910). *Miscellanea Hagiographica Hibernica*, Charles Plummer (Brussels 1925).

*Martyrology of Oengus*, ed. Whitley Stokes (London 1905). *Martyrology of Tallaght*, ed. R.I. Best and H.C. Lawlor (London 1931). *Martyrology of Donegal*, ed. John O'Donovan and J.H. Todd (Dublin 1864).

*The Metrical Dindshenchas*, ed. Edward Gwynn (Dublin 1903–35, 5 vols). *Early Irish History and Mythology*, T.F. O'Rahilly (Dublin 1946). *Old Irish Personal Names*, M.A. O'Brien (*Celtica* 10, 1973). *Borrowed Elements in the Corpus of Irish Personal Names*, Brian Ó Cuív (*Celtica* 18, 1986). *Myth, Legend and Romance*, Dáithí Ó hÓgáin (New York 1991). *The Life and Legend of St Patrick*, Ludwig Bieler (Dublin 1949). *Laoithe na Féinne*, Pádraig Ó Siochfhradha (Dublin 1941). *The Dream of Oengus*, Francis Shaw (Dublin 1934). *The Calendar of Óengus*, Whitley Stokes (Dublin 1880). *Acallamh na Senórach*, ed. Whitley Stokes (Leipzig 1900: *Irishe Texte* 4). *The Birth and Life of St Moling*, Whitley Stokes (London 1907). *The Voyage of Máel Dúin*, H.P.A. Oskamp (Groningen 1970). *Cath Maighe Mucrama*, Máirín O'Daly (Dublin 1975). *Compert Con Culainn*, A.G. Van Hamel (Dublin 1933).

*Táin Bó Cuailnge from the Book of Leinster*, Cecile O'Rahilly (Dublin 1970). *The Voyage of St Brendan*, John J. O'Meara (Dublin 1978). *Early Christian Ireland*, Máire and Liam de Paor (London 1958). *Celtic and Early Christian Wexford*, Edward Culleton (Dublin 1999). *Settlements of Celtic Saints in Wales*, E.G. Bowen (Cardiff 1954). *Ancient Irish Tales*, T.P. Cross and C.H. Slover (London 1897). *Over Nine Waves*, Marie Heaney (Dublin 2000).

*Irish Names*, D. Ó Corráin and F. Maguire (Dublin 1981). *The Irish Saints*, Daphne Pochin Mould (Dublin, London 1964). *Irish Names for Children*, Laurence Flanagan (Dublin 1993). *Irish Personal Names, Co. Donegal*, J.C. Ward (*Gaelic Journal*, ix, no. 104, Feb. 1899). *Irish Personal Names, Co. Antrim*, P.T. McGinley (*ibid.*, no. 105, March 1899). *Irish Personal Names, Oirghialla*, S. Ó hAnnabháin (*ibid.*, no. 119, 1900). *Dictionary of First Names*, Patrick Hanks and Flavia Hodges (Oxford 1996). *Dictionary of Saints*, Donald Attwater (London 1965). *A Calendar of Saints of the Diocese of Ferns*, Séamas de Vál, unpublished, 2000.

# NOTES ON PRONUNCIATION

MÁIRE NÍ CHIOSÁIN

## PRONUNCIATION

The pronunciations provided strive to be representative of common pronunciations. There are, of course, other variants of some of these names which generally reflect dialectal variation. The pronunciation of each name is given in phonetic transcription. The phonetic transcription is given in square brackets. The following is a guide to the pronunciation of the symbols used:

### Consonants

*Broad and slender consonants*

Irish has what are traditionally called broad and slender consonants. The slender (palatalised) consonants involve a raising of the front of the tongue body which can result in a short 'y' sound following the consonant. In Fionn, for example, a short 'y' sound is produced between the consonant and the vowel; this is represented by [$^{j}$] or [j]: [f$^{j}$ʌn̪]or [fjuːn̪]. In Cearbhall there is a shorter 'y' sound between the first consonant and the vowel, represented by an apostrophe after the consonant: [k′aruːl̪]. The latter notation is that conventionally used to represent slender/palatalised consonants in Irish.

Slender 't' and 'd' are represented here as [t′] and [d′]. The pronunciation of these sounds can be more like [t$^{s}$] and [d$^{z}$]or [t$^{ʃ}$] and [d$^{3}$], e.g. Réiltín [reːl′t′iːn′], Deorán [d′oːrɔːn̪].

The slender/palatalised counterpart of 's' is represented using the symbol [ʃ] which is pronounced like English 'sh', e.g. Seán [ʃɔːn̪].

[k] is used to represent the initial sound in Caitríona [kat′r′iən̪ə] or Ciara [kiərə]. In the case of broad [k] and [m] before [iː] there is a short (vocalic) transition from the consonant to [iː]. This is represented here using [$^{ə}$], e.g. Caoimhe [k$^{ə}$iːv′i] (compare with English *key* [kiː] where no such transition occurs), Maolíosa [m$^{ə}$iːl̪iːsə] (compare with English *meal* [miːl] where no such transition occurs).

*Dental consonants*

Irish has dental consonants which are produced by placing the blade of the tongue against the back of the upper teeth. This is represented using the symbol [ ̪]. Examples containing dental consonants include Dónal [d̪oːn̪əl̪], Tuathal [t̪uəhəl̪], Seán [ʃɔːn̪], Lugh [l̪uː]. (Compare the Hiberno-English pronunciation of the initial consonant in ***think*** and ***this*** which is typically a dental consonant.)

*R-sounds*

R-sounds are represented using the symbols [r r′] (though the sounds are generally approximants and, as such, would be represented in IPA transcription by [ɹ]).

Slender/palatalised [r′] is pronounced with the tongue higher than for English r, for some speakers almost like the final consonant in English mira*ge*, e.g. Lasair [l̪asir′].

*Other symbols*

The following phonetic symbols are also used:
[ŋ], [ŋ′] as found in Aonghus [eːŋgəs] (compare English *anger* [aŋgər]) Aisling [aʃl′iŋ′] (compare English *sing* [siŋ])
[j] as found in Iubhdán [juːd̪ɔːn̪] (compare English *use* (verb) [juːz])
[ɣ] as found in Dubhghlas [d̪uːɣl̪əs]

**Vowels**

Irish has long and short vowels. Length is represented here using a colon, e.g. [oː iː]. The quality of short vowel in particular is influenced by neighbouring consonants. The following is a guide to the symbols used in the transcriptions using English words to illustrate the sounds in question. Two transcriptions are provided for the English words, the first using the same system as is used for the Irish words, the second using the appropriate symbols from the International Phonetic Alphabet (IPA).

iː as in Aoife [iːfə] (English: *see* [siː], IPA [si])
eː as in Éamonn [eːmən̪] (English: *say* [seː], IPA [se])
ɔː as in Ciarán [kiərɔːn̪] (English: *awe* [ɔː], IPA [ɔ])
oː as in Dónall [d̪oːn̪əl̪ ] (English: *show* [ʃoː], IPA [ʃo] )
uː as in Úna [uːn̪ə] (English: *boo* [buː], IPA [bu])
au as in Labhrás [l̪aurɔːs] (English: *how* [hau])
iə as in Liam [liəm] (English: *be a* .. [biːə], IPA [biə])
uə as in Nuala [n̪uəl̪ə] (English: *do a* .. [duːə], IPA [duə])
i as in Cillín [kil′iːn′] (English: *miss* [mis], IPA [mɪs])
e as in Nessa [n′esə] (English: *nest* [nest], IPA [nɛst])
a as in Aisling [aʃl′iŋ′] (English: *cash* [kaʃ], IPA [kæʃ])
ɑ as in Anraí [ɑn̪riː] (English: *honour* [ɑnəɹ])
ʌ as in Colm [kʌl̪əm] (English: *cut* [kʌt])
u as in Brandubh [brɑn̪duv] (English: *would* [wud], IPA [wʊd])
ə as in Ciara [kiərə], Dónall [d̪oːn̪əl̪ ] (in unstressed syllables) (English: *alive* [əlaiv], Tallaght [talə])

## Stress

Stress is typically on the first syllable of a word in Irish. However in Munster dialects when the second syllable contains a long vowel (usually indicated in the spelling by a 'fada'/grave accent, e.g. á, é), the syllable containing that vowel is stressed. Stress is generally not marked in the transcriptions; however, in the few instances where it is marked, this is done by placing [ˈ] *before* the syllable in question. Where there is possible variation this is indicated, e.g. Tomás [t̪ əˈmɔːs] (stress on the second syllable, typical Munster pronunciation) or [ˈt̪ ʌmɔs] (stress on the first syllable, typical Connacht pronunciation), Siobhán [ʃiˈvɔːn̪] or [ˈʃuːwɔːn̪].

# INDEX OF NAMES WITH PHONETIC TRANSCRIPTION

## INDEX OF NAMES

| | |
|---|---|
| AARON (m) | |
| ABBÁN (m) | 'ɑbɔːn̪ / ə'bɔːn |
| ÁDHAMH (m) | ɔːv |
| AGUISTÍN (m) | ɑgiʃt′iːn′ |
| AIBHISTÍN (m) | av′iʃt′iːn′ |
| AIBIGÉAL (f) | ab′igeːl̪ |
| AIFRIC (f) | af′rik′ |
| AILBHE (f) | al′vi |
| AILLINN (f) | al′in′ |
| AINDRÉAS (m) | an′d′r′eːs |
| AINDRIAS (m) | an′d′r′iəs |
| AINDRIÚ (m) | an′d′r′uː |
| AINGEAL (f) | aŋ′g′əl̪ / aŋ′əl̪ |
| AISLING (f) | aʃl′iŋ′ |
| AMHLAOIBH (m) | aul̪iəv |
| ANLUAN (m) | ɑn̪l̪uən̪ |
| ANRAÍ (m) | ɑn̪riː / aun̪riː / aun̪əriː |
| AODH (m) | eː / iː |
| AODHAGÁN (m) | eːgɔːn̪ |
| AODHÁN (m) | eːɔːn̪ |
| AOGÁN (m) | eːgɔːn̪ |
| AOIBHEALL (f) | iːvəl̪ |
| AOIBHINN (f) | iːv′in′ |

| | |
|---|---|
| AOIFE (f) | iːfə |
| AONGHUS (m) | eːŋgəs |
| AONNA (m) | eːn̪ə |
| ART (m) | ɑrt̪ |
| ATHRACHT (f) | ɑhrəxt̪ |
| BAILE (m) | bɑl′i |
| BAIRBRE (f) | bɑr′ib′r′i |
| BAIRTLIMÉAD, BEARTLAÍ (m) | bɑrt′l′imed̪, b′ɑrt̪l̪iː |
| BALAR (m) | bɑl̪ər |
| BEARACH (m) | b′arəx |
| BEARCHÁN (m) | b′arəxɔːn̪ |
| BÉBÓ (f) | b′eːboː |
| BÉIBHEANN (f) | b′eːvən̪ |
| BEIRCHEART (m) | b′er′ix′ərt̪ |
| BEOC (m) | b′oːk |
| BLÁTHMAC (m) | bl̪ɔmək |
| BLÁTHNAID (f) | bl̪ɔːn̪id′ |
| BLINNE (f) | bl′in′i |
| BRAN (m) | brɑn̪ |
| BRANDUBH (m) | brɑn̪d̪uv |
| BREAC (m) | br′ak |
| BREACÁN (m) | br′akɔːn̪ |
| BREACNAIT (f) | br′akn̪it′ |
| BRÉANAINN (m) | br′eːn̪in′ |
| BREANDÁN (m) | ′br′en̪d̪ɔːn̪ / br′aun̪′d̪ɔːn̪ |
| BREAS (m) | br′as |
| BREASAL (m) | br′asəl̪ |
| BREASLÁN (m) | br′asl̪ɔːn̪ |
| BRIAN (m) | br′iən̪ |
| BRÍD (f) | br′iːd′ |
| BRIGHID (f) | br′iːd′ |
| BRIOC (m) | br′ʌk |
| BRÓNACH (f) | bron̪əx |
| BUADHACH (m) | buəx |
| BUANAIT (f) | buən̪it′ |
| CADHLA (m,f) | kail̪ə |

| | |
|---|---|
| CAILÍN (f) | kal′iːn′ |
| CAILLÍN (f) | kal′iːn′ |
| CAIMÍN (m) | kam′iːn′ |
| CAINNEACH (m) | kan′əx |
| CAIREANN (f) | kar′ən̪ |
| CAITERÍNA (f) | kat′ir′iːn̪ə |
| CAITILÍN (f) | kat′il′iːn′ |
| CAITLÍN (f) | kat′l′iːn′ |
| CAITRÍONA (f) | kat′r′iən̪ə |
| CAOILTE (m) | kᵊiːl′t′i |
| CAOIMHE (f) | kᵊiːv′i |
| CAOIMHÍN (m) | kᵊiːv′iːn |
| CAOMHÁN (m) | kᵊiːvɔːn̪ |
| CARA (f) | kɑrə |
| CARTHACH (m) | kɑrhəx |
| CASS (m) | kɑs |
| CASSAIR (f) | kɑsir′ |
| CATHAL (m) | kɑhəl̪ |
| CATHAOIR (m) | kɑhiːr′ |
| CEARBHALL (m) | k′aruːl̪ |
| CEALLACH (m,f) | k′al̪əx |
| CEASAIR (f) | k′asir′ |
| CIABHÁN (m) | kiəvɔːn̪ |
| CIAN (m) | kiən̪ |
| CIANÁN (m) | kiən̪ɔːn̪ |
| CIARA (f) | kiərə |
| CIARÁN (m) | kiərɔːn̪ |
| CIARNAIT (f) | kiərn̪it′ |
| CILLÍN (m) | kil′iːn′ |
| CINNSEALACH (m) | kin′ʃəl̪əx |
| CIONAODH (m) | k′ʌn̪iː |
| CLÍODHNA (f) | kl′iən̪ə |
| CLÍONA (f) | kl′iən̪ə |
| CLODAGH (f) | |
| CÓILÍN (m) | koːl′iːn′ |
| COLLA (m) | kʌl̪ə |

COLM, COLUMBA, COLMCILLE (m) kʌl̪əm, kəl̪ʌmbə, kʌl̪əmk′il′i
COLMA (f) kʌl̪mə
COLMÁN (m) kʌl̪mɔːn̪
COLUMBÁN (m) kʌl̪əmbɔn̪
COMHDHÁN (m) koːɔn̪
COMHGHALL (m) koːl̪
CONALL (m) kʌn̪əl̪
CONÁN (m) kʌn̪ɔːn̪
CONCHÚR (m) krʌhuːr
CONLAO (m) kʌn̪l̪iː
CONLAOCH (m) kʌn̪l̪iəx
CONN (m) kʌn̪
CONSTANS (f)
CORMAC (m) kʌrmək
CRÍOSTÓIR (m) k′r′ist̪oːr′
CRÓNÁN (m) kroːn̪ɔːn̪
CUÁN (m) kuːɔːn̪
CUARÁN (m) kuərɔːn̪
CUILEANN (f) kᵊil′ən̪
CUMMAÍNE (m) kʌmiːn′ə
CÚNLA (m) kuːn̪l̪ə
DÁIBHÍ (m) d̪ɔːv′iː
DAIMHÍN (m) d̪av′iːn′
DÁIRE (m) d̪ɔr′i
DAIREARCA (f) d̪ar′arkə
DAIRÍNE (f) d̪ar′iːn′i
DÁITHÍ (m) d̪ɔːhiː
DAMHNAIT (f) d̪aun̪it′
DÉAGLÁN (m) d′eːgl̪ɔːn̪
DEALGNAT (f) d′al̪əgn̪it′
DEARCÁN (m) d′arkɔːn̪
DEASÚN (m) d′asuːn̪
DEIRBHILE (f) d′er′v′il′i
DEIRDRE (f) d′er′d′r′i
DÉITHÍN (f) d′eːhiːn′
DEORÁN (m) d′oːrɔːn̪

| | |
|---|---|
| DIARMAID (m) | d′iərmid′ |
| DIL (m) | d′il′ |
| DOIRE (m) | d̪er′i |
| DOIREANN (f) | d̪er′ən̪ |
| DÓNAL (m) | d̪oːn̪əl̪ |
| DONAT (m) | d̪ʌn̪ət̪ |
| DONN (m) | d̪ʌn̪ |
| DONNABHÁN (m) | d̪ʌn̪əvɔːn̪/d̪ʌn̪əwɔːn̪ |
| DONNCHA (m) | d̪ʌn̪əxə |
| DUÁN (m) | d̪uːɔːn̪ |
| DUARTACH (m) | d̪uərt̪əx |
| DUBHGHALL (m) | d̪uəl̪ |
| DUBHGHLAS (m) | d̪uɣl̪ əs |
| ÉADAOIN (f) | eːd̪iːn′ |
| EALLÓG (m) | al̪oːg |
| EAMHNAT (f) | aun̪ət̪ |
| ÉAMONN (m) | eːmən̪ |
| ÉANNA (m) | eːn̪ə |
| EARNÁN (m) | arn̪ɔːn̪ |
| EIBHLÍN (f) | ail′iːn′/ev′l′iːn′ |
| ÉIGHNEACHÁN (m) | ain′əxɔn̪ |
| EILEANÓIR (f) | el′ən̪oːr′ |
| EILEANÓRA (f) | el′ən̪oːrə |
| EILTÍN (m) | el′t′iːn′ |
| ÉIMHIN (m) | eːv′in′ |
| EIRNÍNE (m) | er′n′iːn′i |
| EISIRT (m) | eʃir′t′ |
| EISTIR (f) | eʃt′ir′ |
| EITHNE (f) | ehin′i |
| ÉMER (f) | eːmər |
| ÉNÁN (m) | eːn̪ɔːn̪ |
| EOCHAÍ (m) | ʌxiː |
| EOGHAN (m) | oːən̪ |
| EOLANG (m) | oːl̪əŋ |
| EÓRANN (f) | oːrən̪ |
| ERNÍN (m) | er′n′iːn′ |

| | |
|---|---|
| FACHTNA (m) | faxn̪ə |
| FERGAL, FEARGHAL (m) | fergəl̪ |
| FEICHÍN (m) | fehiːn′ |
| FEIDHLIM (m) | feːl′im |
| FEIDHLIMIDH (m) | feːl′imiː |
| FERDIA (m) | ferd′iə |
| FIACHA (m) | fiəxə |
| FIACHNA (m) | fiəxn̪ə |
| FIACHRA (m) | fiəxrə |
| FIANAIT (f) | fiən̪it′ |
| FINÍN (m) | fin′iːn′ |
| FINNIAN (m) | fin′iən̪ |
| FÍONA (f) | fiən̪ə |
| FÍONÁN (m) | fiən̪ɔn̪ |
| FIONN | fʲʌn̪ / fjuːn̪ |
| FIONNBHARRA (m) | fin̪bɑrə |
| FIONNCHÚ (m) | fin̪xuː |
| FIONNUALA (f) | fin̪uəl̪ə |
| FIONNÚIR (f) | fin̪uːr′ |
| FIONTAN (m) | fin̪t̪ɔːn̪ |
| FÍTHEAL (m) | fiːhəl̪ |
| FLANN (m) | fl̪ɑn̪ |
| FLANNACÁN (m) | fl̪ɑn̪əkɔːn̪ |
| FLANNAGÁN (m) | fl̪ɑn̪əgɔːn̪ |
| FLANNÁN (m) | fl̪ɑn̪ɔːn̪ |
| FLIDAIS (f) | fl′id̪iʃ |
| FRAOCH (m) | friːx / freːx |
| FURSA (m) | fʌrsə |
| GARBHÁN (m) | gɑrəvɔːn̪ |
| GEARALT (m) | g′arəl̪t̪ |
| GEARÓID (m) | g′aroːd′ |
| GEARÓIDÍN (f) | g′aroːd′iːn′ |
| GOBNAIT (f) | gʌbn̪it′ |
| GORMÁN (m) | gʌrəmɔːn̪ |
| GORMLAITH (f) | gʌrəml̪ə |
| GRIAN (f) | g′r′iən̪ |

| | |
|---|---|
| GUAIRE (m) | guər′i |
| IARFHLAITH (m) | iərl̪ə |
| ÍOBHAR (m) | iːvər |
| ÍOMHAR (m) | iːvər |
| IRIAL (m) | iriəl̪ |
| ISIBÉAL (f) | iʃibeːl̪ |
| ÍTE / ÍDE (f) | iːt′i / iːd′i |
| IUBHDÁN (m) | juːd̪ɔːn̪ |
| KERRY (m, f) | |
| LABHRAIDH (m) | l̪auriː |
| LABHRÁS (m) | l̪aurɔːs |
| LAISRE (f) | l̪aʃr′i |
| LAISREÁN (f) | l̪aʃr′ɔːn̪ |
| LAOGHAIRE (m) | l̪eːr′i |
| LAOISE (f) | l̪iːʃə |
| LAOISEACH (m,f) | l̪iːʃəx |
| LASAIR (f) | l̪ɑsir′ |
| LASAIRFHÍONA (f) | l̪ɑsir′iːn̪ə |
| LÍ BAN (f) | liːbən̪ |
| LÍADAIN (f) | liəd̪in′ |
| LIAM (m) | liəm |
| LIAMHAIN (f) | liəwin′ |
| LOCHLAINN (m) | l̪ʌxl̪in′ |
| LOMÁN (m) | l̪ʌmɔːn̪ |
| LONÁN (m) | l̪ʌn̪ɔːn̪ |
| LONNÓG (f) | l̪ʌn̪oːg |
| LORCÁN (m) | l̪ʌrkɔːn̪ |
| LÚCÁS (m) | l̪uːkɔːs |
| LÚGADÁN (m) | l̪uːgəd̪ɔːn̪ |
| LUGH (m) | l̪uː |
| LUGHACH (m) | l̪uəx |
| LÚÍ (m) | l̪uːiː |
| LUÍSEACH (f) | l̪iːʃəx |
| LÚITHIARN (m) | l̪uːhiərn̪ |
| MÁBLA (f) | mɔːbl̪ə |
| MAC CÁIRTHINN (m) | mɑk kɔːr′hin′ |

| | |
|---|---|
| MAC DARA (m) | makd̪arə |
| MACHA (f) | maxə |
| MAINCHÍN (m) | man′ix′iːn′ |
| MÁIRE (f) | mɔːr′i |
| MÁIRÉAD (f) | mɔːr′eːd̪ / mʌr′eːd̪ |
| MÁIRTÍN / MÁRTAN (m) | mɔːr′t′in′/ mɔːrt̪ən̪ |
| MÁNAS (m) | mɔːn̪əs |
| MAODHÓG (m) | m$^{ə}$iːoːg |
| MAOL EOIN (m) | m$^{ə}$iːl̪oːn′ |
| MAOL ÍOSA (m) | m$^{ə}$iːl̪ iːsə |
| MAOL MHÓRDHA (m) | m$^{ə}$iːl̪woːrgə |
| MAOL MHUADH (m) | m$^{ə}$iːl̪wuə |
| MAOL MHUIRE (m,f) | m$^{ə}$iːl̪wir′i |
| MAOLÁN (m) | m$^{ə}$iːl̪ɔːn̪ |
| MAOLCHOLUIM (m) | m$^{ə}$iːl̪xʌl′im′ |
| MAOLMHAODHÓG (m) | m$^{ə}$iːl̪wiːoːg / m$^{ə}$iːl̪viːoːg |
| MAON (m,f) | m$^{ə}$iːn̪ |
| MARCAS (m) | markəs |
| MARGO (f) | margə |
| MATHÚIN (m) | mahuːn′ |
| MÉABH (f) | meːv |
| MEL (m) | |
| MELL (f) | |
| MELLA (f) | |
| MIS (f) | miʃ |
| MOBHEOC (m) | mʌv$^{j}$oːk |
| MOCHAOI (m) | mʌxiː |
| MOCHAOMHÓG (m) | mʌxiːvoːg |
| MOCHUARÓG (m) | mʌxuəroːg |
| MOCHUDA (m) | mʌxʌd̪ə |
| MOIBHÍ (m) | moːv′iː |
| MOLAISSE (m) | mʌl̪iʃi |
| MOLING (m) | mʌl̪iŋ′ |
| MONCHA (f) | mʌn̪əxə |
| MÓR (f) | moːr |
| MORANN (m) | mʌrən̪ |

| | |
|---|---|
| MÓRNA (f) | moːrn̪ə |
| MUIRCHEARTACH (m) | m$^{ə}$ir′x′ərt̪əx |
| MUIREANN (f) | m$^{ə}$ir′ən̪ |
| MUIRÍOS (m) | m$^{ə}$ir′iːs |
| MUIRIS (m) | m$^{ə}$ir′iʃ |
| MURCHÚ (m) | mʌrəxuː |
| NÁBLA (f) | n̪ɔːbl̪ə |
| NAITHÍ (m) | n̪ɑhiː |
| NAOISE (m) | n̪iːʃə |
| NEACHTAN (m) | n′axt̪ən̪ |
| NEASA (f) | n′asə |
| NEASÁN (m) | n′asɔːn̪ |
| NÉIDHE (m) | n′eː |
| NESSA (f) | n′esə |
| NIALL (m) | n′iəl̪ |
| NIAMH (f) | n′iəv |
| NINIAN (m) | n′in′iən̪ |
| NIOCLÁS (m) | n′ikl̪ɔːs |
| NÓINE (m) | n̪oːn′i |
| NUALA (f) | n̪uəl̪ə |
| NUALLÁN (m) | n̪uəl̪ɔːn̪ |
| ÓENGUS (m) | eːŋgəs |
| OILIBHÉAR (m) | ʌl′iveːr |
| OILIFÉAR (m) | ʌl′ifeːr |
| OISÍN (m) | ʌʃiːn′ |
| OISTÍN (m) | ʌʃt′iːn′ |
| ONÓRA (f) | ʌn̪oːrə |
| ÓRÁN / ODHRÁN (m) | oːrɔːn̪ |
| ÓRNAIT (f) | oːrn̪ət′ |
| OSCAR (m) | ʌskər |
| OSNAIT (f) | ʌsn̪ət′ |
| PÁDRAIG (m) | pɔrik′/pɔd̪rig′ |
| PARTHALÁN (m) | pɑrt̪əl̪ɔːn̪ |
| PEADAR (m) | pad̪ər |
| PEIG (f) | peg′ |
| PIARAS (m) | piərəs |

PILIB (m) pil′ib′
PÓILÍN (f) poːl′iːn′
PÓL (m) poːl̪
PROINSIAS (m) prʌn′ʃiəs
RAGHALLACH (m) rail̪əx
RAGHNAILT (m) rain̪il′t′
RAGHNALL (m) rain̪əl̪
RÉAMONN (m) reːmən̪
RÉILTÍN (m) reːl′t′iːn′
RICARD (m) rikərd̪
RÍONACH (m) riːn̪əx
RISTEARD (m) riʃt′ərd̪ / riʃt′ɔːrd̪
RISTERD (m) riʃt′ərd̪
RIOCARD (m) rikərd̪
ROIBEÁRD (m) rib′ɔːrd̪
RÓNÁN (m) roːn̪ɔːn̪
RÓS (f) roːs
RUAIRÍ (m) ruər′iː
RUÁN (m) ruːɔːn̪
SABIA (f)
SADHBH (f) saiv
SAOIRSE (m,f) siːrʃə
SÁRÁN (m) sɔːrɔːn̪
SÁRNAIT (f) sɔrn̪it′
SCIATH (f) ʃk′iə
SEALBHACH (m) ʃal̪əvəx
SÉAMAS (m) ʃeːməs
SEÁN (m) ʃɔːn̪
SEANACH (m) ʃan̪əx
SEANÁN (m) ʃan̪ɔːn̪
SEANCHÁN (m) ʃan̪əxɔːn̪
SEÁRLAIT (f) ʃɔːrl̪ɪt'
SÉIMÍ (m) ʃeːmiː
SEOIRSE (m) ʃoːr'ʃi
SEOSAIMHÍN (f) ʃoːsif′iːn′
SEOSAMH (m) ʃoːsəf

| | |
|---|---|
| SETANTA (m) | sətantə |
| SIBÉAL (f) | ʃibeːl̪ |
| SÍLE (f) | ʃiːl′i |
| SÍNE (f) | ʃiːn′i |
| SINÉAD (f) | ʃin′eːd̪ |
| SIOBHÁN (f) | ʃivɔːn̪ / ʃuːwɔːn̪ |
| SÍODA (m) | ʃiːd̪ə |
| SÍOMÓN (m) | ʃiːmoːn̪ |
| SIONAINN (f) | ʃun̪in′ |
| SOMHAIRLE (m) | soːr′l′i |
| SORCHA (f) | sʌrəxə |
| STIABHNA (m) | ʃt′iəvn̪ə |
| STIANA (m) | ʃt′iən̪ə |
| STIOFÁN (m) | ʃt′ifɔːn̪ |
| TADHG (m) | t̪aig |
| TÁRLACH (m) | t̪ɔːrl̪əx |
| TASSACH (m) | t̪ɑsəx |
| TEAMHAIR (f) | t′aur |
| TIARNÁN (m) | t′iərn̪ɔːn̪ |
| TIARNMHAS (m) | t′iərn̪wəs |
| TÍREACHÁN (m) | t′iːr′əxɔːn̪ |
| TOMALTACH (m) | t̪ʌməl̪t̪əx |
| TOMÁS (m) | t̪əˈmɔːs/ˈt̪ʌmɔːs |
| TRAOLACH (m) | t̪reːl̪əx |
| TREASA (f) | t ′r′asə |
| TUAMA (m) | t̪uəmə |
| TUAMNAIT (f) | t̪uəmn̪ət′ |
| TUATHAL (m) | t̪uəhəl̪ |
| UAINE (f) | uən'i |
| UAITÉAR (m) | wat′eːr |
| UILLIAM (m) | il′iəm |
| ULTÁN (m) | ʌl̪t̪ɔːn̪ |
| ÚNA (f) | uːn̪ə |
| VAUK (m) | |
| VOGUE (m) | |